Shadow Witness

Jenna Ross Thriller Book 3

Judith A. Barrett

Wobbly Creek, LLC

SHADOW WITNESS

JENNA ROSS THRILLER BOOK 3

Published in the United States of America by Wobbly Creek, LLC

2025 Georgia

wobblycreek.com

Cover by Wobbly Creek, LLC

ISBN 978-1-967288-12-0 eBook

ISBN 978-1-967288-13-7 Paperback

Dedication

Shadow Witness is dedicated to the color red and to good friends who laugh with us. And rescue dogs because they're the best.

Previously

I'm Jenna Ross. My sweet Golden Retriever, Katy, and I have been alone since my husband was killed in action overseas five years ago.

When I inherited a failing bed-and-breakfast from my husband's side of the family a year ago, I didn't hesitate to leave my high stress corporate accounting career in the city for the small town of Paisley, Georgia. Katy and I enjoy having room to roam and spending our days together.

I threw all my energy into reviving the inn, hoping I would find a renewed purpose to heal my grief.

From the first day I walked into the inn, my groundskeeper, Ethan Bentley, didn't have a good word to say about anything I did, and the feeling was mutual. We're a little past that, but both of us still have wounds from our past lives we need to mend.

Surprisingly, the bed-and-breakfast soon flourished beyond what one person could manage alone. At the insistent nudging of my chef, Darlene, I hired an operations manager, Morgan Farley, who was a former hotel manager, and a fulltime housekeeper, Wendy.

Architect Shane Lawson and general contractor Clarence Moore repaired my cottage behind the inn and updated an old barn on my property to become an event center. Mr. Moore and his wife, Bobbie, leased the barn from me to establish the event center, but after Mrs. Moore's untimely death, our lawyers got together, and I bought Mr. Moore's fledgling event business.

After Ethan bought Mr. Moore's contracting business, he and Shane updated the Peach Blossom Barn with a heating and air conditioning system so it could be rented any time of year in our unpredictable Georgia weather.

I have always had a gift of feeling someone's joy, sorrow, or anger as if it were my own; my gift however, has an intense side of intuition so sharp that it manifests as visions when I touch certain objects or people. It weighs on me like a burden.

When a former college classmate of mine and her assistant arrived at the inn, I realized she was as self-centered as ever. I soon discovered there was more to her than just annoying lies, and I felt drawn to untangle a web of deceit.

I closed in on the truth thanks to my intuitive senses and the portrait of Nettie Wyndham, the owner of the Wyndham estate in the 1920s, whose quiet presence inspired me.

After I stopped the killer, Ethan and I took the time to talk and agreed to set aside our protective walls that stood between us. It won't be easy for either of us.

Chapter One

Jenna glanced up from her computer and gave a quick wave when Morgan breezed into their shared office from the kitchen.

Morgan closed the door. "Darlene's mad about something."

"Sounds normal to me." Jenna squinted at her spreadsheet.

Katy trotted to Morgan and stretched in greeting then rolled onto her back. Morgan kneeled next to her and cooed while she gave Katy her morning belly rub. Katy moaned in delight.

"Are you ready for the East Coast Genealogy Club?" Morgan kissed the top of Katy's head then rose. "It isn't a very imaginative name, but I guess that's a plus for a genealogy club."

While Morgan hung up her winter coat, Jenna's phone rang. Jenna frowned. "It's Ellie Martin, our caterer."

"Maybe she's calling to confirm the times." Morgan crossed her fingers as she strode to her desk.

Ellie said, "Jenna, I am so sorry, but I have bad news. I just learned our chef is not available for this weekend. Our assistant chef can prepare the main course, and it will be delicious, but we can't manage lunch, the afternoon snack, or dessert unless we can substitute commercial food. My crew will serve dinner and clean up after dinner as planned, so at least that's covered. Do you want me to see if I can find someone to cover lunch and maybe dessert for us?"

"I'll get back to you."

After Jenna hung up, she said, "Morgan, her chef isn't available. I don't know why, but she has a new chef that can fill in, but they can't cover lunch and the afternoon snack or provide dessert."

Jenna rose from her desk.

"Are you going to talk to Darlene?" Morgan asked. "I'll check the reservations."

"Come with me; I might need backup."

Before Jenna reached the door, Darlene burst into the office.

"A friend of mine called me. Did you know the chef for this weekend has skipped town? What's the plan?"

"The caterer just called me; the assistant chef is taking over, but we'll have to provide lunch, the afternoon snack, and the dessert." Jenna said.

Darlene snorted. "Harry Whittaker has been unreliable since he moved back last year from Atlanta. I didn't know she had an assistant chef. Maybe she's been easing in someone new to replace the chef. That's what I would have done. I'll call my sister Nora to help me bake, but I'll have to hide my spare apron. She'll steal it first chance she gets."

Morgan frowned. "The original plan was for the caterer to provide a light lunch, afternoon snack, and a seven o'clock dinner at the barn on Friday and Saturday nights, and the inn would provide happy hour at the barn at six o'clock on Friday and Saturday."

Jenna shook her head. "That might be too much for us to handle. How many people would that be?"

Morgan grabbed her notebook from her desk and opened it. "We'd be serving breakfast at the inn for ten guests, and then lunch and a snack at the barn for eleven club members. In the evening, we'd host happy hour at six o'clock for two couples at the inn and for thirteen people at the barn, and then provide dinner at the barn on Friday and Saturday for thirteen people."

Darlene exhaled. "I have an idea, but I'll swear it was Morgan's. We could make sandwiches on Friday and Saturday morning for sack lunches and add grocery store chips and cookies for the club members. We could also provide prepackaged afternoon snacks. Nora and I can make the desserts for Friday and Saturday night."

"That would work, but how do we manage happy hour?" Morgan said.

Jenna absently tapped the table with her fingertips while she considered the options. "Our contract with the club states Peach Blossom LLC will provide East Coast Genealogy Club the exclusive use of the barn on Friday and Saturday for their event with lunch and snacks included, and we'd also provide happy hour appetizers and dinner. In our phone discussion with the coordinator, we said happy hour and dinner would also be at the barn."

"Couldn't we talk to the coordinator to see if they'd be agreeable if we hosted happy hour at the inn for the East Coast Genealogy Club, and then they can go to the barn for their evening meal?" Morgan asked.

"I suppose we could; it wouldn't be inconvenient for the Peach Blossom Retreat guests, but the members who are staying at the hotel will be driving here, then to the barn, and then back to the hotel."

"But if we don't have a consolidated happy hour, you'd be hosting happy hour here by yourself for the two couples on Friday and Saturday night, and I'd be hosting happy hour for the genealogy club at the barn," Morgan said.

"It's much simpler for everyone if we host happy hour at the inn for everyone, and since the entire East Coast Genealogy Club will be here for happy hour, we'll have the caterer serve dinner at the inn. We'll have to discuss the change in location with the genealogy coordinator to see if we're missing something. We still want the catering crew to serve dinner, don't we?" Jenna asked.

Darlene raised her eyebrows. "Yes, they should take care of serving and cleaning up after dinner, but if we're taking over lunch, we'd need someone to set out the lunch and snacks for them and clean up afterwards, and I don't think it should be you, Boss Lady. Morgan, make me a copy of your list so I'll know how many people we'll have for each meal so I can plan lunch and the evening desserts. Why don't you see if Layla is available? You can't tell her the idea was mine, though." Darlene left for the kitchen with Katy following her.

Jenna exhaled. "I think we have a plan, Morgan. Call Layla; maybe she can juggle her schedule. I'll call the caterer. We'll need to call the coordinator too, since we're changing the location that was specified in the contract."

Morgan nodded. "I'll take care of that."

When Ellie answered, Jenna said, "We'll take over the lunches and afternoon snacks, but we're moving the Friday and Saturday dinners to our dining room at the inn. We'll provide the dessert, and your chef will provide the meals. Your team will set up for the meals, serve, and then clean up after the meals Friday and Saturday."

The caterer sighed. "That's great. I can manage the crew for dinner and try to pitch in to help our chef. Are you certain about lunch? I can ask around to see if anyone else is available."

"No need, and we'll host happy hour at the inn."

"Talking about the inn, I'd like to have a few of your business cards. Last week, I was at the gas station in my work van and a man at the next pump asked me about my catering business. You know, all the usual stuff like who was my chef and where our next engagement was. When I told him about the Peach Blossom Barn, he asked me questions I couldn't answer; a business card would have been nice. He was polite and good looking too. I told him to call you, but I couldn't remember the number; later I kicked myself because I could have given him my number. I wouldn't have minded a call from him. Anyway, I'm afraid I really fumbled that for you."

"That's okay; sounds like he had enough information to call if he was really serious."

"Thanks; I didn't think of it like that."

After Jenna hung up, she shook her head. *Couldn't remember my phone number? Then how did you manage to call me just now?*

"What's up?" Morgan asked.

"Ellie. She has a tendency to spin a tale to make herself look better."

Morgan said, "I was worried we might be premature or overly aggressive in our actions, but I'm not any more. I sent Layla a text. If you have time, can we review the reservations?"

Jenna opened the reservation system on her computer while Morgan picked up a notebook from her desk and pulled a chair close to Jenna's.

After she sat, Morgan opened her notebook and pointed at Jenna's screen while she referred to her notes. "The genealogy club members have reserved six rooms; two of the rooms are for couples, three rooms are for female members, and the sixth room is for the new coordinator, Petra Lenza. She told me her husband might join her on Saturday. I've assigned downstairs rooms to one woman, who can't maneuver stairs, one couple, and Petra. The second couple and the other two women who are members of the club will be upstairs. We have two couples who are friends and not a part of the genealogy club that will arrive Friday, and they will have the two remaining upstairs rooms."

Jenna nodded. "So we have one vacant room downstairs. Anything else I need to know?"

Morgan nodded as she referred to her notebook. "The five other members are staying at the new hotel. Petra said they're the less adventuresome group. I'm not sure what that means."

"I didn't realize how many moving parts we would have when we said we'd take over the Peach Blossom Barn business."

"Neither did I." Morgan chuckled as she showed Jenna a chart she had drawn in her notebook with notes in the margins, words crossed out, and arrows pointing from one section to another. "Like this? I'll clean it up a bit and have copies for you, Darlene, and Layla."

Jenna studied Morgan's chart. "Do we know where the genealogy crowd plans to go for dinner this evening?"

Morgan's eyes widened. "I assumed they would go somewhere as a group, but I don't really know. Do we care?"

Jenna sighed. "I guess we really don't."

Morgan's phone buzzed with a text. She exhaled in relief as she read it then responded to the text.

"Layla's in class and will get back to me when it's over. She said she'd help and asked for details. I told her I'd send her the chart with the meals and rooms schedules."

While Morgan sat at her desk with her notebook and typed on her computer, Jenna mumbled, "I should have done this earlier."

"Did you say something?" Morgan asked.

"Just thinking out loud." Jenna turned on her computer to check the reviews for the catering company.

After a thorough search on the internet, Jenna sighed. *I can't find anything listed for the catering company including on social media.*

She switched to searching for Ellie Martin, but it took a while to find the right one. *She's all over social media, but it's mostly photos of her and her friends. A lot of bitterness over an ex, but nothing about employment or a business.*

She exhaled. *I'll try the chef; maybe the third time's the charm.* When she found Harry Whittaker on a social networking site for the business community, she jotted down the places and dates of his employment for the past two years on her notepad. When she finished, she counted over a dozen different businesses with significant gaps between each business. She tapped her pen on her pad as she wrinkled her nose.

"Morgan, I did a quick internet search on the chef and found a spotty employment record for him. His title was most often cook's helper with a few listed as sous chef, but he didn't last very long anywhere. We might be lucky he's a no show."

Morgan rubbed her forehead with her fingertips. "I should have done that before I jumped so fast to move forward with them."

"We thought it was right."

Morgan nodded. "We won't get caught like that again."

Jenna's eyes twinkled. "We'll make a different mistake next time."

Morgan chuckled. "You got it, Boss Lady."

Jenna stuck her phone into her back pocket then went into the kitchen.

Darlene was standing at the counter. "I have the list of what we'd need for lunches and snacks on Friday and Saturday, and a plan for happy hour for tonight through Saturday."

"What can I do to help?" Jenna asked.

Darlene growled, "Tell Morgan to let me know when I can expect Layla, so she doesn't blast in here and scare me."

Jenna nodded. *Layla roars in on her motorcycle. Darlene knows her hearing is getting worse.* "Ready to go for a walk, Katy?"

Katy trotted to the door and stared at Jenna.

Jenna chuckled. "I know I'm slow."

After she put on her coat and grabbed the keys to the barn, they went outside.

Katy cocked her head as she waited to see which direction they would be going.

Jenna headed toward the barn. "Morgan and Darlene are busy, and I need a walk. I'm sure Morgan has everything under control, but let's see if anything has to be done at the barn before the genealogy club arrives."

Katy dashed ahead on the wide path to the barn. Jenna glanced around then ran at a slow pace as she followed Katy. When she reached the barn, her nose was cold, and she was out of breath.

Jenna put her hands on her knees. After she caught her breath, she laughed and Katy danced.

"I'm improving, girl."

Jenna unlocked the door and went inside the barn and glanced around. The hand-hewn wood floor, the bare, wooden rafters, and the soft patina of the old dining table that served as a sideboard gave the barn its rustic look. In contrast, the custom electric window blinds and pale creamy peach walls set the tone for glam.

Katy explored the barn while Jenna strolled to the handmade cupboard where the large coffee maker and table linens were stored. *I can't wait to see the room with tablecloths.*

Three round tables with five chairs around each one were clustered in front of the wall where the overhead screen was stored.

Jenna smiled. The East Coast Genealogy Club might not need any audio/visual equipment, but it's there if they need it. Morgan wanted the barn to fit any type of event, so Shane consulted with the experts.

"Ready to go back to the inn, Katy?"

Katy trotted alongside her while Jenna jogged toward the inn. "This isn't too bad, is it?"

When they were halfway to the inn's driveway, Katy growled then turned around and sniffed the air. She snarled as she faced the barn.

When Jenna took a step toward the barn, Katy blocked her.

"Is there something there?" Jenna asked.

Katy snarled then barked. Jenna listened as a car drove from the road to the barn.

She shrugged. "It's okay, girl. It's probably Shane doing a last minute check just like we did."

After Jenna turned to stroll to the inn, Katy trotted ahead of her.

When Jenna reached the driveway, Katy yipped at the back door. Darlene opened the door and Katy dashed inside.

Jenna snickered. *Darlene's hearing might not be great, but she's tuned in to Katy's single yip and hears it just fine.*

After Jenna hung up her coat, she went into the kitchen. Katy was sprawled on the floor near the oven, and Darlene was mixing batter.

Darlene glanced up. "I was watching for you to come in. After I get this batter in the oven, Morgan and I are going over the meals."

Jenna poured a cup of coffee and sat at the counter.

Darlene continued, "Nora will be here soon, and we'll bake everything we can this morning. She's picking up her granddaughter this afternoon to spend the long weekend with her. I'd forgotten about that."

Darlene told stories about her childhood adventures with Nora as she poured the batter into the pans, put the pans into the oven, and then washed the mixing bowl and utensils for her next creation.

Jenna smiled. *I wonder if Nora knows she was always the naughty child, and Darlene was the good one.*

While Darlene lined up ingredients next to her mixing bowl, Jenna groaned at the familiar roar of Ethan's truck as it sped up the driveway. *I don't suppose it's possible he's dropping by to say good morning. I'm not ready for more bad news.*

"Want to go outside with me, Katy?"

Katy stared at Jenna with her are-you-kidding-me puppy eyes.

Jenna smiled. "I don't blame you. You do have the best spot in the inn."

She threw on her coat and went outside to wait near the driveway for Ethan.

After Ethan parked, he strode to Jenna.

She smiled at his familiar gait and his mustache she'd grown fond of.

"What are you doing standing out here?" Ethan asked.

Jenna narrowed her eyes. *No good morning. It's bad news.*

"I heard your truck; Darlene has hot coffee."

Ethan put his arm around her. "Aren't you cold? Hot coffee sounds great."

"Are you saying I'm always cold?" Jenna shivered as they reached the back door.

"I count on it." Ethan chuckled as he pulled her closer.

When they went into the kitchen, the heady aroma of warm cinnamon and sugar greeted them.

"I have to snoop." Jenna peeked into the oven. "It's coffee cake."

Ethan inhaled. "Darlene's already gearing up for this weekend, isn't she?"

He glanced around while Jenna poured two cups of coffee. "Where is Darlene?"

"Probably in my office with Morgan. Are you stalling?" Jenna cocked her head as they sat at the table.

"Was I that obvious?" He met her gaze. "I found tire tracks at the barn a few minutes ago that weren't there when I left right before dark yesterday."

Jenna furrowed her brow. "Katy and I walked to the barn this morning to check it out. I didn't see any tracks, but on our way back we heard a car drive up from the road toward the barn. I thought it was Shane. I was going to go back to the barn, but Katy growled and blocked me, which was odd."

"When was that?" Ethan narrowed his eyes. "It wasn't Shane. He's in town meeting with a client."

"I don't know. Maybe thirty minutes ago."

Ethan pulled out his phone and sent a text.

"What's going on?" Jenna asked.

"I don't know," Ethan growled.

Jenna huffed. "Well, who did you text?"

He stared at her. "Shane. Why?"

We were in the middle of a conversation, and you sent a text.

Jenna rose from her seat and dumped her coffee into the sink.

She stared at the dark splashes of coffee on the sides of the stainless steel sink. *I could be offended and run away or be brave and take a chance.*

Jenna rinsed away the coffee and returned to her seat. She gazed at him as she put her hand on his arm. "Because I think I need to know."

Ethan exhaled. "You're right. I asked Shane if we should install a gate at the barn's driveway."

Jenna frowned. "Won't that mean extra work?"

Ethan glanced at his phone. "Shane's going to look into the cost; meanwhile, he suggested I put one of my game cameras along the driveway near the road. What do you think?"

"It would be nice to know if we should be concerned before we do anything."

"I don't think we should worry Morgan."

He's not listening to me; is it because he's worried? "She's finishing up a few things then she'll be busy getting the barn set up. I don't think she'll notice it, do you?"

"Probably not, but could you divert her to something else until I install the camera?"

"I can ask her to make sure the guest rooms are ready. It's something one of us always does before guests arrive."

When the oven timer dinged, Jenna silenced it then hurried to the office door and opened it. "Darlene, the timer went off. Is there something I could do?"

Darlene rushed past Jenna. "I have to check it."

She opened the oven door and lightly tapped on the coffee cakes. "One more minute."

"I'd better be going," Ethan said.

Jenna walked with him to the back door. "Thank you for including me."

Ethan smiled. "Thanks for the reminder."

Jenna returned his smile as she gazed at him then opened her arms for a hug. After a lingering kiss, he left.

When Jenna returned to the kitchen, Darlene was removing the coffee cakes. She peered at Jenna. "You look funny. Is everything okay?"

Jenna rubbed her hands together to keep from touching her mouth that still tingled. *I really enjoyed that kiss.*

"It's cold outside. We're finally getting everything under control."

"Isn't that a relief? Morgan asked Petra if anyone had diet restrictions, and Petra told her not to worry about it because no one in the group will require special meals. I got the impression one or two of the members bring snacks to supplement their meals."

When Jenna went into the living room to check it before any guests arrived, she fluffed the pillows on the sofa, and the wind chimes on the front porch jingled.

Jenna glanced at Nettie's portrait, and Nettie's eyes twinkled.

Jenna sat in the yellow chair and exhaled. "I know the pillows were fine; I just wanted to talk. It was hard, but I didn't snap at Ethan when he said something that felt like he was ignoring me. I took a chance and literally reached out instead; I put my hand on his arm, and he didn't shake it off. That was progress for both of us, right?"

The curtains rustled, and Jenna relaxed as a sense of calm surrounded her. *He's a good man.*

"He is; I appreciate the reminder." Jenna chuckled. "I just quoted him."

Katy trotted into the living room and put her head on Jenna's knee. Jenna stroked Katy's face while she relaxed in the room's calmness.

Katy whined; Jenna jolted out of her reverie and heard a car as it pulled past the inn then parked.

"I wonder if that's Shane, but Ethan didn't say anything about Shane coming here."

When Jenna stepped into the hallway, Darlene rushed out of the kitchen. "Nora texted me; she's at the back door."

Katy followed Darlene; Jenna smiled and continued to the office.

Morgan rose from her desk. "I'm going to the barn after I check the guest rooms unless you've already checked them."

"No, I just checked the living room."

Morgan nodded. "Do you have anything for me?"

"Is your chart finished?"

Morgan tapped her forehead with her palm. "Darlene and I went over it. I've got your copy right here."

Jenna and Morgan sat at the table together. After Morgan reviewed the chart, and Jenna asked a few questions, Jenna said, "I like how we consolidated happy hour with hosting it at the inn. Do you think the guests who aren't part of the genealogy club will feel left out when the majority of our guests remain for dinner?"

"No, I talked to Petra, and we decided the group will leave the dining room after happy hour and relax in the living room."

"That's great," Jenna said.

"Did I tell you Petra plans to be here early in the afternoon? I thought of a few more things I want to ask Darlene, then I'll check the guest rooms."

After Morgan left, Jenna's phone rang. *Ethan.*

She smiled as she answered.

"I'm ready to install the camera. Want to ride over with me? I've warmed up my truck."

"I'll be right out."

A blast of icy wind billowed open her jacket after she stepped outside. She shivered as she pulled the jacket together and zipped it up. *Should have done that before I opened the door.*

She rushed to Ethan's truck and hopped into the passenger seat. The warmth of the heater blew on her feet. "This is much nicer than that frigid wind."

"Thought you'd appreciate toasty toes." Ethan smiled.

Jenna giggled. "Very much so, and that was funny."

Jenna waited in the truck while Ethan pounded a metal fencepost into the ground in the middle of a small stand of trees that had a clear view of the driveway. After he attached the camera to the post, Ethan returned to his truck.

On the way back to the inn, he asked, "Is there anything unusual about this group that's meeting at the barn this weekend?"

"Not that I know of. Petra took over the club this year when the original coordinator wanted to retire. She said most of the members are from North or South Carolina, but all of them are from the East Coast, which is obvious from their club name. They get together once a year to exchange genealogy tips and analyze interesting gaps they have found in genealogy records. The annual meeting gives them a chance to talk in depth about genealogy without boring anyone."

Ethan cleared his throat. "The morning went fast, didn't it? How tied down are you? Would you like to go into town for lunch?"

Jenna side-glanced at him. *Like a lunch date?*

She furrowed her brow. *I'm overthinking this. He's just being nice.*

"I thought you could use a break." He shrugged. "You're probably too busy; forget I said anything."

An all-black fox squirrel sat near the side of the road then raced alongside the truck before it darted up a tree. *He's reciprocating and reaching out to me.*

"That's a brilliant idea. I can't remember the last time I slowed down enough to relax and enjoy my lunch. I usually just grab a bite from the kitchen and eat on the run, or on rare occasions, I sit at my desk."

Ethan chuckled. "I'm the same. I can't tell you how many times I've had a sandwich in one hand while I steered the lawn mower with the other. One of the older cafés in town is only open for lunch, but their daily soup is always good, and you can order a half sandwich with your soup. The owner is the mother of a young man who used to work for Mr. Moore, but works for me now."

"Soup and half a sandwich sounds perfect."

Chapter Two

When they went inside the crowded café, Jenna glanced around but didn't see anywhere to sit.

"Ethan." A man in the back called out and motioned for them to come to his table.

Ethan took Jenna's hand and led her as he snaked his way to the back.

"I was just getting ready to leave when I spotted you and thought you'd like to take my table. Hey, Miss Jenna; have a seat. Can I talk to you outside for a minute, Ethan?"

Ethan glanced at Jenna, and she nodded as she sat down.

As the man rose, a server quickly cleared the table and cleaned the top before she handed Jenna a menu.

Ethan and the man went outside.

While Jenna read over the menu, the conversation of the two women at a table behind her was as clear as if they were sitting at the same table as Jenna.

"Tell me again why it was so important for us to join this club, Wanda." The woman spoke in a melodious South Carolina Lowcountry accent.

Wanda snorted. "It was your idea, Felicia, not mine."

Jenna cringed at the raspiness of Wanda's creaky, low-pitched voice that made her Maryland accent harsh.

Felicia said, "Only because you insisted."

Wanda continued, "Well then, you tell me, why did Petra pick a sleepy town that is barely a wide spot in the road?"

"Did you want to take over the club? I certainly wouldn't want to. Speaking of taking over the group, have you noticed how bossy Vera has become?"

"She gets more obnoxious every year if you ask me; you don't think she'll try to become a member, do you? At least Petra can't win the story competition again this year like she did last year. A coordinator isn't allowed to compete unless we vote to change the rules, which isn't likely."

"I hope nobody brings up any rule changes. Remember four years ago when the discussion lasted for three hours?" Felicia asked.

"If it goes that long, let's walk out. There's no way I'll stick around and listen to a rehash of what we'd already heard twice before and end up missing happy hour and dinner," Wanda said.

Felicia whispered, "I overheard some certain person on the phone and got the impression there's some funny stuff going on with that certain person and the chef."

"That sounds juicy. Who are you talking about?"

Felicia mocked Wanda's raspy voice. "Wouldn't you like to know?"

Wanda yawned. "You think you're funny; you're not. At least we had an excuse to stay in a modern hotel. I couldn't sleep in a house that was over a hundred years old. Can you imagine how creepy that place must be? I'll bet it's a fire hazard too."

"And what's the big deal about a bed-and-breakfast? I'm not interested in sharing a bathroom with strangers. I'll bet they leave their toothbrushes on the sink, and I hear the bathroom doors don't even lock. No, thank you," Felicia said.

"Have you seen Tisha? She never shows up on time, does she? I wouldn't mind if she didn't show up at all; she makes me nervous. I don't see why a cop would be interested in genealogy. Maybe she's investigating someone in the group. If she was investigating you, wouldn't you be worried?" Wanda asked.

"You never get your facts straight. Tisha isn't a cop. She's an investigator or something like that for one of those fancy estate lawyers, but from what I hear, she's not a very good one."

"Whatever; that's like a cop. Did you see the meeting room at the hotel? There is not much to it, but at least it's convenient for us."

Felicia sniffed. "You didn't read Petra's email, did you? We're meeting in a barn."

"That's not funny."

"Don't say I didn't warn you."

Jenna heard the scrape of their chairs when they rose then peered over her menu as they made their way to the register to pay.

One woman was tall and muscular, with carefully styled, short black hair. The other woman was of medium height and weight; her shoulder length hair was dyed bright red.

"It's your turn to pay," the woman with red hair said.

Jenna smiled. *Ah ha. The red-haired lady is Wanda of the raspy voice, and Felicia is tall and is from South Carolina.*

Jenna absently drummed on the table with her fingers. *Would it be mean if I borrowed some goats?*

When Ethan joined her at the table, he said, "I'm so sorry; I didn't expect to be gone that long."

"That's okay. I had entertainment." Jenna told him about the conversation between the two women who sat at a table behind her.

Ethan shook his head. "There's no accounting for taste, is there? Are they even members?"

Their server appeared with their iced tea. "Are you ready to order?"

"Potato soup with half a grilled ham and cheese sandwich," Jenna said.

"Same for me except a full sandwich."

After the server left, Jenna said, "They said they were staying at the hotel, and Morgan told me three female members were staying there. The members who are married are staying at the inn."

"I've been thinking about those tire tracks at the barn; I have a white shirt stuck back in my closet somewhere.

If you need another server, I'm trainable. The potential for weekend entertainment would almost be worth my while to iron that shirt."

Jenna chuckled. "You could be security."

Ethan furrowed his brow. "You know, that's not a bad idea. I have an olive green long-sleeved T-shirt."

"I didn't really mean it; it was supposed to be a joke."

Ethan put his hand over hers. "Maybe so, but I'll feel better."

Jenna glared at him. "If you're security, what's Shane going to be?"

"We'll leave that up to him and Morgan. I vote for Master of Ceremonies. We need a security vest for Katy too. We can't leave her out."

"She'd love that. Can you find a pink one?"

Ethan grinned. "I'll work on it."

When their food arrived, their soup was steaming, and the cheese from their sandwiches had oozed onto the plate.

Jenna spooned up some soup and blew on it. After it had cooled a bit, she tasted it. "Yum. The soup has bacon in it."

While they ate, Jenna asked, "What did you want to be when you were growing up?"

Ethan smiled. "I guess I was a handful at school because I overheard the elementary principal tell Mom to be sure I learned a trade or I'd be on the street. When I was a kid, we played ball in the street all the time, so I was excited. The principal wasn't around the next year, and I was sad because he was my inspiration for my life on the street."

Jenna giggled. "That's where your destiny in streets came from. Look at the driveways and the paths you've created."

"It was meant to be." Ethan finished his sandwich. "What about you?"

"I've always known I felt things other people didn't, so I thought it would be wonderful to travel so I could observe people without having to be social. I decided my perfect career would be a truck driver, but it didn't work out. When I was in the fourth grade, a girl told me I'd never be strong enough to be a trucker. After I thoroughly researched the job requirements and my potential muscle mass given the size of my mother, I came to the same conclusion."

"How did becoming an accountant fit in with your truck driver's soul?"

"I've always loved the predictability of numbers, and accounting worked out because it was like keeping a trucker's log, but I was surprised by how perfect the inn was for me."

Ethan raised his eyebrows. "You have your numbers and different people to observe every week, and for a bonus, you don't have to worry about road conditions. What about the social?"

Jenna sighed. "I'm learning. Darlene nags me, and Morgan gives me her version of gentle suggestions."

Ethan chuckled. "I can imagine."

The server cleared their dishes. "Ready for dessert?"

Jenna shook her head. "No, thank you."

"I'll pass," Ethan said.

When the server removed their ticket from her pad, Ethan deftly plucked it from her fingers before she could set it on the table. "My treat, Boss Lady. I invited you."

Jenna rolled her eyes as she rose from her chair and zipped up her coat. Ethan offered his arm, and they strolled together to the café door then hurried to the truck.

While they waited for the traffic light to change, Jenna said, "Getting away for lunch was a wonderful idea. I haven't relaxed long enough to enjoy a conversation in ages, but it will be my treat next time."

"I can't remember the last time I talked to anyone about something other than work." Ethan chuckled. "My nephew Ryan doesn't count; he talks, and I nod."

"Katy misses Ryan."

"He's in football this year, so it's hard to find an opening in his schedule. I'll remind him he has an open invitation to visit the inn."

Jenna peered at the construction site on the edge of town as they drove past it. "Do you suppose we could get a portable toilet delivered to the barn?"

Ethan burst out laughing. "It would be worth it just to see the look on a certain set of faces, wouldn't it? Shall I borrow a few goats?"

Jenna giggled. "That's hilarious. I wondered where I could get goats while I watched them sashay out the front door."

Jenna pulled out her phone and sent a text. "I asked Darlene which night she was going to prepare her famous goat cheese dip for happy hour."

Jenna read Darlene's reply aloud. "Friday night."

"Tell her to make extra for the hired help."

Jenna snorted. "When she finds out you'll be there, she'll have a bowl just for you."

Ethan smiled as he turned at the driveway. "Darlene and I go way back."

Jenna raised an eyebrow. "I'm waiting for the story."

"Remind me on our next date." Ethan bit his lip as he glanced at Jenna.

Jenna rolled her eyes. "Date? Lunch wasn't a date. I didn't even brush my hair before we left."

When Ethan stared at her, Jenna widened her eyes in her best impression of an innocent look, but her slight smile gave her away.

Ethan laughed. "You got me. I thought for sure I'd crossed a line. Remind me on our first date, and I might tell you the story about Darlene."

Jenna smiled.

Ethan parked in his usual spot and opened Jenna's door. "As soon as Shane's free, we can get together and have our security discussion."

When they reached the back door, Jenna grabbed his hand and shook it. He laughed as she darted inside.

Morgan smiled when Jenna entered the office. "Wendy left right before lunch; she plans to arrive in the morning by nine. Layla will go to the barn tomorrow after her nine o'clock class. She and I will stay at the barn until the meeting ends, and then we'll be here tomorrow evening through dinner because I'm nervous about relying on Ellie's team. Layla will help with lunch on Saturday, so we can discuss any adjustments we'd like to make for the rest of the day."

"I'm really grateful Layla is available."

"So am I. She may bring her cousin Hailey on Saturday. I told her that would be great."

"Ellie made me nervous when she told me she'd manage the crew and try to help the chef," Jenna said.

"I was fine at first with the caterer because she was the one Bobbie had planned to use, but this last-minute switch to a less experienced chef is as bad as the job-hopping chef. I don't know why we didn't think of it earlier, but I'll talk to Darlene about the assistant chef to see what she thinks."

Before Morgan left the office, her phone buzzed a text. She exhaled. "Petra will be here in five minutes, and the rest of the members will be here not long after that."

"I'll take care of our guests while you talk to Darlene." Jenna headed toward the dining room door.

Morgan bit her lip. "Are you sure you'll be okay? I could talk to Darlene later."

"I've done this before." Jenna chuckled. "I'll muddle through."

"I won't be long because I intend to get right to the point, but I might have to listen to a Darlene lecture." Morgan wrung her hands as she headed to the kitchen.

Jenna hurried to the registration desk. *Morgan is really rattled.*

When a woman with light brown hair pulled into a messy bun strode up the walk from the visitor parking lot carrying an oversized suitcase and a shiny red purse that matched her bright red lipstick, Jenna opened the front door.

The woman smiled as she entered the inn. She set down her suitcase on the floor and her purse on the foyer table before she pulled off her red and black striped wool poncho. She wore a short-sleeved, hot pink silky blouse and dark red jeans that were tucked into her western boots.

Jenna returned her smile. "Welcome to the Peach Blossom Retreat; I'm Jenna."

"I'm Petra, and I'm so pleased to meet you." Petra's voice was soft with the slow drawl of North Carolina.

Before Petra reached the registration desk, she exhaled and then scanned the registration area. "I swear your lovely inn is so stress free, I relaxed the second I walked in. You must hear that all the time."

She gazed at the staircase and put her hand on her heart. "Can't you just see a beautiful young woman sweep down the staircase and into her lover's arms? This old inn must be teeming with untold stories."

The chimes on the front porch jingled, and Jenna smiled. "So true. Let's get you registered, and then I'll give you a quick tour before I show you to your guest room."

After Petra was registered, Jenna motioned toward the side door. "The door at the end of the hallway is the guest entrance and exit. Your room key unlocks the door to come in and automatically locks when it closes. It also serves as an emergency exit because it has a push bar to go outside."

Jenna led Petra down the hallway and pointed at the main floor restroom on their way to the dining room. When Jenna opened the dining room door, she said,

"We serve breakfast at seven. Breakfast on weekdays is a continental breakfast, but on Saturdays and Sundays, we provide a full breakfast buffet."

"Our meetings start at eight thirty. How early can the members who are staying at the hotel go to the barn?"

"We would love for them to come here for breakfast."

"Thank you. I'm glad Morgan suggested we have our happy hour and dinner here too. It simplifies herding the club from one location to another, doesn't it? My predecessor warned me the meetings become overly intense sometimes. She recommended a calming atmosphere at the end of each day so everyone can decompress before dinner."

After they reached the living room, Jenna said, "The living room is always available for our guests. We have board games, magazines, and books. The contents of our bookshelves are constantly changing because guests drop off books they've read and take books to read on the road. When it's cold like it is today, we have a fire in the fireplace in the evenings."

Petra wandered around the living room as she lightly touched the sofa, coffee table, bookshelves, and mantle. She froze in front of Nettie's portrait. "She's beautiful," she whispered.

Jenna smiled then motioned toward the hallway. "Are you ready to see your room?"

"Was the young woman in the portrait the original owner?" Petra followed Jenna.

"She and her husband were married in 1920. She saved the estate and many of the surrounding farms from foreclosure when banks began closing."

"Are you related to her?"

"I am through my husband's side of the family." Jenna stopped at Petra's room and smiled. "Use your room key to open the door."

When she opened the door, Petra gasped as she placed her hand over her heart. "My room key opened a portal to the past. This room is gorgeous. I love the peach blossom motif on the coverlet. It's going to be very difficult for me to leave my room. I can't wait to see everyone else's reactions. Even our hard core curmudgeons should be happy."

Jenna waited in the doorway while Petra explored her room.

Petra set down her suitcase then sat next to the window in the soft chair. She sighed. "I suppose I will have to greet the members when they arrive."

Jenna quietly closed the door as she left.

Morgan joined her at the registration desk. "I'm glad I talked to Darlene. I'm sure this is one of those things that everybody in Paisley knows, but Ellie, her sister, and her sister's best friend are the crew, and the chef is her brother. The family convinced Ellie to become a caterer so her brother would have a job. Darlene thinks Bobbie agreed to be Ellie's first customer as a favor to the family."

Jenna raised her eyebrows. "Wow. It wouldn't be so bad if this wasn't our first event."

"I know." Morgan sighed. "It still bothers me Ellie wasn't as experienced as we thought, or hoped might be a better word. Darlene said she learned the assistant chef was Ellie's cousin who attended two years of culinary school at a community college. She called a friend who is an instructor at the college, and her friend said he was an excellent student, which is a plus. I can't believe Ellie wasn't more open about the issues, but Darlene said that family had never been very open. Darlene thinks we'll be okay with the assistant chef. It's surprising Ellie chose a service business where talking with the customers was critical."

"We can't beat ourselves up; what's done is done. I'm glad Layla will be here."

"So am I."

"Petra asked me how early the members who are staying at the hotel can arrive at the barn. I need to tell Darlene I invited the five genealogy club members to breakfast here on Friday and Saturday," Jenna said.

""I'm glad she asked. If we tried to have someone at the barn early just in case, that would cut our staff at breakfast at the inn, and we're skimpy as it is."

Jenna glanced toward the front door. "I hear cars in the driveway."

Morgan smiled, and her eyes twinkled. "My favorite part. I've got this."

While Morgan hurried to the foyer to greet the arriving guests, Jenna went into the kitchen.

Katy trotted to her with her tail wagging. Jenna smiled and stroked Katy's back and ears.

When she glanced up, Nora, who was a younger and lighter-weight version of Darlene, smiled and waved as she stirred a sauce on the stove.

Jenna strolled to Darlene to catch her attention. "I've invited the genealogy members who are staying at the hotel to have breakfast with us on Friday and Saturday."

"I wondered when you'd get around to that," Darlene said. "Nora and I decided a warm lunch would be better than sandwiches and a bag of chips."

"You know that sounds good to me. What do you have in mind?"

"Chili and saltine crackers for tomorrow, and pork stew and tortilla chips on Saturday."

"Won't that be a lot of work?"

Nora laughed and spoke to Darlene in Spanish.

Darlene chuckled. "Nora said I should tell you it's going to be almost too much work for two people, but we'll do our best."

Nora nodded as she grinned at Jenna.

Darlene said, "Actually, it's easier than making sandwiches. I sent Nora to the store so we can make the chili, stew, cookies, and desserts today, then all we have to do tomorrow is heat the chili and set everything out. Same for Saturday. The chili and stew will be self-serve so we don't have to worry about portions."

"What about snacks?"

"We bought snack packs."

"Everything sounds perfect."

Darlene nodded and turned away to check the oven.

When Jenna headed toward her office, Katy padded to the door to the hallway then glanced over her shoulder at Jenna.

Jenna turned back and smiled. "Katy and I are going for a walk."

Nora said, "I'll tell Darlene."

Jenna zipped up her coat and put on her gloves before she and Katy went outside.

"Should this be a long or short walk?" Jenna asked.

Katy trotted toward the path to the peach orchard.

Jenna groaned. "I probably need to stretch my legs, don't I?"

Katy grinned then raced into the woods. When Jenna rounded a curve in the path, Katy popped out in front of her.

When they were on the hill that overlooked the orchard, Jenna gazed at the bare branches. "I was so upset our first Christmas here because I thought all the trees had died, and somehow it was my fault."

She was blinded by tears as she kicked at a stick that was on the ground in front of her. *The last thing I said to Tom was don't come back.*

"I didn't mean it," she cried out.

Katy stared at Jenna.

"I know it makes no sense, Katy, but those were rough times, and I was at my lowest. This time of year always gets me."

Jenna wiped away her tears with her coat sleeve and turned to stroll back to the inn. "Spring was a shock to me when the trees began budding out. Do you remember how I cried in relief because the trees had tiny green leaves?"

Katy yipped and raced into the woods to chase a chattering squirrel that had taunted her.

Jenna whispered, "And then I cried because Tom would never be back, and it was my fault."

Jenna trudged toward the inn with her head down until Katy nudged her hand and barked.

Jenna cocked her head. "What is it, girl?"

After Katy pounced forward, she glanced back over her shoulder.

"Oh, you want to run. Challenge accepted." Jenna ran to the inn with Katy at her side.

Jenna slowed when she saw Ethan waiting for her.

He smiled. "Was it a good run?"

She nodded. "Katy said I needed to clear my head, so we raced, except she stayed with me."

"Shane will be here in just a minute. Is now a good time for us to talk?"

"Yes. Morgan's busy with guests."

As they strolled to the back door, Ethan asked, "Is everything okay? You seem a little down."

"Our caterer and chef aren't as experienced as we thought. Morgan and I made some adjustments so we could supplement any gaps, but I'm still worried about the weekend. Layla will be here to help."

"That's good news; Layla will make a difference, but is Darlene okay with that? She and Layla seemed to have a special relationship that always included fireworks."

Jenna's mouth quivered as she glanced away.

He raised his eyebrows then chuckled. "Don't tell me it was Darlene's idea."

"Good, because you didn't hear it from me."

Before they went inside, Ethan put his hand on Jenna's shoulder. Jenna caught a whiff of his soap, and she sighed at the comforting aroma.

"Tell me what I can do to help," he said.

She gazed at the kindness in his eyes. "I've never felt so overwhelmed; it's like I'm stuck on the railroad tracks in a tunnel, and a train is barreling toward me with its horn blasting. Tell me if you see something I've missed."

Ethan nodded. "I'll have your back, Boss Lady."

Jenna smiled. "That helps."

When they went inside, Jenna resisted covering her ears at the loud chattering voices coming from the reception area.

"Settle down," Morgan called out, and the voices became quiet.

Ethan leaned close to Jenna and whispered, "Morgan's the right one to corral that rowdy group, isn't she?"

When they went into the kitchen, Darlene beamed. "Are you helping us this weekend, Ethan?"

"Sure am. I'm Boss Lady's right-hand man and body guard."

Nora added, "We're having goat cheese dip tomorrow night. Darlene said that was your favorite."

"That cinches it for me; I'll be here all weekend." Ethan smiled.

When they were in the office, Jenna giggled. "Darlene knew she had you at the goat cheese dip."

Ethan shrugged as he strolled to the window and peered out. "Shane's here."

When Shane came into the office, the three of them sat at the table.

Shane opened his briefcase. "Our topic is security, correct? At a minimum, we need surveillance cameras at the inn, the cottage, and the barn. I have a draft of the locations I recommend."

After Shane spread out a survey map of the estate property, he pointed to the small circles he'd added in pencil as locations for the cameras.

Jenna listened intently while Ethan asked questions and Shane answered them. Shane made adjustments to the blueprint as they talked. *I'm understanding more than I expected. Shane's explanations are always excellent.*

"Here's a rough cost breakdown for the installation." Shane handed Jenna a price sheet.

Ethan peered at the sheet and frowned. "That seems stiff."

Shane nodded. "We'll get Adrienne involved. She'll negotiate a good price for Jenna. Did you know she has a law degree? I asked her once why she was a paralegal and not a partner with Suzanne Nelson. She told me she makes plenty of money, has free rein in the office, and doesn't have to dress up for court."

Jenna chuckled. "I believe it."

"So, what do you think, Jenna? Can I send our plan to Adrienne?" Shane asked. "I'm sure she'll have more questions and ideas we haven't thought of, which will probably throw us right back to where we started."

Jenna furrowed her brow. "The best case is that we never need this, but yes, send the plan to Adrienne, and you're right. She'll rip it apart."

Shane nodded. "Do you want to let her know I'll be sending her the proposal?"

Jenna pulled out her phone and sent a text. "Done."

"Then I'm on it." Shane rose. "Thank you, Jenna. I'll be able to breathe easier after we beef up the security here. I'll send you a final copy of my drawing this evening."

"Darlene might badger you for a place to put another refrigerator, Shane, because we're doing more of the catering than we had expected. I'm not convinced we're ready to expand into the catering business."

Ethan raised an eyebrow. "I agree with you, Jenna."

"Sounds like an excellent topic for a team discussion," Shane said.

Ethan followed Shane to the door. "I have a few items about the barn to discuss with you, Shane, if you have time."

Shane nodded, and the two men left.

After Jenna went into the dining room, she heard voices in the living room.

When she strolled into the living room, Katy wagged her tail and smiled as she stood alongside Petra, who was in a conversation with a woman with natural red hair and who was much slimmer than the woman at the café with the bright red hair.

Petra continued, "I love her books, but it must be difficult for a writer with a pen name to keep their real identity a secret. There are so many ways these days to discover someone's real name, aren't there?"

Jenna raised her eyebrows when the woman flinched.

Petra glanced up. "Hi, Jenna. Everyone, this is Jenna, the owner of the Peach Blossom Retreat and the Peach Blossom Barn."

The woman with red hair smiled, and her green eyes twinkled as she examined Jenna's face. "I'm Brittany.

I'm sure you won't remember everyone's name, but we'll remind you. My husband is Stan."

She pointed at the two men who stood in front of the fireplace in an intense discussion. "My Stan is the tall, good-looking man with brown hair and glasses."

Stan glanced toward his wife when he heard his name and strode toward them with an engaging smile.

When he joined them, Stan said, "It's a pleasure to meet you, Jenna. I love the architecture of your inn. You may have remodeled, but you've certainly stayed true to her fine bones."

Jenna returned his smile. "Thank you. That was our goal."

"Have you noticed old houses like this always have a history of unexplained gaps in their lineage and whispers of family misdeeds that would shock our current society?" the other man asked. His dark brown mustache and hair had streaks of gray, and he wore a red and gray striped tie and a khaki sports coat.

Petra chuckled. "Isn't that why we're all interested in genealogy? To find those delicious, glaring holes in the family trees?"

A short woman with impeccable makeup and perfectly coiffed shoulder-length, chestnut brown hair with a hint of gray at the roots sniffed. "I suppose that might be so in your family tree, Petra, but my Ralph has traced both of our families all the way back to the fourteenth century with the expert help of my brother, haven't you?"

The man with the mustache furrowed his brow. "I have?"

Petra rolled her eyes. "Vera, my family tree goes back to pirates that evidently just dropped from the sky. Wouldn't you love to time travel back for just a day?"

Vera snorted. "Don't be ridiculous; there's no such thing as time travel."

Brittany cleared her throat. "Jenna, I read the brochure about the peach orchard and the walking path from the inn to the hill that overlooks the orchard then continues to the orchard gift shop. After being in the car most of the day, Stan and I would love to spend a little time outside. The brochure said it was a twenty-minute walk from here to the hill; is it an easy walk?"

"Yes. The twenty minutes is at a leisurely pace, and the path is more like a smooth park path than a rough trail through the woods. You'll enjoy it."

"Anyone else want to go with us?" Stan asked.

Vera exchanged a glance with the other woman who was taller than Vera but was as round as she was tall.

"What do you think, Lucille?" Vera asked.

Lucille said, "I'd like to wait for Susan and Ivy, so they don't feel like I abandoned them."

Petra raised an eyebrow at her.

"Fresh air sounds good to me," Ralph said.

Vera glared at her husband. "We'll wait with you, Lucille."

"Well, I'd like to go," Petra said. "Give me a second to grab my poncho then I'll meet you at the door."

As Jenna left the living room, Vera tugged on Ralph's sleeve and hissed, "I told you Lucille doesn't trust Brittany, and Lucille is my friend, so we don't like Brittany."

Ralph sighed. "I can't keep track of all your drama. Write it down on a scorecard for me."

Jenna raised her eyebrows. *This might be an interesting weekend after all. I wouldn't mind having one of those scorecards too.*

Chapter Three

When Jenna went into the kitchen, Nora was gone, and Darlene was putting the last of the dishes into the dishwasher.

Darlene pointed at the counter. "Everything is ready for tomorrow. There's your list. It took me three pages, but it's all written out for you. I'll be here at my usual time to make sure there aren't any more last-minute changes. Before we host the next event, I need another refrigerator. Talk to Shane about that."

Jenna picked up the papers and read through Darlene's carefully detailed instructions. "These are very clear, but I'm not surprised because you always give us a straightforward list to follow."

Darlene snorted. "They're perfect until some offbeat twist comes up, which happens all the time around here, then they're useless. I'll see you in the morning. Morgan said to tell you she'll be back before five."

After Darlene left, Jenna went into the office.

When she glanced out the window, she gaped at Lucille and Vera who stood on the walkway in front of the inn. She couldn't hear them, but their noses were inches away from each other, their faces were red and contorted, and their fists were clenched. When Lucille sneered, Vera reached out and pushed Lucille's shoulder. Lucille lost her balance and fell backward onto her ample bottom in the grass.

While Lucille struggled to get to her feet, Vera stormed away toward the guest entrance on the other side of the house. After Vera was out of sight, Lucille's mouth curved into a smug smile as she casually rose to her feet. She brushed off the seat of her slacks then scanned the yard before she strolled to the guest parking lot.

"I thought I was going to have to run outside to help Lucille get to her feet. She's more nimble than I expected, and I got the impression earlier those two were friends, Katy." Jenna shook her head. "I guess I was wrong on all counts."

Jenna returned to her office and was soon lost in preparing the quarterly tax statement.

She was startled when she heard a car roar up the driveway, and Katy barked.

"Nobody speeds on the gravel road like that except Layla and sometimes Morgan, but I'm confused because Morgan always rides with Shane, and we don't expect Layla until tomorrow."

Morgan dashed into the office. "Did you look at Darlene's instructions she left for tonight's happy hour? We should have preheated the oven ten minutes ago."

Jenna followed Morgan into the kitchen and picked up the instruction sheets. "We'll be okay. I'll take over the kitchen if you'd rather prep the dining room."

"Darlene counted on me to do this right," Morgan grumbled. "It's all Shane's fault."

"I'll prep the dining room then come help you. We'll be okay; Darelene always builds extra time into her schedule because she doesn't think we're competent. We should be insulted, except she's frequently right."

After Jenna set out the silverware, napkins, and small plates on the sideboard, she brought the large water pitcher and the ice bucket into the kitchen.

While she filled the pitcher with water and the bucket with ice, Jenna said, "I got lost in my comfortable world of numbers this afternoon. So, what were you doing? I thought you were going to be here earlier."

Morgan clenched her teeth as she opened the oven. "I was apartment hunting."

Jenna raised her eyebrows as she peered at Morgan. *Why is that causing her so much pain?*

When Morgan turned, she met Jenna's gaze and sighed. "We'll talk later, okay?"

It's Shane. Jenna nodded as she carried the pitcher and the bucket of ice to the dining room and filled the water dispenser.

After Jenna placed the chips and dip on the sideboard, Morgan carried a tray of sausage cheese balls to the dining room then returned with a tray of crab cake bites.

Morgan added extra napkins and small plates next to the trays. "Darlene told me we have two appetizers along with the chips and dip because it's almost the weekend, and we have practically a full house."

"It's six o'clock. I'll unlock the door, but you don't have to stay, Morgan, if you have things to do."

"I'll stay. You probably have work you'd like to finish today."

"I don't have anything urgent, and according to Mr. Bentley, it wouldn't hurt for me to practice being social."

Morgan put her hands on her hips. "Is Ethan getting on your nerves? Shane's getting on mine." She exhaled as she dropped her arms to her side and shook them. "I'm ready to be nice; you can open the door now."

Jenna chuckled as she copied Morgan's arm shake. "Okay, nice it is."

When Jenna unlocked and opened the door, Petra strode in with a bottle of red wine and hurried to the drink table. She had changed from her hot pink blouse to a long-sleeved bright yellow sweater with a white collared shirt underneath her sweater. She carried her red and black striped poncho in one hand, and her shiny red purse in the other, and dropped both of them on a table on her way to the sideboard.

While she opened the bottle, Petra said, "I can't tell you how excited I am to have such an inspiring setting for the club's meeting. The former coordinator had planned a change of venue for the club this year and knew someone from Paisley who suggested the Peach Blossom Retreat. I'm a big believer in personal recommendations."

Lucille, Susan, and Ivy stood in the dining room doorway and glanced around. Susan was the oldest of the three and used a cane for balance as she walked.

Ivy had pulled her blonde hair back into a low ponytail and wore an olive green shirt and a brown suede skirt that skimmed the tops of her ankle dress boots with two-inch heels; she carried two bottles of white wine.

Petra motioned for them to join her. "I have a bottle of red wine open, if you'd care to try it."

"We prefer white wine." Lucille sniffed as they entered the dining room.

While Ivy opened a bottle of white wine, Susan examined the appetizers. "This is more food than I expected for appetizers, and it looks delicious." She smiled as she put a sausage ball and two crab cake bites on a plate. "I think I'm going to go home a few pounds heavier after this weekend."

"Pick a table; I'll bring you a glass of wine," Ivy said.

Susan carried her plate to the nearest table then sat facing the door. "I can watch all the action from here."

Petra carried her plate and glass of wine to Susan's table. "May I join you? I'm Petra, the new coordinator."

"Of course; I remember you from last year. I'm Susan."

While Susan and Petra chatted, Ivy joined them. Lucille glowered then sat next to Ivy.

Vera and Ralph came into the dining room. She glared at Petra then filled a small plate with appetizers, chips, and dip while Ralph opened a bottle of wine and poured two glasses.

Vera marched to the table and sat next to Lucille then purposely put her purse with the brand name showing on the chair between her and Petra. Jenna rolled her eyes.

When Stan and Brittany strolled into the room, Lucille sneered; Morgan and Jenna exchanged glances.

While Stan opened a bottle of wine, Morgan leaned close to Jenna and whispered, "Wine? I bought a new one for us to try."

Jenna nodded and then strolled to the appetizer side board and examined the choices. She put a crab cake bite on a plate and sat at the empty table nearest to the kitchen door.

Morgan returned from the kitchen with a glass half-filled with wine and handed it to Jenna before she consolidated the two appetizer trays and carried the empty tray to the kitchen.

After Stan poured two glasses of wine, he handed one to Brittany and then joined Ralph at the appetizer table.

Brittany bit her lip as she turned and scanned the room. Jenna smiled and motioned for Brittany to join her.

"Thanks, Jenna." Brittany exhaled as she sat. "Our room is beautiful. I shouldn't have been surprised by the peach blossoms on the coverlet, but I was. I felt like I'd fallen into a portal and back into simpler, elegant times. I told Stan I'd love for the two of us to visit again in the early fall when the leaves are changing; I'll bet it's beautiful here."

"It really is."

While they chatted, Petra rose to add a splash more wine to her glass then joined them.

Jenna leaned to stretch her back and slowly scanned the room. While Stan talked, Ralph nodded, but his attention was on Vera's table. When he shifted his gaze toward Petra, Jenna did the same and smiled at Petra, who sat across the table from her.

"It is so nice to meet you, Brittany," Petra said. "What are your plans while your Stan and the rest of us scour the branches of ancestral trees?"

"I have a long list, but at the top is the peach orchard tour, so in a way, I'll be researching trees too."

Petra tittered. "You are absolutely delightful; I'm so glad you're here."

Petra's phone chimed. "It's time to head toward the restaurant; I'll let the rest know."

Petra rose and strode to the table where the other women were chatting.

Vera glared when Petra interrupted them.

Petra smiled. "Are you ready to wrap up and leave for the restaurant? Does anyone need a ride or directions?"

"We could hardly get lost in that jerkwater town, and Ralph is our designated driver." Vera sniffed. "We're not in a rush."

Petra smiled. "I'll see you when you arrive then. It's first come, first served as far as seating is concerned, and it might be a little cozy, but the restaurant assured me we'll have enough chairs for everyone."

After Petra left, the women at the table exchanged glances, and Stan winked at Brittany as he strode to her side.

"I enjoyed our visit, Jenna." Brittany rose from her seat, and she and Stan left.

Chapter Four

"Shouldn't we leave so we can sit together?" Ivy asked.

Vera snorted as she patted her hair. "Petra said there would be enough seats for everyone."

Ralph headed toward the door. "I'll start the car's engine, so it will be warm when you're ready to leave."

Ivy furrowed her brow and tugged at her ponytail then rose. "I left my coat upstairs; I'll meet you all at the car."

After Lucille pushed back from the table and rose, she slipped on her coat and helped Susan with hers.

Vera's eyes were wide as they left. She glanced at the empty table and then rushed out of the dining room.

Morgan giggled. "I came in to check on the trays at just the right time. That Petra is slick, isn't she?"

Jenna smiled. "It definitely was a beautiful sight to see how quickly she cleared the dining room. Anyone else would have announced it was time to leave, and no one would have budged for another half hour."

"I'll add that cool technique of mentioning first come, first served, to my tool box," Morgan said.

"What are your plans for this evening?" Jenna cleared the tables and changed the tablecloths for fresh ones.

"I thought we could go off duty and enjoy a glass of wine with our supper of appetizers. We know Shane and probably Eithan will show up for food." Morgan gathered the dishes and trays to take to the kitchen.

Jenna asked, "Are you going to tell me what's bothering you before we have company?"

Morgan muttered, "It's no big deal. I'll set up the coffee for tomorrow."

"Good; then the dining room will be ready for breakfast, and we can relax in the kitchen with a sip of wine while you tell me about it."

"You get really pushy sometimes; you know that?" Morgan grumbled.

Jenna rolled her eyes. "You should talk. I'll pour the wine while you set up the coffee."

When Morgan returned from the dining room, she joined Jenna at the kitchen table. Morgan picked up her glass and took a sip. "I wanted to try a new wine, but I just stood frozen in front of the wall of wine bottles because I couldn't decide which one to buy. A woman appeared next to me and pointed to this wine and told me it was her favorite. Do you believe in wine angels? I think that's what she was."

"What would the wine angel say about your problem?"

Morgan sighed. "She would tell me to quit keeping it to myself."

She took a big gulp of wine. "Shane asked me to marry him."

Jenna furrowed her brow. "And of course you..."

Morgan slammed her fist on the table. "What could I say? I didn't say anything because he was just joking." Morgan's eyes welled up. "It was a cruel joke."

Jenna stared at her. "How could the kindest and most considerate man on the planet joke about marriage?"

"I know; that's what makes it so terrible." Morgan's tears spilled over onto her cheeks. "So maybe he wasn't kidding, but our families are exactly alike, and I can't face a big wedding. Both families will want things to go their way, and Shane will want to be married in the barn, and it will be horrible. The families will gang up on us and plan the most extravagant wedding and reception in the history of civilization."

"What if you and Shane get married in the barn, and your families plan separate parties for you?"

"Two receptions? That's worse than one big messy wedding."

"I agree it was a terrible idea. What if you and Shane come up with your own plan?"

Morgan gulped down her wine and covered her mouth as she hiccupped. "Shane would say we should elope by running away to the barn."

Jenna paused as a car came up the driveway. "He's here. I'll get a fire going in the fireplace. I'll listen for Ethan, and we'll wait for you in the living room."

When Jenna opened the kitchen door to go to the living room, she met Shane who came in from the back door.

"Where's Morgan?" Shane asked. "Is she still mad at me?"

"She's waiting for you in the kitchen. Take your chances."

"Hope it's not an ambush," Shane mumbled.

After she had a small blaze going in the fireplace, Jenna sat in her yellow chair.

"People are a mess, aren't they, Nettie?"

"Everybody except us, right?" Ethan stood in the doorway.

The chimes on the porch jingled, and the shadows from the fire danced around Nettie's portrait as the glow from the fire lit up her blue eyes.

You could have warned me, Nettie.

The wind whistled through the eaves and the chimes jingled louder.

"I didn't hear your truck. You sneaked up on me." Jenna turned her glare from Nettie to Ethan.

Ethan chuckled as he strode to the fireplace and held out his hands for warmth. "I left my truck here when Shane and I went into town. Have you heard anything from Adrienne?"

"Not yet, but I suspect she'll call me in the morning."

Ethan sat in the blue chair that was next to the yellow chair. He patted the yellow chair's arm, and Jenna put her hand on his.

He smiled as he held her hand. "I've often wondered about these two chairs that seem to be outside the conversation circle arrangement of the rest of the room. Your placement wasn't accidental was it? Was the blue chair a companion to Nettie's yellow chair?"

"I think it was her husband's chair. I think they were close friends and enjoyed each other's company. Can you imagine a party with the room full of people, and Nettie and Henry sitting together while they commented on the antics of their guests?"

Ethan scanned the room. "That makes sense. This corner is dark and secluded, and the perfect observation point with the lights low and the fireplace commanding the attention of the room. They would have the advantage of being virtually invisible and definitely would have heard and seen more than their guests realized."

Jenna leaned back and watched the fire as the flames died down and the wood glowed as it dropped embers in the firebox.

"Shall I add more wood?" Ethan asked.

"Thank you; the guests will enjoy the warmth when they come in later."

While Ethan added three more small logs, he asked, "How did today go with the East Coast Genealogy Club?"

"They certainly have plenty of internal drama for a club that should be boring, given their theme of genealogy."

Ethan side-glanced at her. "That doesn't sound good."

"I might be less tolerant than usual because of all the extra catering tasks we have this weekend that I hadn't expected to take on."

Ethan turned in his chair and brushed away a loose stand of hair from Jenna's forehead. "Sounds stressful."

"It is, but talking about it helps, and Morgan sees the same drama, so it's comforting that it isn't just me."

Ethan gazed at her. "Let me know if it becomes too much, and I'll tell Katy, Darlene, and Layla to toss out every single one of them."

Jenna giggled. "They'd do it. It would almost be worth it to watch."

Ethan smiled. "I love it when you laugh. Did you know your entire face lights up?"

Jenna felt her cheeks warm. She returned his smile and fanned her face with her hand. "You're making me blush."

Ethan ran his fingertips down her cheek to her mouth and leaned forward.

"Ahem." Morgan stood in the doorway.

Ethan winked at Jenna and whispered, "Is she still there?"

"Yes, I'm still here. Come to the kitchen; are you hungry? We can eat and talk. Shane has news. Nice fire, by the way."

"Thank you. I added the extra wood," Ethan said.

Jenna rolled her eyes and elbowed him.

"Ouch." Ethan put his arm around Jenna as they headed toward the kitchen. "I suppose I could mention Jenna helped a bit by starting the fire with the kindling I cut."

"You're incorrigible," Jenna said.

"Thank you for noticing," Ethan said.

"Any time."

Morgan shook her head.

When they walked into the kitchen, Shane beamed as he stood behind the counter with the appetizers arranged on trays in front of him.

"We can talk after we eat," Morgan said.

Jenna picked up a crab cake bite and popped it into her mouth. "I ate. You can talk now."

Shane chuckled. "I asked Morgan to marry me last night."

Morgan jumped in. "But my mind immediately jumped to the wedding our families would want, and I freaked."

"You weren't that bad, honey," Shane said.

"Yes, she was." Jenna picked up another crab cake.

Morgan glared. "We would love for our wedding to be at the barn, but I don't have the energy to cater a reception for an enormous crowd, and with our families, any attempt or even a suggestion of trimming the number of invitations would cause a big ruckus and hurt feelings. We'd have to go into hiding."

Shane smiled. "You're absolutely right, honey, but I have a solution."

Jenna cocked her head. *I wonder if he brought a draft.*

She glanced at Ethan, and he squeezed her hand. *He's probably thinking the same thing.*

"There is no solution." Morgan's voice cracked.

"I have a cousin who is a talented wedding planner. We'll turn everything over to her. She's especially skilled at running interference with opinionated mothers."

Morgan exhaled. "We can eat now."

Jenna filled four glasses with sweet tea, and Ethan set them on the table. Morgan moved the appetizers to the middle of the kitchen table, and they all sat down.

While they ate, Jenna asked, "What about a date for the wedding?"

"We'll have to talk to my cousin to check her availability first," Shane said.

Morgan sipped her tea then set down her glass. "I was thinking New Year's Eve."

"My accountant's heart loves the idea, but isn't that a short amount of time to plan an event for the number of people you expect to attend?" Jenna asked.

Morgan shrugged. "We'll see what Shane's cousin says."

"You'll still have some decisions you'll want to make, like flowers and colors," Jenna said.

"That's easy; we'll stick with the Peach Blossom theme."

"That's brilliant." Shane sipped his tea. "How was your day?"

Ethan pursed his lips and shook his head at Shane.

Shane furrowed his brow and cocked his head. "Did I say something wrong?"

Jenna and Morgan laughed.

***

After they ate and cleaned up the kitchen, Morgan said, "Follow me home, Shane. I'll fill you in after I change into soft pants and an over-sized T-shirt."

While Shane and Morgan headed for the back door, Ethan asked, "Are you going to your cottage now?"

"I'd like to check the fireplace first to make sure we won't have any flareups."

"I'll take care of the fire then walk with you to your cottage."

When they went outside, the dark sky was clear. The stars twinkled, and the moon was bright. As they strolled to the cottage holding hands, the dry grass crunched under their feet. Katy darted into the woods while a barred owl hooted.

"It will be even colder tonight with no cloud cover," Jenna said. "I love the gas fireplace Mr. Moore insisted I would need in the cottage. He was right."

"Are you going to be working tonight?"

"I do have some things I'd like to catch up on, but I think I'll turn on the fireplace, change into soft pants and a warm shirt, and read."

Ethan smiled. "Good."

Jenna froze at the sound of a scream and grabbed onto Ethan's arm. "Did you hear that? Something or someone screamed, and it sounded like it came from the path to the orchard."

"It sounded like a predator caught a rabbit to me," Ethan said.

Jenna whistled for Katy, and Katy dashed to her from the back of the cottage. Jenna exhaled. "I'm glad the predator wasn't Katy."

When they reached the cottage, Jenna asked, "Would you like to come in for a few minutes?"

Ethan smiled. "I'd love it, but I think you have a rough weekend ahead of you. Can I have a raincheck for Sunday night?"

"Make it Monday, and I'll cook dinner."

"I'm available on Sunday and Monday; sounds great."

Jenna rolled her eyes. "Pick one."

"Sunday for a debriefing." Ethan leaned down and kissed her. "And then Monday for a meal that's not an appetizer."

"That was pretty smooth." Jenna returned his kiss then unlocked her door. "Good night, Ethan."

Katy dashed inside. After Jenna joined her and locked the door, she listened while Ethan strode away. When his truck engine roared into life, she gave Katy a snack and set up the coffee maker to go on automatically in the morning.

After she changed into her favorite old sweatpants and oversized T-shirt she picked up the book she had started reading two nights earlier and sat in her comfortable chair by the front window.

Chapter Five

A cramp in her leg, a crick in her neck, and a bright light in her face woke Jenna. She groaned and sat up in the chair where she had fallen asleep.

My feet are freezing. Why did I pull off my socks?

She groaned again when she looked at her phone. *Four o'clock. Too early to get up, but too late to get any sleep.*

When Jenna picked up her phone and rose, Katy twitched but didn't wake up. Jenna set an alarm on her phone for six, turned off the lamp next to her chair, and went into her bedroom.

She flopped face down onto her bed then flipped to her back. *I'm too cold; I can't sleep.*

Jenna changed into her flannel pajamas and put on a pair of wool socks. She grabbed her pillow and the quilt from her bed and went into the living room. After she turned on her gas fireplace, she wrapped herself in the quilt and lay back on her sofa and stuffed the pillow under her head. She gazed at the glow of the rock wool in the fireplace, and her eyes grew heavy.

The alarm woke her at six, and she opened the back door for Katy. Katy patrolled the yard and chased a squirrel to a tree then returned for breakfast.

While Katy ate, Jenna took her shower. Her phone rang while she rinsed off the soapy bubbles.

Morgan was breathless. "Did you hear? It's been all over the morning news."

"What news?" Jenna glared at the puddle she was making as she stood naked in the middle of the living room.

"Early this morning, a sheriff's deputy found the chef dead in his car at an abandoned gas station in the next county. He had hooked up a hose to his exhaust and stuck it into his car. No note or anything. I'll be at the inn as soon as I get dressed."

Jenna returned to the bathroom, turned off the shower, grabbed a towel, and hurried back to the living room.

While she mopped up the pool of water, her phone rang again.

Ellie was almost unintelligible as she sobbed. "We just heard my brother died early this morning. We're absolutely devastated. I'm sorry, but we won't be there today or tomorrow."

Ellie hung up.

Jenna stared at her phone then called Morgan. "Ellie called me; we're on our own this weekend."

"Oh, man. I'd forgotten the chef was her brother. I'll be there in half an hour. Are you going to call Darlene?"

"She's probably already at the inn. I'll see you when you get here."

Jenna shivered as she took the wet towel she'd used to clean up her puddle to the bathroom and hung it up then grabbed a clean towel and dried herself.

After she threw on her clothes, she and Katy dashed to the inn.

When they hurried into the kitchen, Darlene gave Katy a bite of sausage then narrowed her eyes at Jenna. "You've obviously heard about the chef. His family is devastated. I have a shopping list for the dinners tonight and tomorrow night, and the grocery store opens at seven. Nora will be here at nine to help me cook and then will leave right after lunch to pick up her granddaughter. We'll cook both meals today, so Nora will have tomorrow free."

Darlene set a cup of coffee on the counter. "You might need this."

Jenna exhaled as she reached for the cup. "How did you know?"

"You're wearing a short-sleeved shirt, no coat, and you didn't brush your hair."

Jenna snort-laughed then took a big gulp of hot coffee. "Maybe I'm going for a new scary look."

Darlene nodded. "So far, so good."

Jenna sipped her coffee. "We had already arranged with Petra to serve lunch and snacks at the barn, and host breakfast, happy hour, and dinner at the inn, so there's no change as far as the club is concerned."

"Good; them getting all riled up would mean more work for us, and we sure don't need that."

Jenna tossed down the rest of her coffee and snatched up the list. "I'll brush my hair and put on a warmer shirt.

The grocery store should be open by the time I get there. Tell Morgan where I went."

Jenna stroked Katy's neck and face then raced back to her cottage. After she brushed her hair and changed into a long-sleeved shirt, she added a flannel shirt as an extra layer and put on her coat.

On her way into town, Jenna scanned the sky and frowned at the dark clouds in the west. *Bad weather is the last thing we need today; maybe it will miss us.*

Once inside the grocery store, she went aisle by aisle as she marked items off her list. While she stood in front of the case with cheese, two women at the nearby luncheon meat case were whispering.

Jenna carefully examined the choices of cheese then compared prices. *Nothing catches my attention like whispering.*

"...not an accident at all," one woman whispered.

"I heard he double-crossed that sketchy out-of-town outfit he used to work for and owed them money, so he took the easy way out."

"Well, I heard he staged the whole thing to gain some sympathy, but it didn't work out like he expected."

"He never was as smart as he thought he was." The second woman pushed her cart toward the milk case.

Jenna moved on to the next item on her list and by the time she was ready to check out, she had filled a cart so high she had to lean to the side to see what was in front of her.

After she paid the cashier, the bagger pushed the heavy cart across the parking lot and loaded the sacks of groceries into her car.

Jenna glanced at her phone. *Eight o'clock. It took longer than I expected.*

She sent a text to Darlene. "On my way back."

Darlene replied. "About time."

Jenna smiled and headed toward the inn.

When Jenna arrived, she spotted Ethan's truck and Shane's car. *Maybe I can get help.*

She sent Morgan a text. "I'm here. Can you help unload groceries?"

Ethan and Shane came out of the back door. Ethan wore a green, long-sleeved collared shirt, and Shane wore a white shirt with a tie and a khaki sports jacket. Jenna smiled. *They're dressed to work at the barn.*

She glanced down at her jeans, Western boots, pale yellow T-shirt under her favorite blue-and-cream plaid flannel shirt. *Guess I'm dressed to work at the barn in my signature style too.*

"Morgan sent us," Shane said.

"You can go inside; we've got this," Ethan added.

When she went into the kitchen, Morgan said, "Breakfast went well, mostly because Darlene made the coffee extra strong on purpose. I told her about their complaining and passive aggressive sniping. Darlene said she'd give them something to complain about. Katy was a hit, of course. She got lots of pets. I have a feeling the kid gloves will definitely come off tonight, which might be entertaining unless it turns into a brawl. We boxed up the snacks for today; they're already in Shane's truck. Are you going with me?"

Shane and Ethan carried in the grocery sacks.

"Is that it?" Darlene asked.

"That's it." Ethan set the last sack on the counter. "I told you we could make it in one load."

Jenna and Morgan exchanged a glance and giggled.

"What's funny?" Shane asked.

Morgan shrugged as she put on her coat.

Darlene pointed to a plastic covered bowl on the counter. "Take that with you, Morgan; it's the leftover pastries from breakfast."

Morgan smiled. "You're always thinking."

Jenna asked, "Are you leaving now? I want to help Darlene put the groceries away."

"Come as soon as you can, then; I'm sure Petra's already at the barn."

"I'll help with the groceries, and then you and I can go to the barn," Ethan said.

Shane glanced at Ethan, who gave a slight nod. "Are you ready, Morgan?"

Morgan smiled. "As ready as I'll ever be. At least Vera won't be at the meeting; maybe her fans will settle down since she won't be there for them to impress."

While Jenna handed the refrigerated items to Darlene to put away, Darlene said, "People are saying the chef did himself in, but don't you believe it. He thought too much of himself to do anything like that."

"Maybe it was an accident," Jenna said.

"No, that wasn't his style at all. Anything he did was to his benefit."

When they had everything put away, Jenna asked, "Is there anything else I can do for you before I leave for the barn?"

Darlene raised an eyebrow. "Leave Katy with me."

"She'd love it. See you later."

After Jenna climbed into the truck, she said, "You don't have to spend the entire day at the barn."

"I won't." Ethan turned on the engine. "Shane and I worked out a schedule."

Jenna bit her lip. *I'd suggest a schedule to Morgan, but that would just be inviting another fiasco.*

She scanned the visitor parking lot as they drove by. "I thought more people would have ridden over together."

"Shane said they aren't a chummy group."

As Jenna and Ethan strolled into the barn from the back door, Jenna spotted Morgan sitting at a table in the dark corner near the back door. Morgan smiled and finger-waved at Jenna.

Jenna strolled to the empty table that was near the coffee and sat down.

Petra rose from her seat and strode to the front of the room as she clapped her hands three times to call the meeting to order.

When the conversations continued, she clapped again three times, and the room quieted.

"I'll begin with our reminder that we are here to discuss genealogy. We will help each other fill in any gaps we've found in our family trees, but our major topic of discussion will be on one of the interesting cases that our members have uncovered. Any other topics that are not related to genealogy will be saved for happy hour. We have a new member this year. Chris is from Maryland."

Petra motioned toward the muscular man with closely clipped reddish brown hair and the physique and tan of a beachside lifeguard. He sat at a table with another man and woman who were staying at the hotel.

The second man was middle-aged and slightly overweight. He had brown hair and a cowlick, and his scraggly mustache couldn't hide the scar at the corner of this mouth. *According to the member roster Petra sent us, that's Arthur.*

The woman's hair was dark blonde and lightly streaked with gray. She was slender and what Jenna's grandma would call delicate-boned, but as she surreptitiously scanned the room, Jenna raised her eyebrows. *That must be Tisha, the investigator Felicia and Wanda talked about in the café. It would be easy to underestimate her.*

Chris remained seated as he waved his hand. "Thank you for the welcome, Petra."

"We always start our meeting with a warm up. We'll go around the room, so each member can share a brief summary of their progress on their family tree search since last year. Notice I emphasized brief." Petra tittered. "Susan, would you like to go first?"

Susan nodded. "I was making excellent progress in tracking down my father's side of the family until I came up against records that had been destroyed in a county courthouse fire in the 1800s. I did find a second cousin, but I'm less familiar with that branch, so I didn't make the progress I had hoped I would."

"That was smart to shift to look for cousins," Stan said. "How did you find second cousin?"

"It wasn't easy, but..."

Wanda interrupted her. "You're supposed to be brief. It's my turn."

"Let her finish her thought, Wanda," Stan said.

Wanda snorted. "You don't make the rules."

"We all agreed to the rules," Petra said. "Our number one rule is to be polite. Finish your thought, Susan."

Susan glared at Wanda. "I went back two generations and found a brother who had moved to Alabama where his wife had family."

Petra smiled. "Well done, Susan. Lucille, you're next; would you tell us about your progress?"

Lucille strode to the front of the room.

Jenna sighed. *I wish I had a book.* She glanced at Morgan who was wearing sunglasses and a wide-brimmed sunhat. *She's napping.*

She shifted her gaze to Ethan, and he raised his eyebrows and pointed to the back door.

Jenna quietly picked up her jacket and met him at the door.

After they were outside, Ethan turned his back to the wind and hugged her. "It was time for a breath of frigid air, wasn't it?"

Jenna leaned against him. "Sure was. Thank you for blocking the wind. I should have worn my wool socks, though."

After a few minutes, Ethan said, "We should go back in before your feet are ice blocks."

"Too late." Jenna smiled. "Thanks for the break."

When they returned inside, Jenna glanced at Morgan. *She hasn't moved. I'm jealous.*

Ethan squeezed Jenna's hand before she tiptoed to her seat.

Tisha said, "Lucille, isn't that the same story the coordinator told two years ago?"

Lucille's face reddened, and the veins in her temple pulsated. She gritted her teeth. "No, it wasn't; are you accusing me of plagiarism?"

Tisha shrugged. "You said it, not me."

Lucille clenched her fists and shouted, "You don't know what you're talking about."

Petra jumped up and strode to the front. "We'll take this offline."

She put her arm around Lucille's shoulder. "We'll talk later, Lucille. No one thinks you were plagiarizing anyone's story."

Tisha snorted, and Petra glared at her as she guided Lucille to her seat between Susan and Wanda.

After Lucille was seated with her back to Tisha, Petra returned to the front. "Let's shift away from our family research for now. Chris, don't you have a story to get our investigative genealogy juices flowing?" She motioned for Chris to join her.

Everyone clapped politely except Wanda and Lucille who exchanged sneers.

As Chris strode to the front, his impeccable posture and his purposeful stride reminded Jenna of Tom. *Military.*

Petra shook his hand then narrowed her eyes at Felicia who paled.

While he told the story of the mysterious disappearance of a toddler twenty-five years earlier,

Lucille scrolled through her phone as Arthur wandered past their table with his cup of water. Lucille showed her phone to Wanda.

Wanda's eyes widened, and she showed the phone to Ivy. After Ivy frowned and handed the phone back to Lucille, Wanda and Lucille whispered and giggled while Chris was speaking.

"I read about that case," Ralph said. "She was the heir to a large inheritance, but all the money went to a distant relative after the girl's parents were killed in a crash outside of Savannah. The relative owned a small contracting company that boomed after the inflow of all her money."

Lucille put down her phone and stared at Ralph. Wanda furrowed her brow.

Chris nodded. "When his company grew beyond the point where it needed his expertise at the helm, he retired but still owned much of the stock. When he and the chairman of the board died in a small plane crash in the mountains of North Carolina, he had no apparent living heirs. His stock was placed into a trust managed by his lawyer."

Wanda spoke out. "Doesn't sound like much of a case."

Chris raised an eyebrow. "You're right; however, a rival company started a rumor the toddler was alive and there was a coverup."

"Wasn't that a movie?" Felicia asked.

Chris nodded. "The rival company was the major investor in that movie."

"Dirty politics," Stan muttered.

"Was it true?" Ralph asked.

"According to the movie, the detective who had worked on the girl's disappearance retired early, but stayed unofficially on the case. He eventually found her through DNA records," Felicia said.

"I saw that movie," Susan said. "The detective discovered her DNA matched with the man who owned a small contracting company."

"Well, then, there isn't any case, is there?" Ivy asked.

Chris met her gaze. "The movie was complete fiction."

Lucille snorted. "So, why are talking about this?"

Chris smiled. "There was never any attempt to verify the connection between the girl's family and the man who inherited the money."

Stan narrowed his eyes. "Has anyone tried?"

Chris shook his head. "Nobody thought of it because of the movie."

"What happened to the company?" Ralph asked.

"The company collapsed from the adverse publicity, and a rival company bought them out for pennies on the dollar," Chris said.

"Thank you, Chris; that was very interesting." Petra rose.

"Did anyone else have a case for us to investigate?"

"I do," Tisha said.

"I don't think we need to hear another one. I make a motion to move forward with Chris's case," Ivy said.

"Wait. I had one to bring up, too," Felicia said. "It's about someone who went into a witness protection program."

"Why don't we take a break first?" Petra said. "A stretch and more hot coffee will keep our circulation going."

Jenna glanced at the back door. Ethan scowled and had his arms crossed.

While the group gathered around the coffee pot and jostled one another for the pastries, Jenna strolled to the back door where Ethan continued to scowl.

She squared off in front of him. "I need a short walk."

Ethan exhaled. "I do too."

As they strolled hand-in-hand toward the path to the inn, Ethan said, "Now I remember why I love heavy equipment and being outside. These people are exhausting."

"No kidding."

"Why are you here?" he growled. "This is Morgan's job as the operations manager, and you know she's perfectly capable of handling it."

That's what the grumpy look was all about.

"Yes, she is, but name one thing that hasn't gone wrong so far with this event."

Ethan snorted. "You got me there."

As they turned back toward the barn, Jenna said, "You don't have to stick around. I'll let you know if anything comes up."

Ethan chuckled. "Sure. Name one thing that hasn't gone wrong so far."

"You're quoting me?" Jenna asked.

Ethan shrugged. "It's hard to argue with the expert."

Jenna rolled her eyes. "I walked straight into that one."

Ethan stopped and put his hands on her shoulders then lightly kissed her.

He gently nudged her. "For a change, it was you, not me; thank you for letting me win one."

As they continued toward the barn, Jenna felt a warm feeling in her heart that she thought she'd never feel again. The wind rustled the treetops. *Told you.*

Jenna smiled.

"What are you smiling about?" Ethan asked when they reached the barn.

Jenna touched her still-tingling lips with her fingertips. "It's a good day, after all."

Ethan beamed as they went inside.

Morgan was near the sideboard; she glanced at them then raised an eyebrow.

When Jenna joined her, Morgan whispered, "These people are worse than first-graders. I never thought I'd sympathize so much with my mother, who was a teacher. If I told her she must have been a saint, she'd be positive I'd lost my mind, but that's exactly what I think."

Jenna nodded. "Are you ready for your turn for a break?"

"I'll sit in the back for a while. We need books here for us to read."

"I wish we'd thought of it earlier. I'll ask Layla to bring a few from the shelves in the living room. Do you have a preference?"

"Whatever Layla brings will be perfect."

Jenna sent a text to Layla, then sat at the table where Morgan had been sitting while Morgan grabbed her jacket, strode toward the back door, and whispered to Ethan.

As Morgan left, Petra said, "Shall we resume our meeting? I believe we had a motion on the floor. Would you repeat your motion, Ivy?"

"That's not fair," Felicia said. "I wanted to talk about the woman who was undercover at a company and turned them in for money laundering then went into the witness protection program."

"Did you want to amend the motion?" Petra asked.

Felicia glanced around for someone else to speak. "Yes. I make a motion to vote between Chris's suggestion and mine."

"Do I hear a second?"

Lucille said, "I second."

"All in favor, raise your hand."

Petra nodded. "It's unanimous, so we'll vote on Chris's story or Felicia's. All in favor of Felicia's, raise your hand."

Felicia, Lucille, and Wanda raised their hands.

"Chris's story?"

Everyone else raised their hands.

"We've selected Chris's story for our competition. If you'd like to participate, write your best story using the information Chris has given us, and be prepared to read your story tomorrow after dinner. After everyone who has written a story has read theirs, we will vote to determine who has written the most impressive tale. We have a wonderful prize for the winner this year; if you don't write, you can't win. Questions?"

Petra scanned the room while the members shook their heads.

"There are no questions, so we'll resume working. I'll set the timer for an hour, then we'll take a stretch break."

Felicia crossed her arms and pouted while everyone else opened their laptops.

Except for the sound of tapping keyboards, and the occasional scrape of a chair as someone rose to stretch or get another cup of coffee, the room was silent.

When the timer chimed, Petra said, "Five minute break."

Stan rose from his chair. "That hour went fast, but I'm stiff. Is it still chilly outside, Jenna?"

"I was glad I wore my jacket when I went out."

Stan nodded then put on his windbreaker and headed for the door.

"I'll go with you, Stan," Chris said.

Lucille walked to the sideboard with her coffee cup and refilled it. After she picked up a napkin and wrapped it around her cup, Lucille returned to her table and whispered to Wanda. Wanda shook her head and tugged at Lucille's sleeve. Lucille sat down.

As Jenna rose, she heard the rumble of a motorcycle as it roared up the driveway then parked next to the barn.

When she turned toward the back of the room, Ethan smiled as he opened the back door, and Layla burst inside.

After Layla set down her backpack on the nearest table and tossed her leather jacket over a chair, she removed her helmet and shook her head. She pushed back the mop of wild, untamable red hair from her face with her forearm. Her tattoos on her upper arms were a sharp contrast to her no-nonsense, dark-framed glasses, and her shirt buttons strained against the fabric in a constant battle to pop free.

When Jenna joined them, Ethan said, "Shane picked up Morgan, and they left just a few minutes ago. Morgan said she wouldn't be long."

"I stopped at the inn before I came here and have a few books in my backpack," Layla said. "Darlene wants Ethan to pick up lunch about eleven-thirty, and she caught me up on what's happened so far; are you okay?"

"I am, especially since our entire team is here."

"I have a paper due on Monday and haven't done anything on it because I've been too busy. I just need an hour with my laptop, and I'll have a complete outline, and then I can write the paper this afternoon and edit tomorrow, so this is perfect for me. Where's the best place for me to sit?"

"The table where you put your backpack is probably best; you'll have a clear bird's-eye view of the room but won't have to listen to catty, irritating whispers."

"Thank you." Layla opened her backpack and pulled out five books. "I grabbed these books from the shelf where guests leave books for others to read. If you don't see anything you like, you'll have to upgrade your clientele." She grinned as she handed the books to Jenna.

"You're a lifesaver; thank you."

Layla scanned the room. "I know her." She strode across the room to Tisha.

Jenna stared as Layla spoke to Tisha, and then the two of them laughed and shook hands. They strolled to a corner away from everyone where they engaged in an animated discussion.

Petra clapped her hands. "Our break is over. Ivy, would you please call in our members who went outside?"

Layla joined Jenna. "She runs a tight ship, doesn't she?" Layla whispered.

Jenna nodded. "I heard nobody else wanted the job when the previous coordinator retired."

"Tisha Holloway was the guest lecturer for our four-week session on investigations. Our professor told us we were lucky she was available because she's one of the best. She told me she remembered me because I asked excellent questions for clarity. Do I sound like I'm fangirling, because I am." Layla giggled.

"I could tell you were having a great conversation. I was dying to eavesdrop."

Layla chuckled. "I was so engrossed, I wasn't aware of what was going on around me. I asked her what she was doing here, and she said her dad's family had always claimed to be related to Doc Holliday. She thought joining a genealogy club would be the quickest way to prove or dispel it. She proved there was no link, but the former coordinator asked her to come to the meeting this one last time, so there would be some continuity of the group. Tisha thinks that's why Stan is here too."

"That's interesting."

Layla sat at her table, and Jenna grabbed a book and hurried to her table. While the East Coast Genealogy Club meeting resumed where they had left off, Jenna opened her book and read.

She was on chapter three when she felt a presence next to her.

Morgan leaned close to whisper. "I got a call from a former colleague who works at the hotel. I'll tell you what she said later. If you want to get some work done at the inn, Ethan will take you, and you can come back with him when he brings lunch. Shane's going to stay with me and Layla until after lunch."

Jenna noticed a folded sheet of paper on the floor near the coffee station. She picked it up and stuck it into her book to save her place.

"Can you take my book, so I don't forget it?" Jenna handed her book to Morgan who slipped it into her computer bag.

Ethan waited for Jenna at the back door. After they were in his truck, Jenna asked, "What are you going to do while I'm working?"

"Shane and I have a contract to build an office for a new doctor on the other side of town. I'm going to check with the crew this morning to make sure they will have everything they need for next week. Shane will follow up on any slips in delivery dates."

"You and Shane work surprisingly well together."

Ethan nodded. "We had a rough start, but we've worked out most of the major kinks. Mr. Moore has become our sounding board. He doesn't want to come out of retirement, but I'm glad he's still willing to share his expertise. He's also a talented negotiator. Shane and I have learned a lot from him. Maybe over time, we can pull him in as a third partner or our advisor. We'll see."

"It would be wonderful to see him again; I've missed him."

"I'll tell him."

After Ethan parked behind the inn, he said, ""Shane and I are supposed to meet with a client this afternoon at two. We've been talking about rescheduling it."

"Don't cancel your meeting. Morgan and Layla will be at the barn, and I'll be at the inn with Darlene. If Morgan was going to be alone, I'd be worried, but she and Layla will be fine." Jenna opened her door. "Let me know if you need more time at your job site because Darlene and Nora can help me load my car, and I can take lunch to the barn."

"I don't expect to be delayed, but I'll let you know if something comes up."

Jenna hopped out and smiled as she hurried to the back door. *He didn't shut me down for offering to jump in for him.*

She continued to smile as she went into the office. Nora waved and poked Darlene.

"Layla is still riding that motorcycle of hers. Did you notice? I told her she was too old to be a dare devil, and she laughed at me," Darlene growled.

Jenna furrowed her brow to keep from smiling. *Darlene has missed Layla.*

"And did you change Katy's food? She's been scratching at her face all morning. "

"I haven't changed her food at all."

Jenna kneeled down next to Katy and examined her face. "It's little red like she's been scratching it, but I don't see a rash. We'll keep an eye on her."

Jenna hurried into her office to check the registrations; before she opened her laptop, her phone rang. *It's Adrienne.*

Jenna crossed her fingers as she answered. "If this isn't good news, you've reached a recording. Beep."

Chapter Six

Adrienne chuckled. "You need to work on your beeping sound. You sounded a little mechanical."

"I was the lowest bidder," Jenna said.

Adriene laughed. "I reviewed Shane's plan; if he ever tires of being in a small town, send him our way. His plan is similar to what I envisioned when we talked about security earlier. I'm negotiating with a company we've used before. They're good and not too pricey. Does the system have to be installed right away? Is anyone in danger?"

"Shane and Ethan are hovering, so we're all quite safe."

"Good; I can get a better price if we aren't dealing with an emergency. I think it could be installed before next weekend."

"That doesn't sound bad at all."

"Are you and Ethan getting along?" Adrienne asked.

"Yes, why?" *Don't tell me you are asking for a friend.*

"There's been some friction there in the past, and Suzanne will ask me. Your lawyer is very nosy; did you know that? I'll probably get back to you before the end of the day for a contract for you to sign."

Adrienne hung up, and Jenna snickered. *Right, Suzanne wanted to know.*

After Jenna checked the online registration system, she strolled through the dining room and into the hallway to look for Wendy.

She heard Wendy humming in one of the upstairs guest rooms. After she climbed the stairs, she found Wendy in Vera and Ralph's room.

Wendy smiled when she saw Jenna. "After this room, I'll dust and vacuum the living room; everything else is done. No one has been here long enough yet to make a big mess other than the eight bottles of makeup scattered on the counter in this bathroom. I left it undisturbed because people are funny about someone else touching their things."

Jenna returned her smile. "Sounds smart to me. Our two couples will be here this afternoon around four o'clock, according to Morgan's notes."

"If you don't mind, I'd like to offer to help Darlene in the kitchen so Nora can spend the weekend with her granddaughter."

"That's really kind of you, and I'm certain Nora will appreciate it. Are you sure?"

Wendy's eyes twinkled. "Absolutely; it's my sneaky way to get a peek at some of Darlene's recipes, especially her warm goat cheese dip."

"That's brilliant."

As Jenna headed toward the kitchen, her phone buzzed a text from Ethan. "I'll be there in five minutes."

When she went into the kitchen, Darlene asked, "Where's Ethan?"

"On his way."

"The chili is in the slow cooker, but it's heavy, so he'll have to carry it to his truck. We have everything else packed and ready to go in a plastic bin that won't be too heavy for you to carry. It has everything you need for lunch and for the snack stuff except for drinks. We put them in a cooler with ice. You can refill the ice and drinks from the Peach Pit. Earlier this morning, Nora and I loaded extra drinks into the refrigerator at the Peach Pit and put two large bags of ice in the freezer there. I can pull the cooler out to the truck, but Ethan will have to lift it into the truck bed."

"I love how organized you are."

Darlene blushed and turned away without a word.

Is she pretending she didn't hear me?

Darlene opened the refrigerator then cleared her throat. "Thank you," she mumbled.

Jenna smiled. *Nora's been coaching her.*

Ethan hurried into the kitchen. "What's the plan?"

Darlene pointed at the large slow cooker. "That's for you. The drink cooler is on wheels, so I'll pull it to the truck, and Boss Lady will bring the plastic bin we packed."

"I can carry the bin and the chili," Ethan said.

"No, you can't. It's my bin because Darlene assigned it to me." Jenna sniffed.

Darlene growled, "Quit your flirting; we're on the clock here."

"Yes, ma'am." Ethan picked up the slow cooker, and Jenna, Darlene, and Katy followed him to the truck.

Ethan put the cooker on the back seat floor then lifted the cooler into the truck bed while Jenna put the bin on the back seat on her side of the truck.

"It's too cold out here." Darlene and Katy rushed inside.

After Ethan parked at the barn, Morgan and Shane came outside. Shane pulled the cooler to the barn while Ethan carried the slow cooker, and Morgan took the bin away from Jenna.

"You know that was assigned to me," Jenna hissed.

"It's my excuse to come outside. Run open the door for Shane and Ethan."

Jenna rushed past the two men and opened the door. Ethan raised his eyebrows as he passed her.

"Morgan needed an excuse to leave the barn for a few minutes," she whispered.

"Understood."

Morgan joined Jenna. "There's one more thing. Go outside with me for a second?"

When they stepped outside, Morgan said, "My friend at the hotel told me a couple of women were waiting for the elevator. One of them said something about unfasten, and the other one told her she was paranoid. My friend reads spy books, so she decided the first one actually said assassin. She hurried around the corner to see who it was, but the door on the elevator closed before she got there. I asked her if there were more women besides our three staying at the hotel, and she said yes. She probably completely misunderstood because she missed the context, and it's a long shot that it has anything to do with us, but I can't help but feel like it goes along with the rest of the odd circumstances around here. Anyway, it gave me the creeps. Let's go back inside; it's cold out here, and I need to get busy."

Jenna returned to her table while Morgan rushed to help Layla.

After Morgan and Layla set up lunch on the sideboard with all eyes on them, Morgan nodded at Petra.

Petra rose from her chair. "Thanks to the Peach Blossom Retreat team, we have a hot meal for our lunch on this blustery day. Put away your papers and computers so you can relax and enjoy your food. We scheduled forty-five minutes for our lunch, so there is no rush."

Felicia lifted the lid on the slow cooker, and her southern drawl intensified. "Oh, my word; it has beans. My family could afford meat, so we didn't have to put beans in our chili."

She put two large pieces of cornbread in her bowl then stopped for a bottle of water before she continued to her seat.

When Wanda sat next to her with her chili, Felicia wrinkled her nose and moved to a table near the front door.

So much for no special meals. Jenna glanced at Ethan, and he motioned for her to join him. She smiled as she strode away from the sideboard.

The two of them joined Morgan, Layla, and Shane at the table in the shadows.

Morgan whispered, "If we told Darlene what Felicia said about beans, there would be beans in everything, including the desserts."

"I'd laugh, except that's true," Jenna said.

"I've always heard that Texas chili is the chili with no beans. She doesn't sound like she's from Texas," Layla said.

"That's an interesting point. Do you think Felicia is the whistleblower in her witness protection story she wanted to tell?" Morgan asked.

"That doesn't make sense," Shane said. "Why would she want to blow her cover?"

Talk to her.

Jenna furrowed her brow. "I have a feeling..."

Jenna went to the sidebar and grabbed a bottle of water and a cookie then strolled to Felicia's table.

After she sat across from Felicia, Jenna said, "I agree with you about beans in chili. My mama's family was from east Texas, and we never had beans in our chili either."

Felicia nodded. "My daddy loved my mama's chili. Mama called us two peas in a pod. I'd never heard of Texas chili until I was in college. I always thought it was how chili was supposed to be made."

"You must have had a great family life growing up."

Felicia nodded. "I asked Mama about her chili, and she said that was the way her mama and her nana made chili. I've searched but didn't find any ties to Texas in our family. Mama always told me I took after my daddy, which is why he trusted me. I was proud to follow in his footsteps."

"That a wonderful story," Jenna said. "If I were you, I'd bring it up sometime. Speaking of stories, I was sorry you didn't get a chance to tell your story about the woman in the witness protection program."

"I really don't know much about it; I just thought it was intriguing."

"How did you learn about the story?"

Felicia bit her lip while she stared at the ceiling for a moment. "I overheard a brief discussion about a person going into the witness protection program at our meeting last year and was fascinated with the idea, so I dug into it. I didn't see who was talking or recognize the voices because we were at a club and there was a lot of background noise. In fact, because of the acoustics, I only caught snatches of the conversation and couldn't even tell if the voices were male or female. Toward the end of the discussion, one person said wouldn't it be something if the true story got out. The second person told them to be careful because too much speculation could be deadly."

Felicia put her hand near her face and bit her thumbnail. She lowered her hand and leaned back as she examined Jenna's face.

Jenna rose her eyebrows. *Only partially true, but a good cover story.* "Now that definitely adds an element of suspense to a great story. Did you do any research?"

Felicia's face brightened. "I actually did quite a bit. Are you interested? I can send you what I've found so far."

"I'd love it."

Felicia pulled out a thick manilla envelope from her oversized tote bag and handed it to Jenna. "This is my backup material; I take it everywhere I go in case I have down time for reading." She rolled her eyes. "I've been collecting it for a while, but I haven't had time to study it thoroughly. I'll send you copies of my research files that are more recent as soon as we get back on our computers. Do I just send it to the Peach Blossom Retreat?"

"That's perfect. I use that email for everything; it makes it so much simpler than trying to check three or four emails every day."

"That's smart. I do the same thing. I know people who have three or more email addresses, and all I can think is why?"

Jenna smiled. "I look forward to seeing what you have so far; I'll send you anything I find, but it may be after the holidays because we are coming up on our busy season."

"That's wonderful to hear. I'm glad your business is doing well."

When Jenna rose, Felicia put out her hand. "I'm really glad we talked; it's been important to me to find someone I could trust."

Jenna held her breath, and they shook hands.

Her mean girl personality is a mask; she's putting everything in order. Why? Jenna was lost in thought as she strolled back to Morgan's table.

Ethan startled her when he asked, "Can I get you some chili?"

He furrowed his brow. "Are you okay?"

"Sorry; I was thinking about Felicia. I can't have any chili because it turns out I'm a third generation no-beans-in-chili person," Jenna said.

Ethan chuckled. "We'll be taking the chili back to the inn. I'll have a bowlful for you to keep your strength up on the way there."

Jenna smiled. "I'd really appreciate that; I've been looking forward to having some chili since early this morning."

"So, what did you learn?" Layla asked.

"I'm not really sure, except I have a genealogy buddy now."

"I wasn't sure if I was supposed to grab a cookie and join you, but then you two looked like schoolmates catching up on the good old days," Morgan said. "You want to drop that manilla envelope in a bag? I have a spare Christmas gift bag in my computer bag."

"A Christmas gift bag? Sure." Jenna blinked.

Morgan opened her computer bag then handed the gift bag to Jenna. "Don't scoff. I hate to throw anything away."

Shane broke the rest of his cornbread into his chili. "I was ready for fireworks."

"Actually, so was I," Jenna said. "I need another cookie."

"I'll get it for you," Ethan said.

When he swaggered to the sideboard, Morgan and Layla exchanged a look. Jenna cleared her throat and glared at them. Morgan shrugged, and Layla giggled.

"We can pack up the chili and cornbread before their lunch break ends, so we won't be disruptive during their meeting. Ethan and I will take the leftovers back to the inn. Our new guests are supposed to arrive at the inn around four o'clock, but we all know how that goes," Jenna said.

Ethan returned with two cookies. "I figured you might want one for the road."

Jenna smiled. "My sweet tooth thanks you."

"The East Coast Genealogy meeting is scheduled to end at three, and from what we've seen of Petra so far, the meeting will end on time," Morgan said.

"I predict there won't be any socializing after the meeting is over," Shane said.

Layla added, "We will have everything cleaned up and ready for tomorrow by three thirty."

After they finished eating, Morgan said, "I'm glad we held back the afternoon snacks, because the cookies are gone. I'm ready to shut down the buffet."

Layla nodded. "Let's do it."

Ethan unplugged the slow cooker then carried it out to his truck. Shane rolled the drink cooker outside and drained the water.

After he brought the cooler back in, he asked, "Should I make a quick run to the Peach Pit for more ice and drinks?"

Morgan nodded.

Layla giggled. "Y'all still haven't come up for a name for the reception center?"

Morgan shrugged. "Actually, we did. Its official name is Peach Suite, with the play on words intended, but we still haven't completely adjusted. If we ever host a wedding, we'll have to practice saying Peach Suite."

"Wouldn't it help if you had a sign on the building?" Layla asked.

Jenna smiled. "You might want to keep that to yourself. Shane wants Ethan to hand-carve a sign. Ethan said the only thing he carves is a turkey at Thanksgiving. Negotiations are currently stalled."

Layla laughed.

When Ethan returned, Jenna asked, "What else needs to go out?"

"We're set," Morgan said.

"If you think of anything we forgot, let us know," Layla said.

Jenna raised her eyebrows.

Layla whispered, "You know; give us a sign."

Jenna coughed to keep from laughing, and Layla turned her back and strolled to the sideboard with her shoulders shaking.

Morgan peered at Jenna.

"Later," Jenna said.

"I'll hang around here and then meet you at the client's office a little before two, Ethan," Shane said.

"Are you ready, Jenna?"

Jenna picked up the gift bag. "Let's hit it."

As they strolled to the truck, Jenna said, "I think I understand hovering better. I was really reluctant to leave Morgan and Layla at the barn."

Ethan nodded. "I know you trust them, but I know how you feel too."

Jenna giggled. "I guess you do."

After they climbed into the truck, Ethan handed Jenna a bowl and a spoon. "Here's your chili."

"Thank you." Jenna took a bite. "This is delicious."

She finished the bowl before they reached the inn.

Ethan side-glanced at Jenna. "Were you implying I hover?"

She smiled. "Sure was."

He sniffed. "You're entitled to your opinion, but I don't see it."

Jenna laughed.

After Ethan parked, he said, "I have a few things to prepare before our meeting, but don't embarrass me by telling Shane. I'm sure he had everything he needed pulled together two days ago."

Jenna picked up the gift bag and gazed at him. "You're different people. You have strengths Shane wishes he had."

Ethan furrowed his brow as they climbed out of the truck then put his arm around her as they walked to the inn.

"Thanks; I'll try to remember that. Our meeting will either be relatively short if the client agrees with our proposal after we answer a few questions, or it could go for two hours or more if they've thought of significant changes to their original request."

"That's why you are partners and both of you have to be there," Jenna said.

Ethan nodded. "Mr. Moore will be on standby to back us up."

When they stopped at the door, Jenna dropped the gift bag and wrapped her arms around his neck as she gazed up at him. Ethan leaned down for a kiss, and Jenna's eyes twinkled as she nibbled on his lower lip.

Ethan chuckled then kissed her with a sweet, slow passion that took away her breath, and she returned his kiss with matching intensity.

When their kiss ended, Ethan lightly stroked her cheek.

"Nice," she murmured.

Ethan nodded. "Very." He picked up the gift bag and handed it to her.

Ethan followed Jenna while he carried the pot of chili and she carried her gift bag and the other leftovers to the kitchen.

After Ethan left, Jenna hurried to the living room to catch her breath.

When she sat in her yellow chair, she leaned back and then glanced at Nettie's portrait.

Nettie's smile was gone, and her face was dark with worry.

Jenna straightened her back. "What is it, Nettie?"

A great sorrow filled Jenna, and tears ran down her face.

"Nettie, tell me who. What can I do?"

The drapes rustled. *Listen to the stories.*

Jenna's tears flooded down her face and soaked her shirt, but she waited. "There's more, isn't there?"

A flash of red blinded her, and Jenna gasped when the great sorrow returned.

As she broke into a cold sweat, Jenna clutched the arms of the chair and sobbed. "All I see is red."

A gust of wind shook the trees, and a tree branch scraped a window. *Stories.*

The red slowly dissipated, but a small piece of the sorrow remained in her heart like a shadow.

Jenna stumbled into the laundry room and washed her face at the sink. After she ran cold water over a clean cloth, she wrung out the cloth and held it to her eyes.

When her eyes no longer burned and she had only a tinge of red in the periphery of her vision, Jenna went into her office and jotted down notes of the stories she'd heard so far.

She stared at her notes. *Is someone close to me the key to a story?*

She frowned as she locked her notebook and the gift back in a drawer. *I need to hear all the stories.*

She exhaled as she turned on her computer. *Was the red a warning or a distraction? Nettie said to listen to the stories.*

Her eyes widened. *Felicia sent me her research notes after all, and we have a new registration.*

She checked the registration and sent a text to Morgan. "New registration. Solo woman will check in today and leave on Sunday."

Morgan replied, "Full house."

Jenna went into the kitchen, and Katy left her spot near the stove greeted her with a grin.

Jenna stroked Katy's back. "I missed you too."

When Jenna sat down at the counter, Wendy nudged Darlene.

Darlene frowned. "What?"

Wendy pointed at Jenna.

"We have another registration. A woman is checking in today and will check out on Sunday." Jenna spoke loudly so Darlene could hear her.

"We can handle one more mouth to feed," Darlene said.

"The room is ready," Wendy added. "I checked it this morning."

"I'll update our registration book after Katy and I take a break."

While they strolled down the path to the peach orchard, Jenna said, "I need to straighten our house; I left it in a mess. I know nobody will see it, but we will when we go home tonight."

When they reached the halfway point, Jenna turned around to jog back. Katy trotted along with her.

After they reached the cottage, Jenna said, "Good run, Katy; thanks."

When Jenna went inside, Katy stayed outside to patrol the backyard for squirrels.

Jenna made her bed and put a load of laundry into the washer then joined Katy in the backyard with her hands in her pockets until she couldn't take any more of the icy wind gusts that found openings around the neck of her coat.

On their way back to the inn, Jenna's phone buzzed a text from Morgan.

"Is Felicia there? She sneaked out a while ago."

After she and Katy went inside, she checked the living room.

She replied to Morgan, "She's not here."

Morgan called. "I didn't see her leave, but Layla said Felicia quietly closed her laptop, put on her coat, and took all her things with her as she slipped out the front door. That was about half an hour ago."

"Did Petra notice?" Jenna asked.

"No, she's sitting with her back to everyone and has been on her computer just like everyone else since the break was over."

"Is anyone sharing stories?"

"Are you kidding? Not at all; everybody is heads down. Petra called for a two-hour work session."

After they hung up, Jenna updated the registration book and then went into her office and stared at her computer.

She replied to Felicia's email. "I may have found something, but I have a question when you have time."

Jenna bit her lip. *Okay, big shot. Find something.*

Jenna pulled out her notebook to take notes while she meticulously traced each branch of the genealogy chart labeled Garrisons and cross-referenced it with Felicia's comments and questions in her document she'd labeled G-Notes.

After an hour, she leaned forward to stretch her back. She froze and stared at her screen. *Did I skip a page?*

She switched her screen to the previous page and zoomed in on the last entry at the bottom of the page. *Married couple with three boys and a girl. All still living, according to the chart.* She wrote the page reference number and the names and birth dates of the couple and their children in her notebook.

She moved to the next page and zoomed in on the first entry at the top. *Married couple with three boys, all are still living.* She wrote the page reference number and the names and birth dates of the couple and their three children in her notebook.

"Something's off," she muttered. "The reference numbers are consecutive, and the names and birth dates match, except Brandi, the three-year-old girl, was not included on the update three years later."

Jenna rubbed her forehead. *Is this just a typographical error?* Who do I know that could explain this to me?

"Correction," she mumbled. "Who do I know and trust that could explain this to me?"

After she shut down her computer and locked the notebook in her drawer, she opened the kitchen door. *Are Darlene and Wendy arguing?*

She slipped into the kitchen and waited for them to notice her.

"You can't send me home," Darlene shouted.

"Nobody is sending you home," Wendy said. "All the cooking and baking is done, and the kitchen is clean. You've written your excellent instructions for the team to follow for the appetizers and for dinner. You were here at five this morning, and you always go home at two, which is nine hours. I was here this morning at nine. I have to catch up on the laundry, but I'll be finished by three thirty."

Darlene picked up the schedule Morgan had given her. "Morgan's schedule says she will be here by three thirty."

"That's perfect, then. I live five minutes from here. I can return at six thirty to help with dinner and can leave at eight thirty after the dining room is cleaned and prepared for breakfast, which will be no later than eight thirty. I'll have worked eight and a half hours today, so you still have me beat."

Darlene jutted out her chin. "I'll have put in more hours than you."

Wendy nodded. "Nobody can work as hard as you do."

"That's right," Darlene said.

Good negotiating, Wendy. Jenna quietly opened the door to the office then let it slam. She strolled to the counter and sat down. "I've caught up on my work for today. Is there anything I can do to help get ready for this evening?"

"Not a thing, Boss Lady," Darlene said. "It's all done. I was just getting ready to leave. We decided Wendy will catch up on the laundry before she leaves, so we've got it all covered."

Jenna nodded. "That's great news."

Darlene put on her coat. "I'll be here at five tomorrow morning, so I can bake the pastries for breakfast."

"I appreciate how hard you work," Jenna said.

Darlene beamed as she opened the refrigerator door and pulled out a small covered dish with cooked chicken. After she gave Katy her chicken treat, she left.

As Wendy headed to the door, Jenna said, "Thanks, Wendy. I appreciate your style."

"I do love working here, Boss Lady."

After Wendy left for the laundry room, Jenna heard a car in the driveway. She hurried to the foyer with Katy at her side and watched as a woman who wore a red wool stocking cap and a red wool overcoat pulled her roller bag that was the size of flight carry-on luggage behind her up the walkway toward the inn.

Jenna felt the knot in her stomach and gritted her teeth. *It's just a color.*

The knot crumbled then disappeared; Jenna furrowed her brow. *I need to talk to Nettie.*

Jenna opened the front door when the woman reached the porch. "Welcome, I'm Jenna."

The woman smiled. "You're Jenna, the owner? You're much younger than I expected. I'll bet you get that a lot, don't you? I'm Amanda. And who is this gorgeous creature?"

Amanda is a cop. Jenna returned the woman's smile. "This is Katy."

"Good girl, Katy. Do you sit?"

Katy sat for Amanda who pulled out a dog treat from her coat pocket and then held it out for Katy.

Katy daintily took the treat then nudged Amanda's hand with her nose. Amanda chuckled then rubbed Katy's ears.

"I apologize, Jenna." Amanda stepped into the foyer and put down her luggage. "I should have asked you first, but when I meet a sweet dog like Katy, I lose all my social skills. My Willow has been gone for a year. She was fourteen years old and had a good life, but I still miss her. She was a German Shepherd; I have a soft spot for big dogs."

Jenna smiled. "No apology is necessary."

After Jenna completed Amanda's registration and gave her the room key and explained the guest entrance.

When Jenna showed Amanda the dining room and explained happy hour and breakfast, Amanda asked, "Do most people show up for breakfast at seven? I'm not much for crowds, so if I came down for breakfast at seven thirty would most of the people be gone?"

"We have one or two breakfast stragglers only occasionally. Our early birds do tend to be a lively bunch, so if you're looking for a quiet breakfast, seven thirty would be your best bet."

"Thank you; I don't mean to sound a recluse, but I do much prefer dogs rather than people. Does Katy have any close friends who could join us for breakfast?" Amanda's eyes twinkled.

Jenna smiled. "Don't give her any ideas. Next is the living room."

Amanda ran her hand along the edge of the fireplace mantle. "The mantle is gorgeous. Is this a working fireplace?"

Jenna nodded. "We frequently have a fire in the evenings when it's cold enough."

"I would think this would be a favorite gathering place for your guests. Are there many guests here this weekend?"

"All our rooms are taken. We usually have a few people who relax in the living room when they return from dinner, but most of our guests enjoy the privacy of their rooms."

"That sounds good to me."

"I'll show you your room; it's on the main floor and overlooks the front yard."

As they passed the stairs on their left, Amanda said, "You don't see many staircases that are this wide. I love it."

When they reached the end of the hall, Jenna pointed to the right. "Your room is right here. Use your key to unlock the door."

When Amanda opened the door, she said, "I've never stayed in a bed-and-breakfast. I was just passing through and overheard someone at the gas station mention the Peach Blossom Retreat. I'm glad I took a chance; this room has a lovely, calming feel to it. Thank you."

"I hope you enjoy your stay." Jenna furrowed her brow as she followed Katy down the hallway.

Jenna stopped at the laundry room. "Our solo guest arrived. Our two couples should be here soon."

Wendy nodded. "This is the first time since I started working here that we've had a full house. I don't know why, but it's exciting. Oh, I found a ring on the floor in the restroom across from the dining room. I'll bet someone took it off to wash their hands and then forgot it. I put it on the kitchen counter."

"Thanks, I'll put it in the safe. No one has said anything yet, but I'm sure whoever lost it will be asking about it soon."

Jenna strolled into the kitchen and stared at the gold ring with the oval cut ruby and three small diamonds on each side of the ruby.

What's your story, ring? No way am I picking you up.

Jenna turned a coffee cup upside down and put it over the ring.

After she went into her office, Nettie's words echoed. *Listen to the stories.*

"Seriously, Nettie?"

The wind chimes on the front porch jingled in the breeze.

Chapter Seven

Jenna trudged into the kitchen and sat at the counter. She sighed then lifted the cup and set it aside.

"Okay, ring; what's your story?"

Jenna lightly stroked the ruby with her fingertip. *Before the secret.*

Jenna furrowed her brow and picked up the ring. *From the times before the secret.*

"I'll put you in a safe place."

Jenna carried the ring to her office and unlocked the drawer at her desk. She set the ring in a corner then pulled out her notebook and added the words, "from the times before the secret." She stared at her notebook then locked it in the drawer before she turned on her computer and dived into reviewing expenses.

Morgan came into the office from the kitchen and stopped to stroke Katy's back. "So, what did Layla say that was so funny after our conversation about Peach Suite?"

"Do you remember when she followed up the Peach Suite conversation by saying I should let you all know if we'd forgotten anything? She whispered to me, give us a sign."

Morgan laughed. "Just when I thought Layla would become a stuffy lawyer, she came up with a line that would have gotten all three of us in trouble."

Jenna laughed with Morgan.

Morgan exhaled. "We needed that. Wendy just left. This afternoon was relatively quiet at the barn, believe it or not. Layla and I decided the story contest is more of a cut-throat fight to the finish than a friendly competition. The prize must be worth a lot."

Katy rolled over for a belly rub, and Morgan chuckled as she sat on the floor next to Katy.

"The prize is a three-day weekend at the Peach Blossom Retreat. Petra purchased it when she paid for the weekend."

"Wow; that's great, but winning must carry significant bragging rights too. Do you know who won last year?"

Jenna laughed. "As a matter of fact, I do. Petra did, but as the new coordinator, she is not eligible this year."

Morgan rose. "I need a stretch break; is it okay with you if Katy and I take a walk?" Morgan asked.

"That's fine; she'll love it."

"Ready to go for a walk, Katy?"

After Morgan and Katy left, Jenna returned to her computer and frowned. "I didn't notice this earlier. The email I sent to Felicia bounced."

Jenna compared the email address to the one Felicia had used to send her the genealogy files. *This is odd. I sent it to the right address.*

Jenna smiled when an email popped up from Adrienne. She downloaded the contract and read it.

Adrienne called her.

"Did you read the contract?"

"I just finished, and it looked fine to me. Do I sign it and send it back?"

"No. I'll send you a secure link with the document for you to sign. How's the Peach Blossom Barn event going?"

"We're limping along. The weekend is a real drain on everyone. I knew I didn't want to get into the event hosting business, and this weekend definitely has not changed my mind. We'll have a debriefing after the weekend's over, but we know we have to find an experienced caterer with a stable staff."

"I didn't have any experience to bring to the table either. I've been talking to my buddies who had excellent suggestions on vetting caterers and on the language we should consider for the contract. I'll send you some notes for your debriefing."

"That would be extremely useful. Morgan has experience managing events, so if we have an experienced, reliable caterer, we'll be fine."

After Jenna hung up, Morgan opened the office door. "Our two couples pulled into the visitor parking lot. Katy and I came inside for a drink. Care for some iced tea?"

"That sounds great." Jenna turned off her laptop.

While Morgan poured the tea, Jenna said, "They're coming up the walkway. They sound like a lively bunch."

"My turn." Morgan left the kitchen.

"I feel like I should jump up and do something because it's been so frantic; it's nice to have a quiet break." Jenna sipped her tea.

When her phone buzzed with a text, Jenna sighed. "I guess that was our break."

She furrowed her brow when her phone buzzed with a text from the sheriff. "Is there somewhere private we can talk?"

"My office."

"Not good enough."

Jenna bit her lip. *Doesn't sound good.* "We could meet at my house."

"I'll park behind the cottage and knock on the back door."

Jenna put on her coat. "Come on, Katy."

On her way to her cottage, Jenna sent Morgan a text. "Katy and I will be at the cottage for a bit."

After she unlocked the door, Jenna and Katy went inside; Jenna sat in her green chair next to the window then rose.

"I can't just sit and wait. I'll start a load of laundry; maybe that will make the sheriff show up faster."

While she gathered clothes to wash, she heard the crunch of tires on the gravel as a car rounded the cottage and stopped near her backyard fence.

She tossed the clothes into the washer and smiled as she started the machine. "What do you know, Katy? It worked."

Katy grinned then trotted to the back door.

Jenna opened the door, and the sheriff smiled as he stepped up on the porch. "Did Katy give me away?"

Jenna returned his smile and nodded as Katy slipped outside to patrol the backyard.

"Shall we sit?"

"Good idea." The sheriff sat at the kitchen table.

"Would you like a glass of iced tea?" Jenna asked.

"No, but thanks."

She joined him at the table.

He cleared his throat. "I'm sure you know Felicia Thorton left the barn earlier today. We don't think she'll be back. Why doesn't matter, but Georgia needs to examine the barn, especially the rest rooms. Would Felicia have had access to the Peach Pit?"

"We normally keep the Peach Pit locked, but we've been overwhelmed with work since the caterer dropped out. One of us could have left it unlocked. You mean Georgia as in Bureau of Investigation Georgia?" Jenna asked.

"Yes. We need a story about why Felicia left and why Georgia might be at the inn this weekend, in case any of your team sees her. I was hoping you'd help me come up with something. You know your team, and you've met Felicia and the group. What do you think is a plausible story?" The sheriff asked.

"Is Felicia dead?" Jenna narrowed her eyes.

"Not that we know of."

"Does she have an ex-husband?"

The sheriff's eyes twinkled. "I like where you're going; yes, as a matter of fact, she could."

"Good; do you want me to spread the story that she disappeared to hide from him?"

The sheriff exhaled. "That would be extremely helpful."

. "That's easy; I'll just mention something to Petra, the club coordinator. As far as my team is concerned, Georgia might be here undercover in case the ex-husband shows up because there's a warrant out on him."

"Believable all the way around; I'll fill in Georgia, and she'll be here early tomorrow morning."

"She'll be here all weekend?"

"Saturday morning for sure; I don't know how long."

"And you don't want anyone to see her, right?"

"Yes, we don't know who might recognize her, and if your team sees her, someone else might too. She'll be dropped off as early as possible and picked up before eight."

"How early?"

"She'll be at the barn around midnight. Do you have a hidden key to the barn or one I can get to her?"

"I'll give you a key." Jenna rose and opened her junk drawer and pulled out a key from a clear plastic storage bag.

She added the key to a keychain from a local business and gave it to the sheriff. "The same key works for the barn and the Peach Pit. If someone's on their way to the barn earlier than eight o'clock, how do I warn her?"

"Text me."

Jenna glanced at the green chair. *Secrets.*

"I can do that. Felecia mentioned a case about someone in a witness protection program during the meeting. Did she leave because she knew more than she said?"

The sheriff met her gaze. "That's interesting, but it doesn't have anything to do with why she left, which is not up for discussion."

Jenna glanced at the green chair then outside the front window at the treetops that swayed in the light breeze. *Baloney.*

She narrowed her eyes. *Is that why we have Amanda who was just passing through?*

Secrets.

The sheriff groaned as he rose from the table. "I split some wood for our fireplace when I got home yesterday, and now I'm paying for it."

"I've started jogging again, so I sympathize; what's the actual story with Felicia?"

The sheriff narrowed his eyes. "She's in danger because she knows too much; don't be a Felicia."

The sheriff strode out the back door. Jenna listened as he drove down the driveway.

Jenna narrowed her eyes at the green chair. "I don't believe him either. Was she goading someone?"

She waited for a response that didn't come.

Jenna sighed and opened the back door. "Are you ready to go back to the inn, Katy?"

As Jenna hurried to the inn's back door with Katy at her side, she shook her head. "Can this weekend get any messier?"

Katy growled.

"You're right; I shouldn't have said anything."

When she went into the kitchen, Morgan stood at the counter while she read the instructions for happy hour and dinner.

"I got a call from the sheriff," Jenna said. "Felicia won't be back; she's making herself scarce. They think her ex-husband is looking for her."

"There was speculation along those lines at the barn this afternoon, except I don't remember anyone mentioning an ex-husband. Anyway, no one will be surprised."

Jenna nodded. *That's good news.*

Katy sat and scratched her neck then whined.

"I'm sorry you're itchy, girl. I'll call the vet to see what I can give you."

Katy flopped down on the kitchen floor as Jenna and Morgan went into the office.

Jenna said, "Remember Georgia from the Georgia Bureau of Investigation? She might come here, but she'll be undercover because law enforcement believes the ex-husband might show up, and they have a warrant for his arrest. She'll stay out of sight, so probably none of us will see her. If we do, we have to ignore her."

"Darlene will be sad that she can't hunt down Georgia to feed her."

"That's a good point. Be sure to stress that we don't want to blow Georgia's cover. Let me know if Darlene decides to try to find Georgia anyway so I can step in, or you might hint you could ask me to smuggle food to Georgia. I'm not sure when or even if she'll be here, but she may be gone sometime on Sunday. If the ex-husband shows up, I need to know, so I can get word to Georgia."

"I'll talk to Darlene, Wendy, and Layla."

Jenna nodded. "Tell me about the two couples."

Morgan rolled her eyes. "The young women were best friends in college, and they married brothers less than six months ago. Annie is black and reminds me of my cousin who is always bubbly. Quinn is more serious and looks a lot like Layla, except she's blonde. I didn't catch the husbands' names, but it doesn't matter because they are identical twins, and I'd never call them the right name anyway except by accident. The four of them are full of energy and are here on an adventure to have an old-fashioned weekend like people did back in the day twenty years ago, which is a direct quote. It kills me because they're probably only two or three years older than Layla. You won't believe their plans. I hate to admit it, but I actually liked their ideas, except I'd tweak their plan to be a little less athletic and a little more pathetic."

Jenna giggled.

"Thank you." Morgan curtseyed. "They're going to power walk to the peach orchard tomorrow morning for the tour and homemade peach ice cream, and after they have lunch at a quaint café in downtown Paisley, they're going to rent kayaks. On Sunday, they plan to get up early and drive three hours to hike to a waterfall for a picnic. I dared my knees to creak when I went up the stairs to show them to their rooms."

Jenna shook her head. "I'd work in a power nap in the afternoons, wouldn't you?"

"Absolutely. I like how you think, Boss Lady." Morgan smiled. "They really are delightful people and very refreshing after spending a day with professional grumps, but they made me feel so dang stodgy, which is on me, not them."

Morgan's phone buzzed with a text. "Shane said they got the contract. Isn't that exciting? He said there were only a few changes, so after the contract was signed, they began discussing the details of the schedule."

Jenna's phone buzzed with a text from Ethan. "Success."

She laughed and showed her phone to Morgan.

"He didn't bore you with details, did he?" Morgan snickered.

"What's your plan for this evening?"

"Wendy and Layla will be here at five thirty. I thought you and I could focus on happy hour while they take care of dinner. Maybe we could let Wendy go home early while you, Layla, and I clean up after dinner."

"You might have a fight on your hands. Wendy and Darlene have a little competition going over who works the hardest," Jenna said.

"Thanks for the warning. I'll ditch the idea of sending her home early. What do you think about celebrating the new contract after dinner? We'll have extra baked goat cheese dip, and Shane can pick up a bottle of wine for us."

"Let's plan a big celebration in the middle of the week."

"That's brilliant. I'm off on Tuesday. I'll cook dinner, and Shane and I will bring it here, and we'll have a big celebration after happy hour."

"That sounds wonderful; you check with Shane, and I'll see if Ethan's available."

"For you? He'll be available." Morgan glanced at her computer. "I want to check the reservations for next week."

"I'll get a head start on setting up for happy hour."

"Bad idea; Layla and Wendy will be here at five thirty, and they expect to be in charge of setting up. You and I are the supposed to be the gracious hosts. Why don't you relax, so you don't snap at anybody. Although, that's more my style than yours, but you know what I mean."

"This weekend has already destroyed my ability to relax."

Morgan opened her computer bag and handed Jenna her book. "Here; this will work."

"I'll give it a try."

Jenna stopped in the kitchen. "Katy, I'm going to relax in the living room with a book."

Katy stretched then followed Jenna into the living room. While Jenna started a fire in the fireplace, Katy flopped down next to the yellow chair.

After the fire caught, Jenna added a log and then sat in the yellow chair.

She gazed at Nettie's portrait. "I have heard so many stories today that I had to make a list."

The flames from the fireplace danced and lit up Nettie's face. Jenna smiled as Nettie's eyes sparkled, and then Jenna opened her book where she had put the makeshift book mark.

After she stuck the crumpled piece of paper into her pocket, she leaned back to read.

"Here you are. I see you've already built a fire. How wonderful," Petra said.

Petra strode to the sofa and sat in the middle of it.

"We had a wonderful session this afternoon; today was the best first day I've ever attended. I think the atmosphere of the Peach Blossom Barn was exactly what we needed to get those creative juices flowing."

Petra glanced around then leaned forward. "Were you there when Felicia left? It was quite abrupt."

Jenna raised her eyebrows.

Petra lowered her voice. "She confided to one of the girls at dinner last night that she was worried because her ex-husband has been stalking her. When she was driving to breakfast this morning, she said she caught a glimpse of him in town, and it was obviously preying on her mind. She has gone into hiding for her own safety, poor thing. Of course, no one blames her. Maybe she'll realize how safe she is here and return later this evening so she doesn't miss the rest of our meeting. Husband problems are one thing I never had to deal with, but I do feel bad for Felicia, anyway."

Susan stood in the doorway. "It's close to five thirty, Petra. Did you forget your wine?"

"Goodness gracious, I certainly did." Petra jumped up. "I have a few things to do, but I'll be first in line at six."

Tisha joined Jenna and Susan as Petra left.

Susan shook her head. "Petra does love her wine. I didn't mean to chase her off, but I was shocked she didn't have it with it being so close to happy hour."

"She did seem a little distracted," Jenna said. "I forgot to ask her if her husband was going to be here this weekend so we could plan our meals for tomorrow.

Susan giggled. "Can you see Petra married?"

Tisha chuckled. "No kidding."

Tisha scanned the living room then strolled to the fireplace. "I left the hotel a little early, and I'm glad I did. I may spend happy hour in front of the fire."

Susan pointed to the bookcase. "Did you see the books?"

While they examined the books, Jenna was lost in thought as she quietly left for her office with Katy trailing her. *Maybe Petra has a boyfriend and thought we might be stodgy.*

Katy stayed in the kitchen while Jenna went to the office and put on her coat. "I'm taking Katy for a quick walk, Morgan. We won't be long."

On her way to the back door, Jenna sent a text to the sheriff. "I need to talk. Not urgent."

Her phone rang almost immediately, and Jenna answered as she opened the door for Katy then went outside.

Katy bounded away after a rabbit.

"What's up?" the sheriff asked.

"You know that story we made up about Felicia and her ex-husband? I didn't have a chance to say anything because Petra, the coordinator, just told me the same story."

"Really? Same story?"

"Almost verbatim; it's almost like my cottage is bugged, but Petra didn't mention anything about the possibility of the ex-husband showing up. When I told Morgan about Felicia and her ex-husband, she said there was a lot of speculation at the barn, but she didn't remember hearing any mention of an ex-husband."

"I'll still send somebody over to check, but it might be awhile before I can find someone; although, is Shane there?"

"Not yet, but he will be soon."

"I'll bet he can do it. Ask him to check and get back to me."

Jenna bit her lip then sent Shane a text. "Can you check my cottage for an electronic bug? No need for Morgan or Ethan to know."

Shane replied, "Can do. I'll be there in five minutes."

When Katy returned from her rabbit chase, Jenna said, "Ready to go inside for some water?"

After they were in the cottage, Jenna sat in her green chair while Katy drank her fill.

I need an excuse for Shane to be searching the cottage. She furrowed her brow as she surveyed the room. She glanced out of the window toward the inn. *Red is a distraction.*

She nodded and sent a text to Shane. "Your excuse: I saw a coral snake in the utility room."

Jenna strolled to the kitchen and ran some water in the sink then squealed. "Oh, no. Katy, is that a coral snake next to the water heater?"

Katy stared at Jenna then tilted her head.

Jenna shrieked. "It's a coral snake. Stay back."

Katy nudged Jenna's hand.

Jenna breathed rapidly and loudly with as much drama as she dared while she stroked Katy's neck. *Hope I don't hyperventilate.*

"I'll call Ethan. No, he's in town. I'll call Shane."

She spoke in a shaky voice. "Shane, there's a coral snake under my water heater. Can you help me?"

Jenna swallowed. *Now I'm scaring myself.* "Thanks."

While Jenna waited, she said, "Stay close to me, Katy."

Jenna sat in her green chair, and Katy flopped down at her feet. "Good girl."

When Shane parked in front of the cottage, Katy yipped.

"You're right; it's Shane."

As Shane came into the house, he held an electronic contraption in his hand. "Are you sure it's a coral snake?" he asked.

"It had red, black, and yellow stripes."

He nodded. "I'll check around the water heater."

Shane slowly strolled around the kitchen. He glanced at Jenna and shook his head as he continued his slow search in the living area. When he neared the green chair where Jenna and Katy were, he said, "Wait a minute. I think I see it."

He motioned for Jenna to move away from the green chair. Katy followed Jenna to the kitchen.

Shane stared at the gadget in his hand. "No; I was wrong."

He walked slowly toward Jenna and Katy. He stopped and stared at Katy who was scratching her neck.

He put his index finger over his mouth.

"I think I see it." He moved closer to Katy.

"I found it. It's a king snake, which is a very beneficial snake to have around. Katy and I will take it out back."

Shane went to the door. "Come on, Katy."

Jenna joined Shane at the door, and Katy followed her.

"Are you coming with us, Jenna?"

"Yes. I want to be sure the snake is safely outside and away from the house."

Shane nodded.

After they walked close to the trees, Shane said, "We'll let her go here."

Jenna sighed dramatically. "Bye, snake."

Shane said, "I think Katy's collar is too tight."

"It looks a little tight to me too. Maybe that's why she's been scratching so much."

"Could be. I'll loosen it." Shane removed her collar.

When he held it up, Shane pointed to a tiny box clipped to the collar.

Jenna's eyes widened.

Shane continued, "I hope it's not too loose, but at least it will be more comfortable. How are you doing now, Katy girl?"

Katy stared at her collar in his hand and yipped.

He looped the collar over a tree limb and clicked the fastener closed.

He motioned for Jenna to return to the house. Katy stayed close to Jenna.

After they were inside, Katy flopped down on the kitchen floor with her back to Shane.

"I think I'm in trouble," Shane said. "Katy needs another collar. What made you suspicious?"

"Can I have a raincheck on sharing the details? The sheriff told me you'd be able to find a bug."

"Are you or Morgan in danger?"

"No."

"Then I'm okay with a raincheck."

After Shane left, Jenna sent a text to the sheriff. "Bug was on Katy's collar."

The sheriff called her. "Katy was outside when we talked."

"You're right." Jenna furrowed her brow. "But Katy was with me when I told Morgan I talked to you and that you had mentioned the ex-husband."

"Where's the bug now?"

"It's still on her collar. Shane hung her collar on a tree limb behind the cottage."

"So Katy lost her collar?" The sheriff chuckled. "We'll pick it up." He hung up.

Jenna sent a text to Ethan. "Katy lost her collar in the woods."

Ethan replied, "I'll get her another one."

Jenna hugged Katy. "Ethan will bring you a new collar." She smiled as they reached the back door. *I knew I could count on Ethan.*

The wind chime on the front porch jingled.

When they went into the kitchen, Morgan sat at the counter with the instructions for happy hour in front of her. She glanced at them then stared at Katy. "Where's Katy's collar? She looks uncomfortable."

"She chased a rabbit then came back without it. Ethan's getting her another one."

Morgan nodded then pointed to the instructions. "The baked goat cheese sounds too easy. What am I missing?"

Jenna peered at the paper. "All we have to do is warm it up, so I don't think you're missing anything."

At the roar of a motorcycle in the driveway, Morgan said, "I lost track of time; let's look busy."

"It's Layla, not Darlene, but okay; we need ice water."

Morgan nodded. "I'll pour the water while you get the ice, and then we'll stress over any last-minute details we forgot."

After the dispenser was full of water and ice, Jenna narrowed her eyes at the sideboard. "We may need more napkins."

Morgan opened the sideboard cabinet where spares were stored. "We're running low on forks and napkins."

"Did you turn on the oven?" Jenna asked.

"I don't think I did."

They returned to the kitchen as Layla hurried in, followed by Wendy.

"You haven't done everything already, have you?" Layla asked.

"All we've done is fill the water dispenser," Morgan said.

"We need more napkins and forks," Jenna said.

Wendy turned on the oven then pulled out more napkins and forks and took them to the dining room.

"Do we have enough tables?" Morgan asked. "Should we get two more from storage at the Peach Pit?"

Layla furrowed her brow. "We have more than enough tables for everyone to sit down and eat dinner. Didn't you tell me at least half of our guests stand close to the sideboard during happy hour so they can stroll over and refill their plates?"

"If I ask any more panicky questions, just chalk it up to a case of the nerves and don't answer."

Layla washed and dried her hands. "Darlene told me Nora bought a bottle of grape juice today at the store in case we wanted to mingle without looking conspicuous."

"That's a great idea," Jenna said. "I know I'd feel less awkward about standing around if I had a glass in my hand."

Wendy opened the refrigerator. "There are two oven-safe bowls in the refrigerator; one is marked Ethan and the other, Shane."

"Darlene wanted to be sure both of them had enough goat cheese dip," Layla said.

Wendy chuckled. "These are very generous portions; maybe they'll share."

Morgan smirked. "I doubt it."

Wendy put the happy hour goat cheese dip for the guests into the oven.

At six o'clock Jenna asked, "Are we ready?"

Morgan nodded, and the two of them went into the dining room.

When Jenna opened the door to the hallway, Petra came into the dining room, closely followed by Vera and Ralph.

Jenna smiled as her guests came into the dining room. Petra returned the smile. Ralph nodded, and Vera sneered.

Petra stepped aside and motioned for Jenna to join her in the corner away from the kitchen door.

While Ralph opened a bottle of white wine and then a bottle of red wine, Petra whispered, "Did you hear from Felicia?"

Jenna shook her head. "Have you?"

Petra's demeanor and tone darkened. "No, but she was the chief topic of discussion during breaks today, and some of the club think you know more than you're saying."

"That's interesting; did anyone give a reason they think that?" Jenna asked.

Tisha and Susan appeared in the doorway. Susan paused as she scanned the room expectantly while Tisha strolled to the sideboard.

Petra glared at Jenna. "Ask her."

Chapter Eight

When Susan's glance reached Petra, Petra's face instantly transformed into her professional persona. "There you are. Don't the appetizers smell wonderful? I'll open my bottle of wine and pour you a small glass while you fill your plate."

"Don't bother." Susan strolled to the table of appetizers and peered at the goat cheese. "Warm, creamy feta cheese dip is one of my favorites." She put a dollop on her plate next to her toasted pita triangles.

She moved to the next appetizer. "And what is this? Buffalo chicken tenders with a ranch dipping sauce in these tiny cups?"

Tisha carried her appetizer plate to a table. "That's what I thought, Susan."

Morgan joined Susan at the sideboard. "Close. Buffalo artichoke hearts, and you're right about the dipping sauce."

"Sounds delicious." Susan put two artichoke hearts and one of the small cups of sauce on her plate. "That must be your chef's signature special because I've never heard of it."

She moved to the last platter on the sideboard and chuckled. "Chips and salsa; this must be your chef's nod to the average diner."

Morgan smiled. "Yes, except our chef makes her own tortilla chips and salsa."

Susan chortled. "I should have known; how delightful."

Vera snorted. "What a crock."

"Here's your white wine, Vera." Ralph set down a full glass of wine in front of Vera then strode to the appetizers. He stuck a napkin and a fork in his shirt pocket then picked up two plates.

He winked at Morgan. "No sense in wasting steps to come back for a refill, is there?"

After he stacked appetizers onto both plates to an impressive height, he joined Vera.

When he set the two plates in front of his nearly overflowing glass of red wine, Vera cleared her throat and spoke loudly, "Excuse me; isn't one of those plates for me?"

He put an entire triangle of pita smeared with goat cheese dip into his mouth and stared at her with his brow furrowed as he shook his head. "No." His voice was muffled by pita and goat cheese.

Jenna froze when Vera pushed against the table to rise, but Ralph picked up his glass before the red wine spilled onto the white tablecloth and took a large gulp.

Jenna glanced at Morgan who mouthed, "Whew."

While Vera stormed to the sideboard, Jenna welcomed the two young couples as they wandered into the dining room.

"We didn't know what to expect," one of the young men said.

"This is really nice. The food smells delicious, and you have ice water, which is wonderful," Annie said.

"I'm glad you came," Jenna said. "Our appetizers are buffet. Help yourselves and sit anywhere."

While the young couples pondered the appetizers with their plates in their hands, the rest of the inn guests and the guests from the hotel poured in.

The young couples picked a table where they could observe the room, and Jenna smiled. *They are people watchers. The genealogy club will certainly provide them with a variety of characters to observe.*

Jenna glanced toward the sideboard and blinked at the platters that had been scraped clean.

She darted into the kitchen. "I don't know how they did it so fast, but our poor platters were swarmed, and we're out of everything."

"Seriously?" Layla asked as she put more pitas in the oven to warm. "Goat cheese too?"

"Everything."

"This is our last goat cheese dip," Wendy said. "We're not touching the Peach Blossom reserve or the two marked for Ethan and Shane."

Jenna nodded. "Thanks to Darlene, our house rule is when it's gone, it's gone."

Layla pushed back her hair from her damp forehead. "That takes off a lot of pressure; I love that rule."

Jenna and Morgan scurried to keep the platters filled as the chatter rose to a roar.

Jenna was near the hallway door when the two young couples rose from their table.

Annie stopped on her way out. "Miss Jenna, we didn't know what to expect from a happy hour since we don't drink and have never been to one, but we're definitely fans of the Peach Blossom Retreat's happy hour. Thank you so much, and thanks to your talented chef for the delicious appetizers. We may have trouble eating our dinner, but we'll do our best." She giggled as they left, and Jenna smiled.

Amanda met Jenna as Jenna came out of the kitchen with a platter of buffalo artichoke hearts.

Amanda smiled. "Who knew a genealogy crowd could be so entertaining?" She held out her opened bottle of wine with its cork reinserted. "Is there somewhere I'm supposed to put my wine until tomorrow, or do I take it with me to my room?"

"We don't have anywhere to store it, but we can give you a plastic wine glass if you'd like to enjoy your wine in your room."

"That's really thoughtful of you. A plastic wine glass would be perfect. It seems so uncultured to drink wine out of a bathroom glass, doesn't it?"

"I'll be right back."

When Jenna went into the kitchen, she said, "Morgan, where did we put the plastic wine glasses you ordered?"

"They're right here, Jenna." Wendy strolled to the pantry and pulled out a wine glass.

Morgan opened a lower cabinet and pulled out a white paper sack with a handle and a Peach Blossom Retreat logo sticker on its side. Wendy put the wine glass, a napkin, and a snack packet into the sack.

"You know, if you take that to the dining room, everybody's going to want one," Layla said.

"Who is it for?" Morgan asked.

"Amanda in room four."

"Tell her I'll deliver it to her room as soon as we find where we put them."

"That's a good idea." Jenna returned to the dining room.

"Are you going straight to your room, Amanda? We just bought the plastic glasses and put them in a safe place. Morgan will bring one to your room as soon as she finds them." Jenna rolled her eyes.

Amanda tittered. "I hate to be the cause of any problems."

Jenna smiled. "It's not a problem at all; we're just still getting organized."

"In that case, I'll take you up on it."

Jenna strolled with Amanda as far as the doorway, and smiled as Amanda hurried down the hall with her wine bottle.

Morgan sauntered past the dining room door with the white sack in her hand. She looked straight ahead, but waggled her fingers in greeting at Jenna.

The volume in the room behind her buzzed with excitement. Jenna rolled her eyes. *Is the dramatic nature of this group catching? We may have gone overboard with our clandestine efforts to keep our plastic wine glasses secret. Everybody's too busy having a good time to care.*

Before she turned to go back into the room, there was a distinct, sharp tone of urgency beneath the outburst of laughter. Then Jenna heard the whispers.

"You promised no one would find out."

"You're the leak."

Jenna furrowed her brow. *I didn't hear the voices clearly enough to recognize them; the first one was female, but definitely not Wanda. I couldn't tell about the second person.*

She casually tilted her head to the side to see who could have spoken, but whoever it was must have moved, because there was no one close enough for her to have heard the words so clearly.

Susan, Tisha, Ralph, and Petra are the only ones who have moved from where I last saw them, but so what?

Jenna was deep in thought as she strolled into the dining room. She stopped and tapped her fingers on the back of the nearest chair while she ostensibly scanned the appetizers. *I could use a team meeting, but those three would tell me to back off.*

Layla cracked open the door to the kitchen and motioned at Jenna. *I could talk to Layla.*

When Jenna was in the kitchen, Layla asked, "What's our status for dinner? Is it too early to remove the appetizers?"

"The inn-only guests have left, so removing the appetizers now is a great idea."

"Do we wait until seven for dinner?"

"I'm inclined to say yes, so we aren't rushed."

"That's what we'll do then," Wendy said.

"What are we doing?" Morgan came into the kitchen from the hallway.

"Snatching appetizers out of their mouths and starving them until seven for dinner," Layla said.

Morgan chuckled. "I have a new tagline for us; customer service no one wants to match."

Jenna stared at Morgan. "Do we have a tagline?"

"I hadn't thought of it; we should."

Morgan followed Layla into the dining room.

Wendy checked the oven and then pulled out the vegetarian lasagna. "This can cool a bit, so we can cut it into servings. If I know Morgan, you'll have your tagline tomorrow."

She removed the tray of salmon topped with lemon-herb butter and slid it into the oven.

"Our side dish is lemon risotto with broccoli. Darlene and I decided it would be more efficient to serve the main dishes to our guests individually on Peach Blossom Retreat plates instead of going the buffet route. Nora found the ideal table markers for us." Wendy put a tray on the counter with three-inch tall, bright yellow, numbered plastic tent markers and red plastic checkers. "Morgan created the sign."

Jenna shuddered. *Red checkers.*

She shook off the dread and read the sign. "Take a number with you to your table for salmon with lemon-herb butter and creamy risotto with broccoli or choose a red checker piece for vegetarian lasagna and garlicky green beans."

Jenna squinted at the yellow markers. "They look like evidence markers."

"They are. Nora found them in the thrift store." Wendy smiled.

"I might have said unique, but efficient works too." Jenna chuckled.

"Nora was sad she couldn't find a second color of evidence markers on short notice, but she's on a quest, so we might have them tomorrow."

"The red checkers work," Jenna said.

Morgan carried in the empty platters from the dining room. "We thought Layla and I would set up the markers, checkers, and the sign while you announce the plan for dinner to the group."

A few minutes before seven, Jenna, Morgan, and Layla went into the dining room while Wendy peeked from the kitchen door.

After Jenna opened the door at seven, she stood in the doorway and raised her hand for quiet.

When the group settled down, Jenna said, "We have an unusual way to serve you this evening. You will find the code for your entrée selections at the sideboard, and we will bring your selected entrée to your table. In the true spirit of investigation and winning a competition, you will pick up a yellow evidence marker or a red checker for your entrée."

The group burst into laughter and applauded.

Jenna exhaled in relief as she stepped aside. The noisy group hurried to the sideboard and jostled each other in their rush to grab an evidence marker or a checker.

Layla brought out more ice for the water dispenser. After she poured in the ice, Tisha approached her and the two of them stepped away from the sideboard to chat.

When Tisha returned to the sideboard for coffee, Arthur stared at the evidence marker on the table next to him as he shuddered then put his hands in his lap and squeezed his arms tight against his sides.

Chris whispered to Arthur, and the two of them switched seats so Chris would be sitting next to Tisha.

Jenna raised her eyebrows. *That was strange.*

Brittany and Stan were the last to come into the dining room; while they waited for the line at the sideboard to become shorter, they joined Jenna who stood at a table close to the door.

"This is really fun. Where did you find the yellow evidence markers?" Brittany asked.

"We think they were supposed to be for a crime-themed party. The idea was our chef's, and her sister found the evidence markers at a discount store in town. Our chef wanted to allow each person to order their meal in a way they'd never forget. She didn't want to have a run-of-the-mill buffet."

"It was a delightful idea; you've provided a truly immersive dining experience."

Jenna smiled. "I'll tell her what you said; she'll be thrilled."

"Are you becoming accustomed to our eclectic group?" Stan asked.

Jenna smiled. "Petra called the members who are staying at the hotel less adventuresome. I didn't understand what she meant. Do you?"

"Not really. My only guess is she might have been taking a swipe at Wanda and Felicia because they didn't want to stay at the Peach Blossom Retreat. Tisha might have a better idea."

"It's not really important; it just struck me as odd." Jenna glanced at Tisha who set down her evidence marker at the empty seat at the table where Chris, Arthur, Ivy, and Susan sat.

"From what I hear, that was probably a typical Petra non sequitur," Brittany giggled.

"We're definitely an odd group," Stan said. "There's a little drama going on at the sideboard."

Stan raised his eyebrows as he pointedly glanced toward the sideboard.

While they watched, Susan elbowed Ivy who had blocked the evidence tags.

Ivy glared at Susan. "Back off. I'm trying to decide which main dish I want, and I don't want to be rushed."

Susan snorted. "Contemplate all you want, but hand me a yellow marker. It's only a food choice, not a life or death decision."

"Oh, my; it must have been an intense day," Brittany murmured.

"After spending all day on the computer doing research and writing, this should have been a welcome relief valve, but it seems to be a defective pressure valve so far. Do you think it will come to blows? I guess that would make it a food fight, wouldn't it?" Stan chuckled.

Brittany shook her head. "That was terrible, Stan; you should be ashamed of yourself."

"You didn't have to spend a day being bombarded by the sniping, honey; it was nonstop and always has been, which is why I intended to quit this year. I'll remember my shooting ear protection tomorrow." Stan put his arm around Brittany and squeezed.

"That sounds draining, but I am enjoying the Peach Blossom Retreat," she said.

"Good," Stan said. "Let's enjoy our dinner then adjourn to a more romantic setting and take advantage of the fire we saw in the fireplace."

After they strolled together to the sideboard to select their meals while they carefully circumvented Ivy, Jenna went into the kitchen as Morgan came into the dining room.

Ethan and Shane sat at the counter with their bowls of warm goat cheese dip and toasted pita triangles.

"Here's your appetizer, Boss Lady," Wendy smiled. "Morgan is getting a quick count of the number who have selected salmon. When Layla returns, she'll have the count for the vegetarian meal."

Morgan returned. "Eight salmon."

"Four vegetarian meals." Layla followed her in. "Ivy is still standing at the sideboard, trying to decide."

"I'll talk to her in one second." Jenna tore a pita in half then used it to scoop up goat cheese dip. "Mmm."

"You've probably noticed her personal space is wider than normal," Layla added.

"I wondered about that; thanks for the tip," Jenna said.

Shane put his bowl of goat cheese dip in the refrigerator. "It will be better with wine when we open a bottle later."

Ethan exhaled as he carried his bowl to the refrigerator. "I'd be kicking myself later if I didn't save some of mine too."

When Jenna went into the dining room, she scanned the room as Petra joined Brittany and Stan at their table. *Everyone is seated except for Ivy.*

Jenna strolled to the sideboard and stood near the end as she surveyed the platters and sighed.

"Is something wrong, Jenna?" Ivy had a yellow crime scene marker in one hand and a red checker in the other.

"I'm sorry; I didn't mean to disturb you. Somebody asked for seconds, and I'm not sure if we should do that. We don't have enough for everyone to have seconds, so it didn't seem right to me."

"Both meals look delicious, but I don't see why anyone would want seconds after the appetizers we enjoyed. Who was it?" Ivy glanced around the room then narrowed her eyes. "I'll bet it was Vera. She's really bossy. Have you run out?"

"We only have one salmon plate left, and that's what someone asked for."

Ivy's eyes brightened as she handed the yellow marker to Jenna. "I like yellow, and I love salmon."

"We'll bring it right to you." Jenna smiled.

Jenna hurried into the kitchen. "Salmon for Ivy."

"I knew you could do it." Layla waited while Wendy plated a salmon with risotto then breezed out of the kitchen to deliver the plate.

Layla returned to the kitchen and giggled. "After I put the plate in front of Ivy, I asked her if there was anything else I could do. She asked me to tell Vera there was no more salmon left."

Wendy's eyes widened. "What did you say?"

"I told her I would love to, but it wasn't very kind, and I might be canned. She told me she didn't think Jenna would fire me, but I shouldn't push it."

"Boss Lady does run a tight ship." Morgan's eyes twinkled.

Jenna snorted. "Can you even see me doing that?"

Morgan added, "Layla, I'd tell Darlene what you said, but she wouldn't believe me."

Layla nodded. "I'll come up with a more shocking version for Darlene."

"We'll give Ivy time to eat her meal before we dish up dessert," Wendy said. "Meanwhile, I'm going to tackle cleanup."

Jenna went into the dining room and stood by the door. *Ivy is still eating; everyone else is finished, but no one seems impatient at all.*

Arthur hovered near the drink table and was wringing his hands as Petra left the drink table with a glass of wine and returned to sit next to Brittany. She set down her glass next to Brittany's glass and nodded when Brittany spoke to her.

Why is Arthur so nervous?

Jenna shrugged and returned to the kitchen.

"What's for dessert?" Shane asked.

Morgan put a platter in the dishwasher. "You have to wait or guess because we aren't telling."

Shane handed her two more platters. "See how helpful I am? Give me a hint."

"We went for the obvious," Wendy said.

Shane nodded. "In that case, I'm guessing peach cobbler."

Morgan smirked. "You're wrong; it's warm peach cobbler with peach ice cream from the orchard."

Shane laughed. "Yes, dear."

Morgan gave him a peck on the cheek.

"You are a very smart man," Wendy said.

Layla peered into the dining room. "Ivy must have been hungry; her food is almost gone. Oops, a mishap. I'll be right back." Layla grabbed a bar towel and rushed into the dining room.

When she returned a few minutes later, she said, "Situation handled. Arthur was helping Stan clear their dishes, and he knocked over a glass of water and jostled Brittany and Petra's wine glasses. The water glass wasn't that full, and the tablecloth absorbed most of it, but he was really embarrassed and apologetic. He put their wine glasses back in place, and I have the offending water glass. Brittany and Petra were very gracious and handled it well."

"Can you imagine if that had been Vera?" Morgan rolled her eyes.

Jenna shook her head. "I'd rather not. Let's serve dessert to those who have cleared their plates; maybe those who are waiting for us to clear their plates for them will get the hint."

Morgan frowned at her phone. "Jenna, we just had a request for a reservation for tomorrow, and it's waiting for approval. As soon as everyone has their dessert, I'll check the system."

"I'll take a quick peek," Jenna said.

Wendy dished up dessert; Layla put five bowls of cobbler and ice cream on a tray, and Morgan added spoons they had wrapped in napkins on Layla's tray.

As Jenna hurried to the office with Katy on her heels, Morgan said, "I'll follow you around with the tray, Layla."

"Good; I get to pick my favorites who will get their dessert first."

"Don't you dare," Wendy said. "You'll get fired."

Jenna rolled her eyes as the three of them giggled.

After Jenna pulled up the reservation system on her computer, she frowned at the screen.

"Vera and Ralph's room appears to be requesting early checkout, Katy. Do you think we have a system glitch?"

Jenna searched for more detail. "The room still shows as paid. I'll talk to Ralph after he's eaten his dessert. Maybe I can catch him without Vera."

Jenna turned off her computer and went into the kitchen.

"What did you find?" Morgan asked before she left with another tray of desserts.

"Ralph and Vera's room has a request for early check out on the system. I thought I'd chat with Ralph to see if they've decided to leave tomorrow instead of staying over."

"Give me a signal if you need backup," Morgan said.

When Jenna went into the dining room, Vera was nowhere to be seen, and Ralph stood alone with a cup of coffee in his hand. Jenna joined him.

"Did Vera call it a night?" she asked.

"She got a phone call from her sister and went to our room to talk. She'll be awhile, so I'm relaxing with an after dinner coffee. Our meal was delicious; it was probably the best I've ever had."

"I'm glad you enjoyed it; I'll tell our chef what you said." Jenna glanced around. "Tomorrow sounds like it will be another intense day."

"It will be, and I'm looking forward to it. Vera's not doing as well, though. I think Paisley is a little too slow-paced for her because she wants to leave in the morning. She's trying to convince her sister to pick her up. Vera tried to talk me into leaving, but genealogy is my only activity outside of work. I have the genealogy bug so bad I go to monthly meetings with a local group. We've always met at the library, but the group has dwindled down to me and two ladies in their nineties, so we pretty much talk about the same thing every month." Ralph smiled. "Actually, they do the talking, and I do the nodding. Occasionally Vera's brother pops in, but he does it just to moon over the librarian. He's had a crush on her for a while."

Ralph scanned the room. "This club might be dysfunctional, but no more so than any of the families I've come across in my years of poking at genealogy."

Arthur joined Jenna and Ralph.

He cleared his throat. When he smiled, his scar around his mouth disappeared. "I'm Arthur Mason, Jenna. My salmon was perfect; thank you."

"It's nice to meet you, Arthur. I'll let our chef know what you said. She'll be pleased."

"Let me know if I can help with anything, Jenna." Ralph pointedly raised his eyebrows then slipped out of the dining room.

Arthur stepped a little closer to Jenna, and she frowned at her shrinking personal space. *I caught that from Ivy.*

Arthur said, "You are a good innkeeper. You and your dedicated staff know how to pamper guests and make them feel welcome. I can tell everybody likes it here a lot." He pursed his lips.

Jenna blinked. *He said that like he'd memorized it.* "Thank you; that's nice to hear. I'll let the team know what you said; they'll appreciate it. If you'll excuse me..."

"Certainly. Maybe we can talk more later when you aren't so busy and there aren't so many people around."

Jenna strolled to the kitchen.

When she went into the kitchen, she said, "Morgan, let's look at that reservation request."

After they were in the office, Morgan asked, "Was there something you wanted to talk about?"

"Look at the reservation request."

Morgan furrowed her brow. "I thought something came up, and you wanted to talk. You had that look on your face."

She sat at her computer and turned it on. "Okay, I'm looking at it."

"What's the name?"

"Arthur Mason, so?"

"What do you know about him?"

"Nothing." Morgan gazed at Jenna. "Is that the Arthur in the genealogy club that is staying at the hotel?"

"Yes. Vera wants to leave Paisley, which is why she submitted the early check out request, and Ralph wants to stay. I'm pretty sure Arthur Mason is Vera's brother, and I think the two of them planned for him to take over the room. Vera obviously expected Ralph to leave when she did, but he is staying."

"But why would..." Morgan scowled. "Did he hit on you?"

"Not really, but there was something about him that was off."

"Are you going to say something to Ethan?"

Jenna snorted. "And be the damsel in distress? No, thank you."

"Are we going to ambush Arthur Mason on the way to his car?"

Jenna laughed. "I know you're joking, but did you know I also heard your heart say please, oh please?"

Morgan giggled. "It gave me away."

"How did he act in the barn?"

"Completely focused on his work. He sat at the table with Chris and Tisha, but didn't chat with either of them or anyone else at break. He didn't pay any attention to me or Layla. None of this matters, though; what matters is that there's something I've missed, and you haven't."

"Thank you."

"So, what's our next step?" Morgan asked.

"After Arthur joined me and Ralph, Ralph left, but first he told me to let him know if I needed any help. I'm going to ask him about Arthur in the morning."

"Ralph said that? He seems so serious and gruff."

"I know; I was surprised at how approachable he was. Oh, and I already declined the early check out on Ralph and Vera's room. Would you decline Arthur's reservation request?"

"I'll be happy to, and I can block him too, so he can't make a future reservation."

"That seems a little extreme, but go ahead. We can always remove the block later, can't we?"

"Whenever we like."

After they returned to the kitchen, Jenna asked, "Where's Ethan?"

"He went outside a few minutes ago. He got a text," Shane said.

"I'm ready to leave, Boss Lady. It's eight thirty, and everything is done in the kitchen," Wendy said.

Layla came in from the dining room. "Miss Ivy was the last one to leave. I removed all the tablecloths and put fresh ones out. The dirty tablecloths and napkins are in the laundry room. I'll take care of them tomorrow. I'm leaving too. I don't want to be accused of being an overachiever."

Wendy and Layla linked arms and giggled as they left.

"Well, that's a wrap. Shall I warm the goat cheese dip?" Morgan asked.

"Yes; I'll take Katy out for a quick break. Maybe we'll convince Ethan to come in with us."

When they went outside, Ethan was waiting near the backdoor. "I've been waiting for you and Katy; Layla told me you'd probably be out soon. We need to talk."

Jenna examined his face. *It's bad news.* "Let's walk."

Ethan took Jenna's hand as they strolled toward the cottage. "What will be my excuse to hold your hand while we walk in the summer?"

"I have complete confidence in you; you'll come up with the perfect reason. What did you want to talk about?"

"I can't think of a good way to ease into this, so I'll just tell you. The chef died from a drug overdose; his body was dragged to his car and staged to look like a suicide."

Jenna stopped and gazed at Ethan. "That's terrible news; I feel so sorry for the family."

He put his arms around her. "So do I, and I'm afraid it will be even worse for them in the morning when the news spreads. There are no suspects or even motives other than a possible coverup for a drug deal gone wrong."

"Does the family know?"

"Yes."

"Do we say anything to Morgan and Shane?" Jenna asked.

"I suspect Darlene will come in with the news in the morning; she may have the latest theory, or at least what the family's reaction is. Why don't we wait?"

Jenna nodded. "It's been a rough day for everyone; it would be nice to end the day together on a pleasant note."

Ethan smiled. "Let's go where it's warm, then."

Jenna returned his smile. "You stole my line."

As they dashed for the back door, Katy passed them and pawed the door.

"I'm hurrying." Ethan opened the door, and Katy raced inside.

When they went into the kitchen, Shane sat at the counter while Morgan massaged his shoulders. She abruptly dropped her hands to her side and quickly sat on the stool next to Shane.

Jenna and Ethan exchanged a glance. Jenna covered her mouth to hide her smile, and Ethan winked.

Chapter Nine

After Katy flopped down next to the warm oven, Morgan cleared her throat. "Wendy made a tossed salad, and put the leftover vegetarian lasagna in the oven to warm. She said we should go off duty and enjoy a meal for a change instead of our usual snacking on bits of appetizers."

"Why don't we go completely off duty and take everything to the cottage?" Jenna said.

"And leave a mess for you at the cottage? No, ma'am." Morgan shook her head.

"I have paper plates; we'll be fine."

Morgan glanced at Shane, and he shrugged.

"I think it's brilliant," Ethan said. "If you're worried about any mess, Morgan, I am highly skilled at arranging plates in a dishwasher."

Morgan giggled. "You win."

"I'll be right back." Shane rushed out the back door.

When he returned, he had a large cardboard box. "I had blueprints in the box. They'll ride just fine on the backseat."

After Morgan and Shane loaded the box with the hot food, Ethan picked up the box. "If you can handle everything else, we can go."

"Got it." Shane opened the refrigerator and pulled out the salad and salad dressing while Morgan put the pita triangles in a bowl and picked up their bottle of wine.

When Jenna pulled out the peach cobbler from the refrigerator, Shane grabbed the ice cream.

"I can't believe we almost left the dessert," Shane said.

"That's okay, honey." Morgan patted his hand. "I would have sent you back for it."

After they were in the cottage, Morgan plated the lasagna while Shane pulled out bowls for their salad, and Jenna put the cobbler in her oven to warm.

Ethan turned on the fireplace, and Shane poured three glasses of wine while Jenna poured a large glass of sweet tea.

After the four of them sat at the table, Shane smiled. "This is how normal people have dinner, isn't it?"

"That's what I hear." Morgan giggled.

While they ate, Morgan said, "Jenna, I found an association of event coordinators and applied for membership and was accepted. They have an extensive archive of online help documentation and tutorials, and an informative monthly newsletter. We need an expert running the events at the barn, so I plan to be one."

"That's an excellent idea," Jenna said. "Maybe I should join an innkeepers association."

Morgan nodded. "I thought you should too, so I saved you the trouble and signed you up."

Shane stared at his glass of wine then took a big bite of lasagna. Ethan choked on his tea.

Jenna rolled her eyes. "Why am I not surprised? It's all online, like your association, isn't it?"

"Of course." Morgan sipped her wine.

Jenna narrowed her eyes. *Morgan left out a critical detail.*

After everyone had eaten, Morgan dished up the remaining peach cobbler into bowls while Ethan cleared the table and Jenna loaded the dishwasher. Shane added a generous scoop of ice cream on top of each bowl of cobbler, and the ice cream oozed into the cracks of the warm cobbler crust and chunks of peaches.

Jenna ate half of her cobbler then leaned back. "I think I'll have warm soupy cobbler for breakfast tomorrow."

While Jenna covered her bowl and put it in the refrigerator, Morgan finished her cobbler then yawned.

"It's only a little after nine, but I'm tired," Morgan said.

"Do you want to ride home with me, honey?" Shane asked.

"No, I'll follow you so you can drop me off in the morning."

After they left, Ethan helped with the dishes.

"I'd better get going too, so you can rest up for tomorrow." He put his arm around Jenna as she walked with him to the door.

"I'm happy Morgan found a group that will help her streamline the process for hosting events. I felt like we'd been pushed barefooted into a snake pit."

"It would have been a tremendous challenge for anyone to take over the catering at the last minute, but I'm impressed with how well you managed it."

Ethan kissed her sweetly then gazed into her eyes. She met his gaze and parted her lips as he leaned down for a kiss. She wrapped her arms around his neck to match the intensity of his passionate kiss.

When they broke away, Ethan smiled. "Good night, sweet thing."

After he left, Jenna peered out the window to watch as he swaggered to his truck.

"I'm a little too wired to relax, Katy." Jenna sat at her computer. "I wonder if there's anything to that story about the man who owned the contracting company."

Jenna's first search results echoed the movie script except didn't identify the source as fiction. She changed some details and searched again.

After an hour of going down rabbit holes that led to another completely unrelated rabbit hole and then another, Jenna revised her latest search to include unsolved cybercrimes.

She stared at her screen. *This is the third one I've found, but it more closely parallels what Felicia sent me.* She blinked her blurry eyes. *I'll bookmark it too.*

"Ready to go outside, Katy? It's bedtime."

Jenna put on her coat and opened the front door. She glanced at the inn. "The lights are still on in Petra's room, Katy. It looks like everyone else has called it a night."

A gust of wind whipped around the cottage and caught her off guard. She shivered and zipped up her jacket.

Jenna gazed at the stars and smiled. *Ethan called me sweet thing.*

When Katy dashed back to the front door, they went inside. Katy followed her to the bedroom. After Jenna changed into her pajamas, Katy flopped down on the orange cotton area rug next to Jenna's bed and was lightly snoring as Jenna turned off her light and pulled up the covers.

Jenna was basking in the sun as her rowboat in the middle of a small lake in the woods gently rocked with the rise and fall of the lake's barely discernible waves.

She woke when Katy growled then barked as she scrambled to the front door.

Jenna jumped out of bed and padded to the front window. "I don't see anything."

She slipped her bare feet into her boots and put on her jacket. When Jenna opened the door, Katy raced out and quietly disappeared into the darkness.

Jenna whistled and called Katy. *I hope it was a rabbit and not a skunk.*

"Katy, here, girl. I'm freezing." Jenna exhaled. *My pajamas are not the warmest thing I could have worn outside.*

She listened as she stood in the front yard in the dark and gazed at the night sky. *I never get tired of seeing the stars.*

Jenna shivered as a car crept up the driveway then parked in the visitor's lot.

When she heard Katy trotting back to her, Jenna glanced at the inn. *Petra's light is still on.* As she stared, the light went off.

After she and Katy went inside, Jenna checked her phone. *Three o'clock.* She yawned as she removed her jacket and kicked off her boots.

"Let's go back to bed."

Katy followed Jenna to the bedroom.

When her alarm chirped, Jenna grumbled as she turned it off. "I have to change the alarm sound; it's too cheerful."

She tossed off the covers and slipped her feet into her slippers. "I feel like I just climbed back into bed."

After she and Katy padded to the kitchen, Jenna poured a cup of coffee then opened the back door for Katy who trotted outside. Jenna showered, dressed, and made her bed.

She hurried to the kitchen and put her leftover peach cobbler and melted ice cream in the microwave. When she opened the back door, Katy dashed inside from the far corner of the backyard.

Jenna checked the weather and enjoyed her warm soupy peach cobbler and tepid coffee while Katy ate breakfast. "It will be as cold as it was yesterday, but we have a pretty good chance of rain this afternoon."

When she stepped outside, Katy dashed to the path that went to the peach orchard. Jenna shrugged as she followed her.

While she strolled along the path, she gazed at the horizon in the east as the sky slowly turned from dark indigo to pale pink and orange.

Katy popped out of the woods and grinned.

"Are you ready to go back?"

Katy dashed toward the inn, and Jenna jogged along the path.

On her way to the inn, Katy barked.

Jenna smiled. *That was her bark for Darlene.*

When she stopped to catch her breath before she went inside, her phone buzzed with a text from Ethan. "Are you at the inn?"

"Yes."

"Good. I'll see you there in five minutes."

When Jenna went into the kitchen, Darlene pointed at a cup of coffee on the counter. "That's yours. It's almost cool enough for you to drink. There weren't any leftovers in the refrigerator. Wendy and I will have to double my recipes for tonight."

"Actually, there was more than enough for our guests. We took the leftovers to my place last night for our version of an impromptu dinner party. There's still a partial serving of peach cobbler left in my refrigerator. I forgot to bring it with me. I'll be right back."

"Leave it," Darlene growled. "We're doing a completely different menu today, and we don't need any leftovers cluttering the refrigerator."

"What's our menu?"

"Garlicky sesame tofu and broccoli over noodles and baked chicken breasts smothered with baby spinach in a creamy cheese sauce. I wanted to call it Kiss Me Tofu and Last Gasp Chicken, but Wendy told me I'd have to get your approval."

Jenna laughed. "I love it, but no. What about the appetizers for happy hour?"

Darlene beamed. "Wendy and I are a team; it's her turn to be in charge of the appetizers. You can check with her."

Jenna raised her eyebrows. "Well done, chef."

Darlene turned to the stove and growled, "Don't you have work to do?"

Jenna hid her smile as she picked up her cup. *Compliments embarrass her. Too bad.*

Katy remained in her spot in front of the oven while Jenna took her coffee into the office. *I don't want to get in Darlene's way.*

When she heard Ethan's truck come up the driveway, Jenna returned to the kitchen with her empty cup in her hand. Darlene raised her eyebrows and refilled the cup before Jenna reached the coffee pot.

"Ethan is here," Jenna said.

Darlene smirked. "I knew that."

Jenna stared at Darlene. "You heard his truck?"

She pointed at Katy who stood with her nose against the door to the hall. "Katy told me."

When Ethan came into the kitchen, Darlene handed him a cup of coffee.

"Thanks, Darlene. Who told you I was here?"

Darlene chuckled. "Boss Lady did after Katy told me."

Ethan set down his cup and rubbed Katy's belly. "Good girl."

"What brings you here so early?" Jenna asked.

"I have that receipt I owe you." Ethan picked up his cup.

Receipt?

"Let's go into the office, and I'll take care of it."

Ethan followed Jenna.

When they were in the office, he said, "I knew you'd go with along with my receipt excuse. I got a call from the sheriff this morning. Let's sit at the table."

"He called you this early?" Jenna examined his face as they sat. *Not good.*

Ethan sipped his coffee then set his cup on the table. "A housekeeper at the hotel found Felicia's body in a stall in their women's restroom near their pool around midnight. Someone had cut her throat. The sheriff didn't go into detail other than to say the housekeeper didn't notice the blood on the floor until after she wiped down the door and cleaned the sinks, so the sheriff is pessimistic about any useful evidence."

Jenna shuddered. "That's horrible."

Ethan nodded. "The sheriff wants to talk to you. He'll be by later this morning, but he said he'd text you first."

Jenna gazed at him. "Why did he call you?"

Ethan glanced at the door and scooted back his chair. "Umm. It was too early to call you."

Jenna narrowed her eyes. "The door's too far away for you to escape before I tackle you."

Ethan chuckled as he rose from his seat. "You would do it too."

Jenna giggled as she stood. "You'd never know what hit you; I'd hang on like a fierce baby possum. So, tell."

He laughed. "You win. The sheriff thinks you know something, and he's afraid someone else is thinking the same thing."

"What am I supposed to know?"

"He didn't say; he just wanted me to stay close."

Ethan narrowed his eyes. "You still carry your pistol, right?"

"Oh, yes." Jenna patted her waistband with her right hand.

"Good." Ethan reached for her and wrapped his arms around her. "Sheriff's orders."

Jenna smiled and leaned against his chest.

Morgan burst into the office. "Hey, y'all. Nice to see you two getting along." She giggled as she sat at her desk.

Jenna's eyes twinkled as she smiled at Ethan. He kissed her lightly and gave her a squeeze before he stepped away. "I'll be around."

After he left, Morgan said, "So, besides morning smooches, what's on our agenda for the day?"

"Darlene and Wendy have two entrées for our dinner guests, Garlicky sesame tofu and broccoli over noodles and baked chicken breasts smothered with baby spinach in a creamy cheese sauce. Darlene suggested we serve every guest their meal at their table like we did last night. It will be a little harder on Wendy and Layla because neither main dish is a casserole, but we'll be serving hot meals. Think we can do it, or do we break out the burners?"

"The yellow evidence markers and the red checkers worked well for us last night; we can do it, and we know they'll handle it because the meals were Wendy's idea," Morgan said.

"Red for the tofu, and yellow for the chicken. Can you take care of the sign?"

"I'll do it. What else do we have?"

"My number one goal is to get through the day without quitting my job."

Morgan snorted. "I'd tell you the Boss Lady can't quit, but you'd take that as a dare. I liked your idea of the club going to the barn after breakfast instead of waiting around here. Layla and I will go to the barn as soon as she gets here, and I expect her a little before seven. We'll have plenty of time to get the coffee going, check the thermostat, and set up the sideboard for the morning. Will you and Wendy be okay with breakfast? Layla could stay if you need extra help."

"Wendy and I can handle it; it's buffet, so we'll basically be replacing empty platters with full platters and monitoring the coffee. Just let me know when you're leaving. Will you need anything from the Peach Pit?"

"No, I don't know where anything is. We'll have to spend a day there sometime to inventory what we have and to put things in order. I'd like to add it to our work calendar; we might have time next week. Shane told me he put things on shelves where they fit. I wouldn't say I cried, but I did have something in my eye for a minute or two."

Jenna sat at her computer. "Everything may feel out of control, but our guests seem happy except for Vera, and every organization has to have a Vera, don't you think? We are carefully tracking our expenses, which will help us price our services appropriately in the future. Do you think we're understaffed?"

"Absolutely. Our biggest problem is the danger of burnout for you, me, and Darlene. We couldn't maintain this pace week after week; although, that's where I'd like for us to be, eventually. We can't rely on Layla because of school, and if we lose Wendy to the kitchen, you and I are back to finding a new housekeeper."

"Wendy may prefer the kitchen, but I'll talk to her after the weekend," Jenna said. "At least you and I know first-hand what all has to be done, which I think will be a tremendous benefit for us."

"I do too. The event management association requires new members to have managed at least one event, and I can see why. I've managed a few simple events, but I never saw the complexities we've been facing. I'll see if there's anything Darlene needs for me or Layla to do before we go to the barn."

"Is Layla coming here or straight to the barn?"

"She's coming here; we'll go to the barn together in my car. I was going to ride with Shane, but I didn't want to bother him with driving me back and forth between the inn and barn."

"I'll be there later; it depends on how much Darlene lets me help clean up after breakfast."

"Don't forget your computer bag; your book is in it."

Jenna picked up her computer bag and put it and her coat on her desk. "Thanks for the reminder. You saved me from a trip back to get it. I really don't need my computer bag because I can't focus long enough to get any work done, but I can definitely get wrapped up in a good book. What about you?"

"I'm taking my computer so I can hide behind the screen, but I'll be like you and reading my book."

"Wendy's loading the utility cart." Jenna hurried into the kitchen.

"What needs to be done, Wendy?"

"I started the coffee machine and finished filling salt and pepper shakers. Darlene said that would relieve some of the backup at the sideboard. The salt and pepper sets and bowls with pats of butter can go on the tables. I put the toaster on the sideboard, but Darlene decided on biscuits instead. We decided to set up two coffee stations with the creamers, sugar, and artificial sweeteners, so I'll take care of that."

"I like it. The guests can pour themselves a cup of coffee then go to a coffee station to doctor their coffee the way they like it."

"Are you talking about the coffee stations?" Darlene asked. "That was Wendy's idea. We tossed around ideas to streamline the buffet and decided the biggest traffic jam was at the coffee machine."

"We should have time to roll the silverware inside napkins. What do you think, Boss Lady?" Wendy asked.

"If we have time, I think it's a great idea."

"I can help roll until Layla shows up. Do we put them on the tables?" Morgan asked.

Jenna furrowed her brow in thought.

Wendy hurried to Darlene. "Do we put the rolled silverware on the tables?"

"No, let's see their reaction to rolled silverware first," Darlene said. "Have a basket with rolled silverware at the beginning of the line next to the plates and set the silverware stand at the end so you can see what works best."

Jenna raised her eyebrows and nodded.

"Yes, chef," Wendy said.

"Morgan and I can get the dining room set up, Wendy, if you want to help Darlene."

Wendy smiled. "I want to, but this is the stage where I stay out of her way while she waves her magical wooden spoon and pulls everything together at the last minute."

Jenna chuckled. "You're right. Let's get to it then."

At five minutes to seven, Jenna heard Layla's motorcycle roar up the driveway. She sent a text to the sheriff. "Morgan and Layla going to the barn in ten minutes. Privacy guaranteed in the Peach Pit."

He replied almost immediately. "Got it. Naptime in the Peach Pit office with the blinds down and the door locked. Sound okay?"

"Perfect."

Layla breezed into the kitchen. "I smelled the bacon before I reached the back door."

Darlene growled, "Don't bother us; we're busy people."

She pointed at a sack on the counter with her wooden spoon. "There's two egg and bacon biscuits for you and two for Morgan in that brown sack; now get to work. You're slowing down the rest of us."

Layla laughed and hugged Darlene who grumbled, "You're in my way."

Morgan grabbed her computer bag, and then she and Layla rushed out of the kitchen.

"That girl pushes my buttons," Darlene said.

"Yes, chef," Wendy whispered.

After Jenna and Wendy carried the platters to the sideboard, Jenna said. "It's seven o'clock, and time for me to unlock the door."

"And for me to disappear." Wendy went into the kitchen when Jenna unlocked the door.

Jenna's eyes widened at the crowd in the hallway. *They're so quiet; they need coffee.*

Petra was pale and had dark circles under her eyes as she came into the dining room, and her voice was weak. "I passed the word to the club that we'll go to the barn right after breakfast. We all appreciate it, Jenna."

Jenna nodded. "It only made sense."

"It's your fault we're all here so early, Jenna," Tisha said as she passed Jenna and beelined to the coffee. "Bacon is a powerful magnet. We could smell it from the hotel."

Jenna smiled. "Our devious plan worked.'"

When the line at the sideboard moved along with no hold ups, Jenna exhaled in relief.

"That was an enormous sigh." Amanda smiled.

Jenna returned her smile. "We're always in such a flurry to set out all the food while it's still warm and at the precise moment for me to unlock the door, it's a relief to slow down and watch our guests enjoy their choices."

"I heard about Ivy's moment last night, and it sounds like you handled it beautifully. I talked to her and Susan later and was surprised to learn they are actually very close friends and quite delightful. Susan told me in confidence, of course, that sometimes Ivy irritates her." Amanda chuckled. "I did learn they are definitely united in an intense dislike of Vera. Sometimes people just rub others the wrong way, don't they?"

Jenna tilted her head as Amanda hurried to the end of the short line for breakfast. *Sounds like Vera and I were the only ones that thought Vera was the leader of that little group.*

After Amanda filled her plate, she glanced around the room for an empty table.

Brittany waved. "Come join us."

Amanda smiled. "Thank you. I didn't want to encroach on anyone."

Stan chuckled. "We'd enjoy your company. Encroach away."

"So, what are your plans for today?" Brittany asked when Amanda sat down.

The noise and energy in the room grew as the group filled their plates and sat down to eat. Wendy and Jenna quickly replaced empty platters with scrambled egg, biscuit, bacon, and pancake platters, and then Wendy removed the empty small bowls and replaced them with small bowls of freshly cut fruit.

While Ralph waited behind Quinn and her husband so he could fill a second plate, Lucille slipped into his seat next to Vera.

Conspiracy?

Jenna rushed into the kitchen for three more small bowls of pats of butter. She carried the bowls to the tables near Vera.

Vera whispered, "I got another note saying I better be gone before tonight. The first note said I knew something I shouldn't know about Felicia."

"Well, when Felicia left, you did say she was a close friend who confided in you."

Vera growled, "I was just trying to be compassionate."

Lucille furrowed her brow. "Somebody must have taken you seriously, but if you want to go home, I'll take you."

"You'd do that for me?" Vera's voice quaked. "Maybe I could stay until after dinner. Last night's dinner was wonderful, wasn't it?"

"My night vision isn't very good; we'd have to leave before the meeting starts or at the very latest, right after lunch."

Vera sighed. "I don't want to miss dinner."

Lucille glanced at Ralph who had set down his full plate while he refilled his coffee before returning. "I better go. You'll have to tell me if we're leaving before I go to the barn."

Lucille quickly returned to her seat.

"What were you and Miss High and Mighty talking about?" Ivy asked.

Lucille snorted. "Nothing you'd care about."

Jenna picked up the empty bacon platter on her way to the kitchen with the empty butter bowls.

"Any more bacon?" she asked when she went into the kitchen.

"That's it," Wendy said.

When Jenna returned to the dining room, Petra had finished eating and joined Jenna near the kitchen door.

Petra said, "I'd like to get a head start in case Morgan could use any help at the barn. I absolutely adore my room. It is so restful. I quickly fell asleep not long after I went to my room last night and didn't wake until my alarm went off at six."

Jenna nodded. "That's wonderful to hear."

When their guests began drifting out, Brittany joined Jenna near the kitchen door.

"Y'all are absolutely magical; the platters were always full. I would have seen how you did it, except I was too busy enjoying my breakfast." Brittany smiled. "Please tell your chef the food was delicious."

"I will." Jenna returned her smile.

As Lucille, Ivy, and Wanda were leaving, Lucille said, "Go ahead; I'll catch up in a second."

Lucille glanced around the room then hurried to Jenna and lowered her voice. "I think I might have misplaced a ring. It's not really all that valuable except to me; it was my mother's. Her birthstone was a ruby."

Lucille tightly squeezed her eyes then a small tear slid down her cheek. "I don't really remember her, but maybe that's why the ring is so important to me."

Careful.

"We'll keep an eye out for it. Do you have an idea where you might have left it?"

"I thought I'd left it in my room, but I can't find it. It was a little big for me, so I suppose it could have slipped off anywhere."

Jenna glanced at Lucille's hands. "I'm really sorry. I'll ask Wendy to check the hall and the common rooms with extra care when she cleans this morning."

"Thank you; I'd appreciate it."

After Lucille left, Jenna shook her head. *I don't mean to be judgy, Lucille, but you couldn't get that ring on your finger unless it was your pinky, and I'm not even sure about that.*

She started to lock the door and then realized Arthur remained standing near the coffee station.

She cocked her head. "I almost locked up; I didn't see you."

"Will you be at the barn again today?" he asked.

"I plan to be there later."

"That's good because we all need friends to watch our back."

Jenna peered at his serious face. "Do you have a friend watching your back?"

Arthur nodded. "Chris is my friend."

"I would think Chris would be a great friend."

"He is. We're your friends."

"Thank you. Do you like staying at the hotel?"

"Yes. I have a television in my room, so I can watch old movies." Arthur stared at his feet. "I have to go. Chris is waiting for me in the hall."

"It's okay for you to go."

"Thank you."

Jenna locked the door after Arthur left. She leaned against the door and exhaled. *What an unusual man.*

He's a friend.

Jenna wrinkled her nose as she headed to the kitchen. *Really?*

When she went into the kitchen, Jenna said, "I'm going to take a brief break."

"You deserve it," Wendy said.

"Did I tell you what I heard this morning?" Darlene asked.

Wendy tilted her head. "No, what?"

"A friend of mine who works nights at the hospital and told me Petra went to the emergency room last night and told them she accidentally took too much of her heart medicine. My friend said they pumped her stomach and kept her for observation for a couple of hours then released her."

"I'm glad she didn't claim food poisoning," Wendy said.

Darlene nodded. "That would have been a nightmare."

Jenna strolled to the living room and sat in the yellow chair.

"What's going on, Nettie?" she whispered.

Secrets.

"I know, and it seems like secrets are everywhere, but who can I trust?"

Ethan.

"I'm getting there. What about the guests? Arthur? Chris?"

Yes.

"Brittany?"

Help her.

"Anyone else?"

Jenna jumped at the sudden crack of a nearby lightning strike that was accompanied by a deafening boom of thunder that shook the windows. "Got it. I'll be careful."

As Jenna strolled back to the kitchen, she furrowed her brow. *I wonder who the true owner of the ring is.*

She rushed back to the living room and stood in front of Nettie's portrait with her hands on her hips. "Does the ring belong to Brittany?"

A gust of wind jostled the wind chimes.

Jenna felt her face grow warm. "You're right; I already knew that."

The chimes jingled again.

"I'm glad I could entertain you," she mumbled as she headed back to the kitchen.

Chapter Ten

Jenna went from the kitchen to her office and grabbed her coat and computer bag then returned to the kitchen. "Let's go outside before the rain starts, Katy."

The distant rumbles became more frequent and louder while Katy investigated the yard and then took care of her business. Jenna watched the black clouds march from the west toward the inn.

After Katy dashed back to the inn and barked at the door, Darlene opened the door.

"It's going to be a dreadful storm, Boss Lady. You better get moving. There's a brown sack inside your computer bag for you and Ethan." Darlene handed Jenna her computer bag and a dry towel, and Katy trotted inside.

As Jenna headed toward her car, a sudden gust of wind and rain sent her running. After she jumped into her car, Jenna turned on her windshield wipers and drove through the rain toward the barn.

By the time she reached the driveway, Jenna had turned on her windshield wipers to their highest setting and was clutching the steering wheel to lean forward in her seat so she could see the driveway and avoid going into a ditch. She could barely see the front of her car hood despite the wipers' frantic pace to clear the relentless downpour from the windshield. Jenna parked as close to the barn's back door as she could.

After she turned off the engine, she jammed the towel between her computer bag and her chest as she reached for the door handle. *Do I wait or go on the count of three?*

Her car door jerked open, and an enormous umbrella blocked her view. "Let's go," Ethan growled.

Jenna clutched her computer bag close to her chest like a parachute and jumped out; Ethan grabbed her up with one arm before her feet hit the ground and carried her to the barn door as it swung open.

"Hurry up; I'm getting wet too," Morgan shouted over the storm.

Ethan released Jenna after they were inside, and the room erupted in applause and cheers while Morgan pulled the door closed.

After the club members settled down and returned their attention to their computers, Jenna set her computer bag on the table in front of her and exhaled. "That was remarkably harrowing for me and coordinated on your side."

Morgan put the open umbrella in the corner to drip dry. "Darlene texted Ethan and told him you were on your way, and Petra loaned us her umbrella."

Layla brought Jenna a cup of coffee. "I poured it when Ethan got Darlene's text. It must have been pretty gnarly driving in that torrential rain."

"It's definitely not anything I'd want to do again any time soon." Jenna shivered as she handed the towel to Morgan. "This is from Darlene; you need it more than I do."

Jenna took off her coat and draped it over a chair.

Morgan dried her face and arms and then handed the towel to Ethan. "Your turn."

"I didn't get all that wet." He handed the towel to Jenna.

Jenna draped the towel over a chair and shrugged. "It's here if we need it."

Jenna pulled out two wrapped biscuit sandwiches from the sack inside her computer bag and handed them to Ethan. "These are for you."

She carried her coffee and computer bag to the same table she had claimed as hers the day before.

After Jenna sipped her coffee, she pulled out her wrapped biscuit sandwich and scanned the room. Arthur raised his palm in a quick wave, and she smiled and copied his palm wave.

Layla joined her and whispered, "New friend?"

Jenna shrugged. "Something like that."

Tell Ethan.

When Layla returned to the table with Morgan, Jenna ate her biscuit sandwich and downed her coffee.

After Jenna rose and hurried to the sideboard, she refilled her cup and poured a cup for Ethan.

She smiled as she carried the two cups to the back where Ethan still stood.

Jenna set the two cups down at the table closest to the back door and sat down. "Care to join me in a cup of coffee?"

Ethan moved a chair close to hers and sat with her. "What did you want to tell me?"

Jenna rolled her eyes. "Maybe I was just being nice and brought you a cup of coffee."

She wrapped her hands around her coffee cup. "Too hot to drink, but a great hand warmer."

Ethan chuckled then sipped his coffee. "Mine's perfect. I forgot about your reputation for being social and outgoing."

Jenna furrowed her brow. "Isn't that redundant? I had a chat with Nettie today. I'm supposed to trust you; how am I doing?"

Ethan gazed at her. "Rapidly improving."

She met his gaze. "Thanks. I have only two friends in the genealogy club I can trust, according to Nettie."

"Two?"

"Arthur and Chris."

Ethan set down his cup and gaped at her. "Nettie said that?"

She nodded. "She was very adamant there was no one else, and I have more to tell you, but it can wait."

Ethan put his hand on her arm. "I can't."

Tell him.

"Wendy found a ruby ring in the restroom. It's part of a secret, but that's all I know. Lucille told me this morning she lost a ruby ring, and it must have slipped off her finger."

Ethan glanced at Lucille and frowned. "The ring's too small for her, isn't it?"

"Yes."

"Where's the ring?"

"Locked in my office. Can we talk later?"

Ethan nodded then downed his coffee and returned to his position near the back door.

Jenna picked up their cups and carried them to her table. She pulled out the book from her computer bag.

When she opened her book, the makeshift bookmark slid out and onto her table. Her eyes widened as she read it. "She has to go."

Jenna exhaled. *Is this "go" like leave, or "go" like die? And who is she?* Jenna rose and stretched then strolled to the back where Ethan stood.

She stood next to him, and he put his arm around her.

She gave him the slip of paper, and he leaned close while she whispered, "This was on the floor yesterday. I picked it up without reading it and stuck it into my book to mark my place."

"What do you think it means?" he mumbled.

"I don't know. Something completely innocent or sinister."

Ethan nodded and stuck the paper into his pocket.

Jenna exhaled then told him what Morgan said about the "unfasten" or "assassin" conversation at the hotel.

"Are we seeing monsters around every corner?" she asked.

Ethan kissed her ear. "Does Morgan know about the ring or the note?"

Jenna giggled then rubbed her ear. "That tickled. No, she doesn't."

"Then it's just you and me that see the monsters."

Jenna peered at him. "That's comforting."

I'll bet Nettie's laughing.

"Sorry; I was trying to be light-hearted. Seriously, thanks for telling me."

Jenna nodded. She bit her lip as strolled back to her seat. *I need time with no interruptions to focus on what Felicia sent me.*

After she sat down, Jenna scanned the room. *I have time right now.*

Jenna pulled out her notebook and her computer. She examined the first record of the Garrison family with the sudden appearance of a baby girl and took notes.

She exhaled. *Was there a typographical error, and the girl was listed on the wrong record? Does that explain why she appears with this family only once?*

She turned the page in her notebook to a fresh page. *Maybe it will help if I move on to the next record.*

The next family record began in the late 1700s. She raised her eyebrows. *Prentice is the same last name as the man who owned the contracting business, according to Chris.*

She scrolled through the next ten pages associated with the Prentice family. *If I were in my office, I could print these and spread them out on my table. I'll do that later.*

The next document was a copy of a census page from twenty-five years ago for a couple named Garrison. The man's occupation was listed as teacher, and the woman's was homemaker.

The document that followed had a cover sheet titled "Baby Girl Doe."

Jenna read the first few pages and raised her eyebrows. *This is a contract between a law office representing an anonymous client and the Garrisons for an adoption. I wonder if Adrienne would review this for me.*

She sent Adrienne an email. "I have a copy of an old contract from one of the genealogy members that looks like it's for an adoption. Could you give it a quick review and send me your thoughts?"

Adrienne responded immediately. "Fire away."

Jenna rolled her eyes as she attached the Baby Girl Doe document to her email. "I thought you wouldn't see the email until Monday. It's not urgent."

Adrienne replied, "It's you; it's urgent. Call me when you have time to give me the backstory."

Jenna peered out the window at the rain that still hadn't let up then checked the weather radar on her phone. *It will be clearing soon; thank goodness. I'm ready to leave.*

Jenna turned off her computer and stretched her back then joined Ethan.

She spoke softly so she wouldn't disturb anyone. "When did Shane leave?"

Ethan continued to scan the room. "Not too long ago; he'll be back in time for lunch. I can leave when he returns. Are you as antsy as I am?"

"Probably. How can you take standing the entire time? Aren't you wearing out?"

"I walk around a little; it's not as bad as if I were sitting."

Petra rose then surveyed the club members before she strode to the front. "Let's take a five minute stretch break. It looks like the rain might break before lunch."

"I need to walk around," Jenna said.

Ethan nodded.

Jenna strolled to the window near her table and watched the rain dance with the leaves on the trees. When Arthur joined her at the window, he said, "People talk like I'm not there."

Jenna examined his face. "Does that bother you?"

He glanced at her then turned his attention back to the rain. "No. Lucille showed Wanda a photo that was supposed to be Vera with the toddler. Wanda told her it had to be a fake because Vera wouldn't know how to hold a baby, and they laughed. Wanda asked for a copy. Lucille said Petra gave it to her, so she didn't know if she was allowed to share it. I could tell the photo was fake."

"Why did Petra do that?"

"Someone who scares her told her to make Vera leave, so Petra told Lucille that Vera was the toddler's nanny and was in danger here. We don't know yet who Petra is afraid of or why Vera has to leave, but Chris said I should tell you what I heard."

"Do you think the toddler is supposed to be the one that disappeared?"

"The photo is not real, so it doesn't matter what I think of it. I think Petra wants Vera to leave, so she convinced Lucille that Vera is in danger."

Share with your friends.

Jenna nodded. "Katy woke me in the middle of the night, and I didn't go back to sleep for a long time. I think Petra was away from the inn until three o'clock this morning because I heard a car return and then her bedroom light that had been on when I got up went off. One of our chef's friends told her Petra was at the hospital because she accidentally took too much of her heart medicine."

"I never have trouble sleeping." Arthur returned to his table.

Jenna listened to the rain pounding the roof and the wind whistling around the corners of the barn. *I wish I could say that.*

After Jenna returned to her table, Petra said, "Time's up; back to your seats, please. Our next break will be at lunch."

Jenna opened the next file after the contract. *This is a birth certificate for Briana Prentice. It's interesting that it includes the tiny footprints. I wonder if they still do that. Felicia must have worked for years gathering all these documents.*

Jenna frowned. *What was the name of the original investigator?*

Jenna began a new search.

Her phone buzzed with a text from the sheriff. "Naptime over. I have the key."

Jenna peered out at the rain that had slowed to a shower. "Good."

After an hour, Jenna found the investigator's name in the archives of a long defunct newspaper and stared at the name. *Thorton. I'd bet a nickel he had a daughter named Felicia. Peas in a pod.*

Jenna saved the article she'd found and exhaled as she shut down her laptop. When she glanced outside, she smiled. *The clouds are clearing, and the only drops of water are from the trees.*

She glanced toward Morgan who tapped her wrist.

Jenna nodded. *Shane will be here in just a few minutes with lunch.*

She slid her computer into its bag and joined Ethan at the back door.

Morgan checked her phone and motioned for Layla to follow her.

"Lunch must be here," Ethan said.

Morgan and Layla hurried to the back door, and Ethan followed them outside. Jenna shrugged and held open the door for Ethan who carried in the large pot of stew. Shane followed him in with a cooler, and Layla carried a cardboard box.

Morgan was empty-handed; she sniffed. "I closed the trunk."

Jenna nodded. "It's almost important as holding the door."

Morgan giggled. "I was planning to be grumpy; you just ruined it, Boss Lady."

"My job."

"You don't need to come back this afternoon; we'll be fine."

"Okay; text me if you want me here."

Ethan joined Jenna at the back door. "Ready to go?"

"Absolutely."

Ethan followed Jenna back to the inn.

After they parked and headed toward the back door, Ethan asked, "Are you planning to return to the barn this afternoon?"

"I don't think so; Morgan doesn't expect me back. I have to check registrations and a few other administrative chores, and then I'll fill in where I can to help Darlene and Wendy so Darlene can leave on time."

"I have to work on a project today because we're a couple of guys short. If you have any problems, Shane said he'd be on standby." Ethan held the door for her, then left.

When Jenna went into the kitchen, Jenna inhaled a tantalizing chocolatey, toasty aroma, and Katy danced.

Darlene laughed. "Isn't that a wonderful way to be greeted?"

"Sure is." Jenna stroked Katy's back and rubbed her face. "It smells good in here. Are you baking something chocolate, or is it a surprise?"

"We're having chocolate sheet cake with fudgy chocolate butter cream frosting and vanilla ice cream."

"That sounds scrumptious. Where's Wendy?"

"She's straightening rooms. Are you ready for lunch? I saved some stew for you."

"That would be great. I'll let Wendy know I'm here."

Jenna heard the vacuum in Susan's room. When Jenna appeared in the open doorway, Wendy turned off the vacuum.

"We need to talk," Wendy whispered. "Can I come to your office in a ten minutes? This is my last room."

Jenna nodded then returned to the kitchen. Darlene pointed to a small bowl on the counter. "That's pork stew, and do you want a warmed flour tortilla? Do you want hot or cold tea?"

"Hot tea, please, but the stew is plenty for me. Thanks for the small bowl."

"You never eat much at lunch, and I don't like to waste food. If you want more, you can have it."

Jenna took a small taste of stew. "It's not too hot, thank you."

"Anytime." Darlene set the cup of hot tea on the counter then turned to the sink and grabbed a large pot to scrub.

After Jenna ate her stew, Darlene whisked away her bowl before Jenna could rise to put it into the dishwasher.

Darlene said, "We made more cookies for lunch. Would you like a cookie to go?"

Jenna smiled. "I never turn down one of your cookies."

Darlene handed her a saucer with two cookies. "Here you are."

Jenna slung her computer back strap over her shoulder then balanced her saucer on her cup as she went into her office.

She removed her computer from its bag and plugged it in to charge then turned on her desktop computer to check the registration system.

Jenna approved a registration for the following week then peered at the screen. "Why don't I just remove the block we put on Arthur real quick?"

Jenna growled as she poked around. "It shouldn't be this hard. Where's the help button or whatever?"

She glowered at her computer and closed the system when Wendy came into the office from the kitchen.

"Are you okay?" Wendy asked.

"I was fighting with my computer; you probably saved me from another hour of doing the same thing over and over and getting more and more frustrated." Jenna exhaled. "Let's sit at the table. My computer needs a time out."

After they sat at the table, Wendy said, "I had a minor run in with Vera. While I was cleaning Lucille's room, which is next to hers, she came into the room and shouted at me for touching her things. I immediately ushered her out of Lucille's room and finally understood she thought she was missing a lipstick. We went to her bathroom together, except I stayed in the doorway. I noticed a drawer that was not quite flush and asked her to check the drawer. The lipstick was there, but then she accused me of hiding it so she would leave it behind. From the state of her room, I think she was packing. Anyway, I did not clean her room and told her I would not be going into her room at all until tomorrow after they left. I suggested she have a conversation with you about her lipstick and her room. I'm worried she'll leave a bad rating for the inn."

"What a stinker," Jenna said. "Are you okay?"

Wendy exhaled. "I am now. I've never been around anyone so hateful."

"She was completely out of line; I'm really sorry you had to deal with her, but you did everything right from not letting her stay in Lucille's room to not going into the bathroom and telling her to report her issue to me. I'd heard she might leave today, and it sounds like she is. If you'd like to stay in the kitchen for a while, I'd like to talk to her before she bolts, and don't worry about a bad review. We have enough glowing reviews that if she gives us a low review or rating, it will reflect on her, not us."

Wendy's eyes welled up. "Thank you. I feel better."

When Jenna followed Wendy into the kitchen, Katy whined.

"I'll take you outside, Katy; I need some fresh air myself."

"That's okay, Wendy. I can take her."

Wendy smiled. "I know, but I really do have to stretch my legs and breathe in some bitingly cold air."

Wendy put on her coat.

"Are you taking Katy outside?" Darlene asked.

"I could use the walk," Wendy said.

"Well, so could I. Can you hold down the fort by yourself, Boss Lady?" Darlene growled.

Jenna pursed her lips to keep from smiling, but her eyes twinkled. "I'll do my darnedest."

"My coat's by the back door. Let's go before she changes her mind," Darlene said.

After the three of them went outside, Jenna climbed the stairs and tapped on Vera's door.

When Vera opened the door, Jenna peered past her. An open suitcase was on the unmade bed with a pile of clothes spilling out the sides.

Vera growled, "Are you here to throw me out?"

Jenna tilted her head. "Why would I want to do that?"

Vera stared at her, then her eyes welled up, and tears flowed down her cheeks. "Because I was ugly to Wendy."

Boo hoo.

Jenna nodded. "After you calm down, you could write her a pleasant note of apology. Wendy is a kind-hearted soul and never holds a grudge."

"It wasn't that bad." Vera's whiny voice grated on Jenna's ears.

Jenna suppressed a shudder. "Up to you. Are you leaving?"

Vera glowered. "Yes. Lucille offered to take me home today because this was not the pleasant place it was supposed to be. She's been telling me all along that I shouldn't be here, and we even had a big argument about it."

"I'm sorry you feel that way. Aren't you going to stay for happy hour and dinner then leave? Surely you don't want to eat gas station food on your way home."

"Lucille said she can't see well enough to drive at night, so I don't have any choice. I have to leave now."

"I'm sorry you're leaving, but it was a pleasure to meet you, and we hope to see you again soon."

Jenna carefully closed the door as she left.

Brava.

Jenna smiled as she went down the stairs. "Thanks."

When she reached the end of the hall, she glanced toward the back door. "If I go outside, they'll think I'm hinting they have to come in." She hurried to her office.

She sat at her desk and turned on her computer. "First things first. I'll check reservations, but I'll let Morgan unblock Arthur."

She pulled out her notebook and jotted down Felicia's father as the lead investigator on the disappearing toddler case and added Felicia as picking up on the investigation.

"But why did she?"

Peas in a pod.

Jenna furrowed her brow. "I wonder if there are any pictures of the Prentice family."

She rubbed her hands together and began her search.

Jenna frowned at the photos in the newspaper articles she found after the crash where the parents had been killed. *These are all the same black and white snapshot. I want a family photo that's in color.*

She read the articles then read the obituaries. "Ah ha. Their joint funeral was held at a church. I wonder if the church had a member directory."

She found the church, but their member directory was available to members only. *How do I gain access?*

She sent a text to Morgan. "How do I get access to a members-only church directory?"

Morgan responded, "Become a member? Give me a minute."

Jenna stared at the phone. *Maybe I shouldn't have texted that.*

"I was just kidding."

"I knew that. See you later."

Ten minutes later, Morgan called.

"Hey, Shane wants to know how urgent this is. Can it wait until after dinner?"

"Of course."

"Good, then while the guests are eating dinner, he'll go home and then, you know, come back. What's he looking for? What about Ethan?"

"I need a directory of church members with photos. I'll text the details to Shane. I'll tell Ethan later, but for now, I don't think anyone needs to be a part of this except Shane, you, and me."

"Your call, Boss Lady, but for the record, I completely agree with you." She hung up.

Good friends.

Jenna nodded. "I don't know why it's important for me to see a photo of the parents, but it is."

She sent the text to Shane with the name of the church, the name of the parents, and the date range of two years before Briana was born to two years after her disappearance.

Jenna opened the folder where she had saved all the documents from Felicia and went to the next two documents, which were newspaper articles about the missing toddler.

The first article was from the local paper and was dated the day after Briana disappeared. Jenna's stomach churned as she read.

Toddler Disappears

Authorities Seek Public's Help

Local authorities are investigating the mysterious disappearance of two-year-old Briana Prentice, who vanished Saturday afternoon during a family birthday party at Sweetwater Park.

According to witnesses, Briana was last seen playing near the park's rose garden shortly before 3 p.m. while her parents helped unload presents and prepare refreshments nearby. Several guests believed she had gone to the playground with other children and their parents, but within minutes, she could not be located.

"We've searched the entire area, including the surrounding woods and creek," the local sheriff said. "At this time, we have no evidence of foul play, but we are treating this as a potential abduction because of the suddenness of her disappearance."

Dozens of volunteers joined law enforcement in an overnight search. Police dogs were brought in from neighboring counties, but no scent trail was found beyond the park's eastern fence.

Briana is described as having strawberry blonde hair, blue eyes, and was last seen wearing a yellow sundress with white sandals.

Anyone with information is urged to contact the Sheriff's Department immediately.

The second article was a follow-up from an Atlanta newspaper five years later. Tears welled up in Jenna's eyes. *This is horrible.*

Five Years Gone Without a Trace

The Vanishing of Briana Prentice Still Haunts a Small Georgia Town

It was a sunny spring afternoon in a small town in middle Georgia, when two-year-old Briana Prentice disappeared without a trace. Five years later, there are still no answers. There are only questions, fading flyers, and a family frozen in time.

Five years ago today, Briana attended her cousin's birthday party at Sweetwater Park, a popular local gathering spot. In a matter of minutes, the toddler went from giggling near the rose garden to simply being gone. No witnesses, no screams, no signs of struggle; just an open gate near the service road and a community desperate for answers.

Despite exhaustive searches, national media attention, and a $50,000 reward offered by a private donor, no viable leads ever emerged. The local sheriff's department, once optimistic, now admits the case has gone cold.

"We followed every tip, every theory," said Chief Investigator Tom Thorton, who led the original investigation. "We still hope someone, somewhere, knows something. All it takes is one phone call."

Theories abound from an opportunistic abduction, a kidnapping gone sour, even whispers of human trafficking, but none have yielded evidence. The Prentice family remains private, no longer speaking to reporters.

Today, a faded yellow ribbon still flutters from a tree in front of the Prentice home. Locals leave flowers at the park each year on the anniversary.

"Someone took her," says a retired schoolteacher who was at the party. "But after all this time, we've finally accepted that she'll never be found."

As the fifth anniversary passes, the name Briana Prentice remains etched in the hearts of the town's residents as a haunting reminder that even the smallest towns can harbor the darkest secrets.

After she read the articles, Jenna turned off her computer as despair enveloped her like a cold fog and tears slipped down her face. *Their hope dwindled then withered into nothingness.*

She sniffled and wiped away tears with a tissue, but the tears were relentless. *Tom Thorton refused to give up and passed his relentless determination to find Briana on to his daughter.*

Jenna grabbed another tissue and went to the living room.

She sat in her yellow chair. "It's so sad, Nettie. I don't want to read any more because Tom Thorton failed to find her, and Felicia devoted her life to the futile search."

Find her.

"You have more faith in me than I do."

Jenna closed her eyes and leaned back in her chair as her despair was replaced with a glimmer of hope.

You're close.

Jenna gazed at Nettie's portrait. "Okay, Nettie. I'll keep reading and searching."

She stopped at the doorway and glanced over her shoulder. "There's still more sadness ahead, isn't there?"

A tiny glowing red ember in the fireplace caught her eye.

Jenna sighed. "Distraction."

Yes.

Jenna walked slowly down the hall while she was in deep thought. *It's sad, but Nettie gave me hope.*

She exhaled when she reached the kitchen door. "Quit moping," she muttered.

She thought about Ethan's grin when she asked about a pink security vest for Katy and smiled. "Now, I'm ready."

When Jenna opened the door to the kitchen, the sweet aroma of peaches swirled around her, and then she heard Darlene's angry voice, and she paused. *Do I really want to go in there?* She shrugged and went into the kitchen.

Chapter Eleven

"You win," Darlene growled. "It's not what anyone else would do, so we'll do it."

Wendy's face was solemn. "You're right, Darlene. No one else would dare do it."

"Then check the peach cupcakes; we want them to be moist, not dried out."

Darlene's face brightened when she saw Jenna. "Boss Lady, we'll have three dessert choices for tonight."

"What are the choices?"

"Chocolate sheet cake with fudgy chocolate butter cream frosting, peach cupcakes with whiskey buttercream frosting, or vanilla bean cupcakes with peppermint crunch frosting."

"They sound delicious, but won't three desserts and two entrées be an impossible amount of work?"

"Of course, but we dropped our original idea to have ice cream with the cake to simplify the desserts." Darlene beamed.

"It would be too much work for anyone else," Wendy added.

"I'll stay out of your way, but if there is anything else I can do to help, tell me."

"Will do, Boss Lady." Wendy smiled.

Jenna absently nodded as she strolled toward her office and thought about Felicia's files. *Nettie said I'm close; maybe I am, but I still don't see it.*

Jenna's phone rang after she closed her office door.

When she answered, Adrienne said, "I've never seen an adoption document written quite like that. It actually gave me the shivers because it read more like a real estate or service contract. I asked Suzanne to look it over, and she didn't like it at all. From a legal standpoint, the Garrisons accepted financial responsibility for the health and education of a child named Brandi, who was three years old, which is technically what an adoption is. Brandi's original birth certificate was from a hospital that had gone out of business. The Holloway law firm had a lot of political clout in those days. Mr. Holloway himself must have pulled strings to get the state to recognize the hospital record as a birth certificate so they could issue a replacement that recorded the Garrisons as the parents. Do you have a copy of the hospital record?"

Jenna furrowed her brow. "I might. I haven't seen it yet, but I haven't been through all the documents."

"When you find it, we'd like to see it. If you don't find it, let me know."

"Okay. I have the copy of the genealogy records of the Garrisons. Brandi Garrison appears as a three-year-old only in the year she was adopted. Nothing before, and nothing since. What could that be?"

Adrienne snorted. "Some type of clerical error is my guess. Send what you have to me, and I'll dig into the Garrison family a little."

"Okay, and I'll watch for the hospital birth record."

After they hung up, Jenna sent Adrienne the Garrisons' genealogy records that she had and the link that Felicia had included.

Jenna rubbed her forehead. *Felicia gave me the records for two toddlers. Briana Prentice disappeared when she was two years old. The same year, three-year-old Brandi Garrison was adopted by the Garrisons. Did she think Brandi could be Briana? Is Brandi's birth certificate buried somewhere in Felicia's files?*

I need pictures. Jenna scanned through the rest of the documents. *No pictures; no birth certificate. Nothing.*

She sent Adrienne a text. "I need a photo of three-year-old Brandi Garrison and a copy of her birth certificate."

Adrienne responded, "I'll work on it."

"Back to the Prentices," Jenna muttered as she pulled out the overstuffed manilla envelope Felicia had given her.

When she opened the envelope, the papers were so tightly packed that she couldn't get a hand hold to pull them out. *These are really stuck.*

She pulled out her scissors and snipped a triangle on a corner so she could grab a few sheets. When she tugged, the old envelope ripped down the side, and an eruption of papers scattered across her desk and onto the floor. Jenna gaped at the pages of handwritten notes and picked up a page from her desk.

She read the first paragraph of the tight, neat handwriting and moaned as she glanced at the pages on her desk. *Mr. Thorton documented at the level of minutia and his meticulous handwriting shows it, but at least he added what look like chapter titles and numbered the pages.*

By the time she reached the end of the page, her eyelids had grown heavy and drooped. *My eyes need a rest.*

As she gathered up the papers that had fallen onto the floor, her eyes widened when she uncovered a photocopy of a birth certificate for Briana Louise Prentice, that included tiny inked baby footprints. *Mr. Thorton was certainly thorough. This must have been the source of the birth certificate Felicia included in her document.*

She set the birth certificate on her desk then collected all the papers from the floor and dropped them into a file folder along with the torn envelope.

After she slipped the birth certificate and the papers from her desk into a second folder, Jenna exhaled and then stared at the folders on her desk. *I need a break.*

Jenna dropped the folders into the file cabinet and picked up her coat.

When she went into the kitchen, Wendy said, "You're dragging, Boss Lady."

Darlene narrowed her eyes and frowned. "You need a glass of ice tea and a cookie."

Jenna draped her coat over a kitchen chair then sat at the counter. "I'm not sure what's worse, mental or physical exhaustion."

Wendy nodded and put a glass of tea and a cookie on a napkin in front of Jenna.

Jenna sipped her drink and ate her cookie while Wendy emptied the dishwasher, and Darlene added ingredients to her mixing bowl.

"Sometimes a change of scenery helps me," Wendy said.

Jenna finished her tea. "That's a good idea. How about a walk, Katy?"

Katy rose from her spot in front of the oven then stretched while Jenna put on her coat.

Katy trotted to the kitchen door; after Jenna opened it, the two of them strolled to the back door then outside.

"Let's take the path to the orchard and see if we feel like jogging back."

Katy dashed into the woods while Jenna strolled along and gazed at the clear sky and the lingering leaves in the trees waving in a light breeze. She breathed in the cold air and exhaled as Katy trotted out of the trees ahead of her.

When Jenna reached Katy, the two of them strolled along together to the hill overlooking the orchard. Some trees still had a few colorful autumn leaves, but most of the trees were bare and ready for their winter dormancy.

"I understand why Mr. Thorton had Briana Prentice's birth certificate because he was searching for her, and Felicia would have it if she was trying to retrace her father's trail. But why did Felicia have the Garrison genealogy records? Was she researching her own project before her father died? I would have expected her to pick up where her father left off, but now I can't get Brandi Garrison out of my head. Clerical errors aren't unheard of, but what else could it be if it isn't a slip on a keyboard?"

Jenna stared at the orchard then sighed. *I have no answers.*

"Ready to go back, Katy?"

Katy trotted alongside Jenna until they came to the curve. Katy grinned then raced toward the inn, and Jenna chased after her.

Before Jenna was within sight of the inn, Katy barked. Jenna chuckled as she shifted from running to jogging. *That little sneak called Darlene to let her in for her treat.*

A mockingbird serenaded Jenna as she neared the inn. Jenna slowed to a walk as she listened, and her breathing returned to normal.

Before she went inside, she stopped at the back door and glanced at the trees and the sky while she inhaled the cool air. "Thank you for the song, bird."

She watched as the mockingbird flew away. *Back to work.*

When Jenna went into the kitchen, she glanced at the counter, and her eyes lit up at the sight of the cupcake and its white frosting with bits of red and white peppermint candy to add color, flavor, and crunch.

"Wow, the cupcake is gorgeous."

"It's still warm, so the frosting might be oozy, and the cupcake itself will probably be crumbly, but you're our tasting guinea pig, not the fashion police." Wendy smiled.

Darlene added, "We gave you two napkins and a knife and fork so you wouldn't have to take a shower before dinner. We have everything ready for this evening. There are only a few things left to do. It's after two thirty; you owe me five minutes overtime, Boss Lady."

"You got it."

Darlene stood at the door with her arms crossed while Jenna cut the cupcake in half then scooped up frosting and cake with her fork.

After Jenna took a bite, she said, "Wow. This is absolutely delicious, and I love the peppermint crunch."

Darlene nodded. "Now I can leave; we passed the Boss Lady test."

"Thank you for the cupcake. Be safe; we'll see you in the morning."

Darlene waved as she left.

"How was your walk?" Wendy put away the clean baking pans.

"Katy ran, and I kind of ran. I needed the fresh air to clear my head; the weather's still cold, but it's a gorgeous day."

Wendy said, "Vera and Lucille left. Lucille told me she'd be back soon because she was taking Vera to meet her sister."

"That's surprising."

"I planned to lie low while Vera was here; since she's left, that takes off a lot of pressure."

"I agree. She probably has redeeming qualities that we just missed while she was being such a pain."

Wendy chuckled. "I'm sure you're right, Boss Lady. Since Vera isn't here, I'd like to clean Ralph's room. Is that okay with you?"

"That's a great idea. I'll be in my office."

Jenna carried her tea and cupcake to her office and printed the Prentice genealogy records. While she listened to the printer whir and click as it crank out page after page, she took a few bites of her cupcake.

Jenna cocked her head and put down her fork. "Must be after three. Cars are pulling into the guest parking lot. It won't be long until Morgan and Layla will be here."

Jenna continued reading page after page then stopped. *It's almost too hard to read, but I feel like there's something here that's nowhere else.*

She carried her empty glass and her plate with half of a cupcake on it into the kitchen.

Wendy said, "We have vanilla cupcakes for Morgan, Layla, Shane, and Ethan as a reward for their hard work this afternoon. Darlene hid five peach cupcakes in the refrigerator for y'all to have tonight."

"You and Darlene spoil us, and we love it," Jenna said.

"Want me to wrap up the other half of your cupcake, Boss Lady?"

"I'd appreciate it."

While Wendy transferred Jenna's cupcake to a container, she said, "It didn't take me long at all to straighten Ralph's room. I didn't vacuum, but I did run the dust mop over the floor. I felt terrible about a guest room with an unmade bed."

"I'm glad you thought of it."

Red spots appeared on Wendy's cheeks. "Thank you."

I have questions.

Jenna cleared her throat. "I just remembered I need to update the registration book for next week."

Wendy set the container in the refrigerator. "I think all our schedules have been knocked off-kilter."

Jenna left the kitchen with Katy at her side and strolled to the registration desk and brought up the system.

While she updated the registration book, Susan and Ivy came inside. Jenna smiled as Ivy hurried up the stairs, and Susan continued toward her room, but both of them ignored her.

I'll try again. "How did today go, Susan?" Jenna asked.

Susan turned around and gazed at Jenna then smiled. "I think the rest of them were working on the challenge because it was almost eerie how quiet it was this afternoon."

She was surprised when I spoke to her. Jenna returned her smile. "I'm sorry I missed that. You said the rest of them; you didn't write anything for the challenge?"

"I never do. Ivy freezes sometimes, and thank you so much for helping her at dinner last night. I'm not always patient with her, and I make it worse. Anyway, I've always read Ivy's submissions for her. I'd feel funny if I won because I'd worry I didn't do justice to hers. Vera told me I coddled Ivy, but I told her we all need a friend we can count on even if our friend wasn't perfect."

"I agree with you, and I think you're a good friend. Did Felicia have any friends?"

"I don't think she really did, but she seemed quite content with that; she was a very focused person."

"What about Petra?"

"I don't trust her; she doesn't have any friends here, that's for sure. She and Tisha are very much alike." Susan gazed at Jenna. "You're observant and very perceptive, so I'm sure you've seen how shallow they are."

Jenna raised her eyebrows. "You're pretty perceptive yourself."

Susan chuckled. "It's my gray hair and the cane. I fall into the class of elderly and infirm, which gives me invisibility in the eyes of most people. It's actually quite useful."

"That's really interesting; I never thought about that before. I think I might be a little jealous." Jenna's eyes twinkled.

"It will take you a while to get there." Susan tittered.

"Who do you think will win the competition?"

"Of course, I'm prejudiced. Ivy has a wonderful twist to her story, but I don't discount Stan. He is a talented storyteller and writer. This may be his last year with the club, which I think will be a loss. He and Brittany are delightful people." Susan shifted her weight and leaned more on her cane.

"I'm sure you'd like to relax before this evening. I enjoyed talking to you." Jenna smiled.

"You too." Susan returned Jenna's smile and continued to her room.

Jenna furrowed her brow. *Interesting observation about Tisha.*

When Jenna heard two women laughing as they stepped onto the porch, she raised her eyebrows, and Katy thumped her wagging tail against the registration desk. *Laughter isn't a sound I've heard very often this weekend.*

Brittany and Amanda came inside still chuckling. Both of them carried enormous shopping bags that were loaded to capacity.

"Hi, Katy." Brittany set down her shopping bags and stroked Katy's back. "You're a sweet girl."

Brittany rose and smiled. "Hi, Jenna. Amanda and I had the greatest day. We started off at the peach orchard for the tour, but in the middle of our tour, our guide raced ahead of the storm to get us back to the gift shop."

"It was the most thrilling ride I've ever had." Amanda set down her bags and gave Katy a treat from her pocket. "Our guide was an octogenarian and drove like a seasoned stock car racer."

"Annie, Quinn, and their husbands were at the gift shop when we returned from our wild ride. They are really delightful."

Brittany glanced at her shopping bags. "I guess you can tell we spent the entire morning in the gift shop until the storm cleared. In between our efforts to buy out the store, the owner set up chairs for the group and presented an impromptu lecture on peach trees and the history of the town of Paisley," Brittany said.

"It was absolutely delightful. I seriously doubt all the town's shenanigans he recounted were factual, but he was definitely entertaining." Amanda peered in her shopping bags. "Oh, no; we forgot to buy peaches."

The two women roared with laughter, and Jenna grinned.

After they settled down, Brittany said, "We ate lunch at a charming café in downtown Paisley. You'll never guess what we did this afternoon. Go ahead, guess." She pursed her lips and glanced at Katy.

Brittany just told me what they did, but I will not ruin their fun. Jenna furrowed her brow in thought. "Went shopping?"

Amanda chortled. "No, we spent the afternoon at the dog park."

Brittany beamed. "It was Amanda's idea; we met the sweetest dogs."

Before she headed toward her room, Amanda slipped another treat to Katy then added, "And their people were pretty okay too."

After Amanda's door closed, Brittany gazed at Katy and then cooed softly while she scratched Katy's ears.

Brittany smiled as she picked up her bags. "After I put these in my room, can we talk for a bit if you have time?"

"Sure. We can go into the living room and relax, if you like."

"That's perfect. I wouldn't mind putting up my feet."

While Brittany went to her room, Jenna updated the registration book that Morgan, Darlene, and Wendy used as a quick reference.

Brittany smiled as she came out of her room, and Katy trotted to the living room while Jenna and Brittany followed her.

When they walked into the living room, Katy had already stretched out near the yellow chair.

Brittany smiled. "There's something about a cold fireplace that I just love. When I catch a whiff of old wood smoke with the trace of acrid creosote, it reminds me of an old cabin in the woods."

"Sounds like you have a wonderful memory of that cabin in the woods."

Brittany stared out the window and shrugged. "Not really; sometimes my imagination gets away from me."

Jenna motioned toward the sofa. "Make yourself comfortable, Brittany; put the ottoman wherever you like. I'll sit in my yellow chair after I get our fire going for this evening."

While Jenna started the fire, Brittany said, "I'm amazed at how easy it is for you to start a fire."

"We always set it up in the morning. I enjoy having it ready to go when we light it, and it's how my dad always did our fireplace when I was growing up."

Brittany's face darkened.

I gazed at my fire as the kindling caught fire. *She can't talk about her family, can she?*

No.

I sat in my chair and smiled. "So what type of dog did you like the best at the dog park?"

Brittany giggled. "You read my mind. There was a sweet English springer spaniel named Lily that I absolutely adored. Her owner told me English springer spaniels are great for families, but they do need space to run, which is perfect because we have two acres of fenced-in yard at home."

"That's wonderful. I love big dogs, but I guess you can tell."

Katy wagged her tail.

Brittany gazed at the fire. "I've been a recluse for ages and have enjoyed being alone during the day while Stan is at work. My days are filled with gardening, yard work, and reading, so I've never felt lonely or missed having a friend around until I met Lily at the dog park. Even though I've been satisfied with my quiet life, I always knew there was something missing."

Jenna rose to reposition a piece of kindling that had shifted.

Brittany exhaled. "While I threw the ball for Lily, her owner said I had a hole in my heart that a dog would fill."

Katy rose and wandered to Brittany.

When she put her head on Brittany's knee, Brittany giggled and stroked Katy's neck. "I guess Katy agrees."

Jenna said, "Dogs and other people, even strangers, sometimes see things about us we don't see ourselves."

Katy grinned at Brittany then returned to her spot near the yellow chair.

Brittany smiled. "Stan has been asking for a dog for ages, so he'll be happy when I tell him about Lily."

Jenna swallowed hard. "I don't know what I would have done without Katy. I'm not great with the casual social stuff. Katy has helped me so much because people talk to her, which takes the pressure off me."

Brittany raised her eyebrows. "I could take my Lily to dog parks and talk about her, couldn't I?"

"Katy and I love to go to dog parks when we have the chance."

Brittany giggled. "I guess I'm getting a girl dog."

"It sounds like you and Amanda had a very productive day."

"It was an amazing day for a recluse, and I really enjoyed Amanda's company. When I told her I didn't really socialize, she told me I just hadn't met the right people. When she sneaked a treat to Lily, I understood what she meant."

Brittany stared at the fire and was lost in thought.

Jenna looked up at Nettie's portrait. *She's at a decision point, isn't she?*

Ya think? Nettie's portrait seemed to side-glance at Jenna.

Jenna covered her mouth to keep from laughing at herself, and the chimes on the porch jingled in the wind.

Brittany stopped at the doorway. "Could I ask a favor?"

Jenna smiled. "Ask away."

"Is it possible Amanda could attend the dinner tonight so I'll have someone to sit with during their meeting and ceremony? I planned to leave before their awards ceremony because if I'm there, it kind of restricts him from socializing."

Cousin.

Jenna nodded. "Tell my cousin Amanda she's more than welcome to attend dinner with you."

"Your cousin?" Brittany smiled. "Okay, I can't wait to tell her. Amanda understands my recluse side; I think she'll be tickled to be your relative and to sit with me."

A passing cloud hid the sun as Brittany glanced at Nettie's portrait then rushed out of the room.

"Suggesting a cousin was a brilliant idea, Nettie; did you see how her eyes lit up?"

More.

Jenna stared at Nettie's portrait. "You're right, Nettie. There was something more important that she decided not to bring up after all."

Jenna scowled as she strolled to the kitchen. *What could it have been?*

Jenna exhaled to shift gears as she went into the kitchen.

Wendy smiled as she put on her coat. "It's time for me to leave; I'll be back at five thirty. Be sure to tell Darlene I left on time."

Morgan followed Jenna into the kitchen. "We will. We have a changing of the guard here, don't we?"

After Wendy left, Jenna asked, "How do you feel about being part of a conspiracy?"

"I'm in," Morgan said. "Who do we ambush?"

Jenna snickered. "That might be later. Amanda, our guest in room two, is my cousin and will be attending the dinner tonight. Brittany feels a little left out as a nonmember, and she and my cousin hit it off today."

"Got it." Morgan narrowed her eyes. "So why didn't your cousin have dinner with us last night?"

Jenna frowned. "I don't know. She's not my favorite cousin?"

Morgan snorted. "That's awful. I've got something better. I heard she had a date last night with an old boyfriend."

Jenna exhaled. "Much better. This is why we do conspiracies. Anything interesting at the barn?"

"You may know this, but Lucille left about an hour ago. According to Petra, Lucille said she didn't feel well. After she left, Wanda wanted to check on Lucille and loudly fretted about it, which was very annoying. Petra finally told Wanda Lucille was fine and had her permission to take Vera to meet her sister in the town north of Paisley. I know this because Petra spoke in her stage voice whisper, so everyone heard it except Ralph who had gone into the men's room, but now that I think about it, he might have too."

"Any idea why Vera was so determined to leave?"

"According to Wanda, somebody hurt Vera's feelings, and Susan said she hoped it was her."

Jenna nodded. "That does sound like something Susan would say."

"And one more probably minor thing, Shane told me Tisha asked Chris if he'd be interested in collaborating and he said no. I thought it was pretty late in the day for something like that. Shane said he got the impression she didn't mean the competition. All that drama is really exhausting. Layla and I were happy when three o'clock arrived. What about you?"

"I updated the registration book, and that's about it. I still have a lot of paperwork to do."

"I planned to go into town with Shane. Should I stick around?"

"I don't know why. Go ahead. If anyone needs me, my number is on the registration desk and on the brochures in the rooms."

"I'll be back by five."

"Layla and Wendy will be here before five thirty because they're overachievers, so don't stress about getting back."

"Thanks."

After Morgan left, Jenna sighed. "I forgot to tell her about the cupcakes, Katy."

Jenna sent a text to Morgan. "You and Shane have vanilla cupcakes with peppermint crunch frosting for your afternoon snack in the refrigerator."

"Thanks. We haven't left yet. I'll run back inside and grab them."

Jenna went into the office, and Katy followed her. "Crisis averted." *I wish they were all that easy.*

While Jenna spread out the pages she had printed, she glanced at Detective Thorton's stack of papers.

"I wonder if there's anything about a ring in his notes."

Jenna pulled out pages from the folder. After she finished scanning each page, she marked it with a red check at the top. As she scanned a page, the word *tragedy* jumped out at her.

He must be referencing the crash that killed the Prentices.

Jenna furrowed her brow. The article didn't say anything about surviving family members. *Why not? What's the old saying? Cherchez la femme? No, that doesn't fit. I'm already looking for the woman, actually a girl.*

Jenna muttered, "I remember. It's follow the money."

Jenna and returned to the handwritten pages to follow the money.

When she picked up at the page with the word *tragedy* on it, she continued reading.

Midway down the page, she screamed, "No!"

Her heart ached, and she was blinded by tears as she reread the paragraph.

"According to bank records, one week after Briana disappeared, the Prentices moved five hundred thousand dollars to a new bank account under an assumed name, Price. They wired three hundred thousand dollars to an offshore bank two days later and then wired the remaining two hundred thousand dollars to a different offshore bank three days after that."

Jenna slammed her fist down on the desk in frustration. *They paid the ransom. Twice. No Briana.*

She continued to scan each page carefully until her eyes burned from reading. *It's only a little after four thirty.*

"Let's walk around the house, Katy."

Jenna put on her coat, then she and Katy went out the back door. When they were outside, Jenna shivered. "Maybe strolling around the house isn't such a great idea after all. I need to exercise to stay warm. Let's jog down the driveway to the visitor parking lot and then walk back up the hill."

Jenna watched the bank of clouds moving in from the west darken as she jogged down the hill. *We may get more rain this evening.*

When Jenna stopped at the parking lot to return to the inn, Katy gazed down the hill toward the road. After Jenna headed up the hill at a jog, she heard a car turn in the driveway. Katy dashed to catch up with her, and they continued together at Jenna's slow jogging pace.

After they reached the inn, Jenna stopped to catch her breath. "I wasn't fast, but I jogged the entire way from the parking lot."

As they headed to the back door, Jenna rolled her eyes at a familiar voice.

Chapter Twelve

"After my sister decided not to pick me up after all, I can't believe you wouldn't take me home. We were practically halfway there," Vera shouted.

"You can't be here. You should have stayed there and waited for someone to pick you up." Lucille shouted in return.

"You don't make any sense," Vera screamed.

Lucille's angry retort didn't carry quite as clearly.

"Oh boy, Katy. I'm not sure what Lucille said, but she's definitely not happy, either, is she? We'll have to warn the team." Jenna and Katy hurried inside.

Jenna stopped in the kitchen and sent a group text to Morgan, Wendy, and Layla. "Vera's sister bailed. Vera and Lucille are back and are arguing."

Morgan replied, "I'll get us ear plugs."

"Let's go in the office, Katy; it's time to follow the money."

When Jenna turned on her computer, she had an email from Shane. "No luck with the church records, but I found two photos of the Prentices with their baby."

Jenna opened the attachments.

The first photo was in black and white and was grainy, but it was of a man and woman in their mid-thirties posing with big smiles in front of a lake cabin. They were dressed in flannel shirts and jeans. The woman held a baby who wore a pair of bib overalls with lace around the hems and a warm jacket over a T-shirt. The baby appeared to be six months old and had no hair, but she wore a baby-sized tiara on her head.

Jenna examined the lake cabin and smiled at the two rocking chairs on the front porch and the brick chimney on the side. *It wouldn't be a cabin if it didn't have a rocking chair and fireplace.*

The second photo was in color at the same cabin and must have been taken the following summer because the laughing mother was in a blue short-sleeved shirt and tan shorts, and the baby, who was closer to a year old, wore a pink shirt and pink shorts. The baby's strawberry blonde hair was flyway, fine baby hair that looked like a static electricity experiment. Her too-small baby-sized tiara perched precariously on top of her head. *That is so cute. She must have loved her tiara.*

The father beamed as he stood behind them with his hand on his wife's shoulder, and his light red hair sparkled like fire in the bright summer sun.

A wave of sadness swept over Jenna. *They were a happy family, and then their baby was gone.*

Jenna peered at the baby's shirt. *Is she wearing a gold chain necklace with a charm or pendant on it?* Jenna enlarged the photo, but the detail was lost. *That didn't help. Now it almost looks like a ring on the gold chain. It was probably just a design on her shirt.*

She put the pages of the Prentice genealogy charts together and pulled out Mr. Thorton's notes. *I've only read half of his notes. He didn't quit after the ransom was paid because Briana was not returned.*

She found the section in his notes dated after the death of the Prentices. Their fortune went to a distant relative of Mitchell Prentice, Gerald Prentice.

I've grown used to Mr. Thorton's handwriting; I'm moving a lot faster through his notes.

Jenna checked the genealogy chart. *Gerald Prentice was a second cousin, which is why the newspapers didn't bother to mention him. So far, so good.*

She continued reading Mr. Thorton's notes and then stared at the page in front of her. *He quit trying to find the baby. Why? Did he think the baby was dead?*

Jenna brushed away her tears for the abandoned baby and paced from her desk to the window and back while she read.

After four more pages, she stopped pacing and sighed in relief. *He's following the money so he can search backwards and find the baby. Gotcha, Mr. Thorton. I'll follow the money. We'll find the baby.*

Jenna found Mr. Thorton's notes about Gerald Prentice who died in a plane crash, and his company was managed by the Hollinger Law firm.

Jenna's eyes widened. *The Hollinger Law firm was listed as one of the employers of Harry Whittaker, but he had a dozen employers in Atlanta. Is it really significant or a coincidence?*

Mr. Thorton's notes continued with three pages of allegations of misappropriation of funds and questionable practices against the Hollinger Law firm.

Whoa, Mr. Thorton did not approve of the Hollinger Law firm.

When Jenna picked up the next page, she frowned and double-checked the page numbers. *This is the next page of his notes according to the page numbers, but the date at the top jumped back to before Gerald Prentice died.*

After she read a few lines, she squealed. "According to his notes, Mr. Thorton discovered Brandi Garrison was an intern at Gerald Prentice's firm before Gerald Prentice died, Katy."

She searched through Felicia's documents again. *No other mention of Brandi Garrison.*

Jenna texted Adrienne. "Brandi Garrison was an intern at Gerald Prentice's company a year before he died in a plane crash. Are there any records of her employment there?"

"Same Brandi Garrison who disappeared from the genealogy records?"

"Who knows?"

Jenna scanned the next five pages of Mr. Thorton's notes and frowned. *That was the only page that mentioned Brandi Garrison. Now we're back to following the money of the Prentice Trust through the Hollinger Law firm.*

Morgan rushed into the office. "Did you get Shane's email? He was happy he didn't have to break the law. He found the photos on the social media of a former neighbor of the Prentices. Are you going to help with happy hour? It's getting close to five thirty, and Wendy and Layla will be here any minute."

Jenna glanced at her phone. "Wow; time got away from me; I'll be right there."

"I just got here, so both of us need to scramble so we don't get caught slacking on the job. Wendy and Layla will take care of the kitchen, so the dining room is mine, and the shmoozing is yours."

Jenna put her papers in the file cabinet and locked it then shut down her computer. "Since it will take at least two of us to keep up with the food with the number of guests we have, and your gift of social graces probably got fried at the barn this afternoon, maybe we should warn everybody to be on their best behavior or no dessert."

Morgan giggled. "That's the best idea you've had since you hired me. Maybe I should change the menu sign to add that."

As they went into the kitchen, Jenna asked, "Do you know what the appetizers are?"

Morgan smirked. "I sure do; I stopped long enough to read the instructions. Our hors d'oeuvres for this evening are carrot and green bell pepper sticks with olive oil and sea salt crackers and a whipped goat cheese dip, which is a different recipe than last night's warm goat cheese, blue cheese and pear flat bread, and Darlene's salsa with tortilla chips because it was so popular last night. Wendy left us instructions, but she'll be here in a ten minutes if we have any questions."

Jenna read the instructions. "Wendy took it easy on us, didn't she? All we really have to do is pop the flat bread into a hot oven to give the crust an extra crisp and a slight char before we put it on the platter."

"Right, and I have a feeling she'll do that while we're doing everything else. I have the signs ready for the meal." Morgan pointed to her feet. "You'll notice I'm wearing my old running shoes, so I'm ready too."

Wendy and Layla giggled as they came into the kitchen. "We didn't arrive until five thirty if Darlene asks," Layla said. "We thought about waiting outside, but it's too cold. What do we need to do?"

Jenna and Morgan exchanged glances.

"Morgan has our signs ready; other than that, we haven't done anything," Jenna said.

"I was about to make coffee, and Boss Lady was on her way to load up the utility cart."

"I'll pull together the ice water," Layla said.

"Good recovery," Jenna whispered when Morgan went past her on her way to the pantry for the coffee container.

"I had cousins," Morgan said.

After fifteen minutes, the dining room was ready for guests.

Jenna glanced at her shirt and groaned, "I'm still wearing the flannel shirt I put on early this morning."

"If you want to change, you have time," Morgan said. "If you're a few minutes late, I can unlock the door for happy hour."

"I have a spare shirt," Layla said.

Jenna blinked. *There's no way I could fill out Layla's shirt.* "Thanks, Layla, but if I run, I can grab something real quick, change, and be right back."

Jenna hurried outside then raced to the cottage with Katy on her heels. After she opened her closet door, she didn't waste time in turning on the light as she grabbed a shirt that buttoned down the front. They dashed back to the inn.

When they went into the kitchen, Jenna stared at the shirt she had pulled from the dark closet. "It's my new red blouse. I've been saving it for a special occasion since last spring."

"Just change; you've got four minutes," Morgan said.

Jenna went into the office and changed into the red blouse.

She grumbled, "Was this your idea, Nettie? Am I supposed to be dangerous or a distraction?"

Ask Ethan.

"Can you imagine poor Ethan trying to decide which answer was the right one, Nettie?" Jenna giggled, and a gust of wind jangled the wind chimes.

. When she returned to the kitchen, Morgan whistled. "That's a wonderful color for you, Jenna. You should wear red more often."

She's right.

"Two minutes," Wendy said.

"The sideboard is set up with appetizers for the first wave," Layla said. "Go."

Jenna exhaled as she and Morgan strolled into the dining room; she unlocked the door at six o'clock and smiled at the two young couples who were waiting at the door.

"It's nice to see you," Jenna said.

"More than you know," Morgan mumbled.

"We had so much fun at happy hour yesterday that we didn't want to miss a thing tonight," Annie said.

Her husband added, "We went to the wine shop before we left Paisley and bought a bottle of wine. The owner was extremely helpful. He said if we didn't like it after all, we could put it on the table with the wine glasses, and it wouldn't go to waste."

Jenna chuckled. "I'm sure he's right."

After they selected their appetizers, they selected a table and set down their appetizers. One of the young men took the wine bottle to the drink table, but struggled to open the bottle. Morgan joined him. While she whispered instructions, the man nodded and followed her directions.

When the cork popped out of the bottle, Annie, Quinn, and his brother applauded, and he beamed. "It's easy when you know how, isn't it? Thank you, Morgan."

He carried the bottle to their table, and Morgan followed him with the four wine glasses he had put on the table. After he poured a small amount into each of the glasses, they toasted and then goaded each other to take the first sip.

Morgan joined Jenna at the door. "This is how a happy hour is supposed to be."

"I'm starving because I didn't have a decent lunch." Vera's voice carried from the top of the stairs.

"You'll feel much better after a glass of wine and the amazing chef's appetizers," Ralph said.

"We all hope so," Morgan whispered before she disappeared into the kitchen.

Jenna muttered, "Scaredy cat."

Chris and Arthur beat Ralph and Vera into the dining room.

"Hello, Jenna. Did you have a relaxing afternoon?" Arthur asked.

Jenna smiled. "I don't know if I'd call it relaxing, but it was productive; thank you for asking. I caught up on this month's finance records for the Peach Blossom Retreat."

Chris smiled. "Catching up on a backlog of work is an impressive accomplishment."

Arthur beamed and nodded.

While they headed to the sideboard, Vera and Ralph came in.

"Nobody's here." Vera's shoulders slumped.

"You'll be among the first to try tonight's appetizers," Jenna said.

"If you decide to go back for seconds of your favorite later, no one will know. Isn't that how it works, Jenna?" Ralph asked.

"That is precisely how it works. Vera, try all of them so you can spoil yourself with your favorite the second time; everybody deserves to be spoiled once in a while."

Vera straightened her back and lifted her chin. "Exactly."

She marched to the appetizers and filled two plates. Jenna smiled. *Smart lady. She's not getting short-changed on appetizers tonight.*

When her plates were in danger of spilling over, she headed toward Ralph.

He pointed to the table occupied by Chris and Arthur. "Your glass of white wine is on the table, Vera. You'll be a rose among thorns."

Ralph chuckled as he strode to the sideboard. He picked up two plates and began filling them.

"That's right, a rose." Vera pushed her hair behind one ear.

Jenna raised her eyebrows as Vera's usual sour face softened, and her mouth twitched into a weak smile.

Jenna heard voices in the living room. *Another argument?*

Jenna stepped into the hallway.

"You haven't paid me," Lucille said.

"You'll get paid when you deliver," Petra hissed.

Jenna stepped back into the dining room as Petra rushed out of the living room.

When Petra strolled into the dining room with her laptop and a bottle of wine, she scanned the room.

"How was your day, Petra? Will we be hearing your story tonight?" Jenna asked.

Petra narrowed her eyes. "Why do you think I wrote a story?"

Jenna blinked. *What set her off?*

Petra sighed. "Excuse me for being snippy. I hit a spell of writer's block because it's not quite finished. Of course, I'm not eligible to win or even read mine aloud to the group, but it was a challenging exercise, and I hated to just sit around while everyone wrote their little stories."

Petra chuckled. "Let's let this be our secret just between us girls, okay?"

Petra scanned the room and grimaced when she saw Vera sitting next to Chris.

Petra cocked her head. "I have an idea; maybe I can leave it as a cliffhanger. No one else would do anything that daring."

Petra hurried out to return to the living room.

"Have you changed your mind? Are you going to pay me, after all?" Lucille asked.

"Let's talk," Petra said.

Jenna raised her eyebrows.

When their voices lowered to whispers, Jenna moaned. *Can't you talk any louder?*

A few minutes later, Petra returned to the dining room and hurried past Jenna. She set her laptop next to the drink table and then opened her bottle of wine.

Petra casually strolled to the table where Vera, Ralph, Chris, and Arthur sat and stopped near Ralph. "How's everybody doing?"

Vera stared at her.

"Are you joining us?" Ralph asked.

"Yes, thank you." Petra set her glass on the table next to Ralph then collected her laptop and sat down.

While Petra sipped her wine, Vera and Chris chatted. Ralph and Arthur rose and strolled to the sideboard.

Jenna joined them and scanned the platters.

"I told myself I'd save room for the main dish and dessert, but here I am." Ralph chuckled.

"Will you be reading your story this evening?" Jenna asked.

"Yes, but the competition is fierce."

"Who do you think will win?" Jenna asked.

"I'm never sure, but Ivy is a strong possibility."

Jenna raised her eyebrows. "Really?"

Ralph smiled. "People underestimate her, but she's a formidable writer."

Vera's phone beeped to announce a text.

She frowned and hurried to join Ralph and Jenna at the sideboard. "My sister changed her mind and contacted Lucille. Jenna, would it be possible to pack up my dinner so I can eat on the road?"

"Chicken or tofu?" Jenna asked.

Vera's eyes widened. "You'd do that for me? Chicken, please."

"We'll do you up right, Vera. Should we prepare a to-go dinner for Lucille too?"

"Oh yes. Chicken, I think, but I'll check."

Vera sent a text, and her phone beeped.

"Chicken. I was right." Vera smiled.

"I'll get your bag for you and carry it out to Lucille's car," Ralph said.

"We have cupcakes for dessert. Would you like a peach or peppermint crunch cupcake?"

"Peach."

Jenna smiled. "Okay. We'll send the same for Lucille."

Jenna hurried into the kitchen. "Vera and Lucille are leaving after all. Can we package two chicken dinners to go with two peach cupcakes?"

"On it," Wendy said. "I think we have some clamshells for to go meals somewhere. Layla, would you pull together plastic knives and forks and napkins?"

Layla pulled a plastic sack out of their stash in the pantry then filled two to-go coffee cups with ice water while Wendy slipped the two chicken dinners into clamshells and found smaller containers for the cupcakes.

After the meals were packed, Jenna said, "I'm impressed. I'll talk to Vera then carry their meals out to Lucille's car."

Morgan said, "I'll go with you."

Jenna shook her head. "Stay here and take care of our guests. I'll be gone less than five minutes. I'll take Katy and my phone, and I have my carry piece. Ralph will carry Vera's suitcase to Lucille's car, so I'll have an escort on the way back."

Morgan nodded. "Be sure to tell Shane and Ethan I tried to go with you if you get into trouble."

Jenna hurried into the dining room.

Vera stood alone as she waited in the doorway for Jenna. "Ralph is getting my suitcase and my warm coat for me."

"Morgan is pulling your food together. I'll meet you out front with your to go meals," Jenna said.

When Jenna rushed back into the kitchen, Layla wore her warm coat and held the bag with the meals.

"Wendy is kicking me out of the kitchen," Layla grinned.

Jenna threw on her coat. "You people are sneaky, but we don't have to empty the kitchen. I'll be walking back with Ralph; he's carrying Vera's suitcase for her."

"You win." Layla removed her coat and handed her a flashlight. "Here."

"Thanks." Jenna took the flashlight. "Let's go, Katy."

As they went out the back door, Jenna said, "I think I just heard Ethan's truck turn in the driveway."

Katy wagged her tail.

When they met Ralph and Vera at the driveway close to the front of the house, Jenna said, "I have a flashlight. Do you want to carry it, Vera, so you can see where you're going? I'll follow you, but Katy and I have walked the driveway in the dark hundreds of times."

As they headed down the driveway, Vera said, "You've treated me with only kindness while I've been here even though I've been a bit difficult a time or two. I'm really sorry, and please tell Wendy I'm sorry I snapped at her."

"I'll tell her; she'll appreciate hearing it. Thank you." *An apology from Vera even if it is by proxy will be a shock to Wendy.*

Before they reached the visitor parking lot, Ethan pulled over.

Jenna hurried to the driver's side. "Lucille is giving Vera a ride to meet with her sister, so Vera can go home. Ralph and I will return in just a few minutes."

Ethan nodded then roared up the driveway.

Lucille was sitting in her car with the engine running. Ralph put Vera's suitcase in the backseat then gave Vera a kiss on the cheek.

"Be safe," he said. "Text me when you're with your sister and when you get home."

Vera nodded as she returned the flashlight to Jenna then climbed into the car.

When Jenna handed Vera the sack with the meals, she inadvertently leaned against Lucille's car and then jerked back her arm and clutched it to her chest as she coughed from the acrid stench of burning rubber mixed with plastic and gasoline. "It burned me; it's on fire."

Ralph frowned. "What?"

Jenna coughed again. "I know this doesn't make any sense, but would you take Vera to meet her sister? Please, it's important for her to be with you."

Ralph examined Jenna's face. "I don't understand, but give me five minutes to grab my keys and coat."

Ralph sprinted up the road.

"What's going on?" Vera asked.

"Ralph wants to take you to meet your sister," Jenna said.

"What about me?" Lucille slammed her hand on the steering wheel. "I can't go back inside because I'm supposed to take Vera to meet her sister. I'll drive behind Ralph so I can at least say I did."

Ethan's truck headed toward them from the inn. When he stopped, Ralph jumped out.

Ethan opened his back door and patted the back seat. Katy leaped into the truck.

After Ralph helped Vera out of Lucille's car, Vera climbed into their car with her sack.

Ralph handed Jenna a file folder with papers inside. "Would you read my story for me if I'm not back in time? Vera would blame herself if my story wasn't included in the competition."

"I'd be glad too."

Before he closed the door, Jenna said, "Vera, you've got my number. Text me when you reach your sister."

"Wait. I've got the two meals," Vera said.

Jenna shrugged. "One for you and one for your driver."

Vera chuckled. "You're right."

"I like the way you think, Jenna," Ralph said.

After Ralph closed his door, Jenna rushed to Lucille's car and stood near the driver's window.

Lucille glared at her then sighed as she lowered her window. "What?"

"I read there's some kind of recall with your car model that just came out. Some cars have suddenly caught fire, and they aren't sure why yet. If the engine temperature suddenly rises even a little, or if you smell melting plastic, pull over immediately and get out."

Lucille furrowed her brow. "A recall? I hadn't heard about it, but thanks, I'll pay attention to the temperature gauge, and if I smell anything, I'll pull over."

Jenna exhaled as she released her grip on her arm and watched Ralph then Lucille pull out of the parking lot and head down the driveway toward the road.

Ethan joined her and put his arm around her. "Are you okay?"

Jenna exhaled as they strolled together to his truck. "I think so. Ralph will take care of Vera now, but I'll feel better when I know Lucille is safe."

Ethan opened the passenger door for Jenna. While she climbed in, he said, "Do you want to talk about it?"

Jenna met his gaze; the concern she saw in his face warmed her heart. "Yes, but it will have to be later."

After he parked in his spot close to the back door, Ethan brushed her hair away from her face with his fingertips and smiled. "Are you ready for the latest drama?"

Jenna sighed. "What is it?"

"I don't know; let's go see."

Jenna snickered. "Might as well unless we can think of somewhere else we'd rather be."

As they headed to the back door, Ethan said, "What about you, me, and Katy in a cabin at the mountains?"

"It's cold in the mountains."

"Maybe so, but wouldn't you rather be cold at the mountains with Katy, me, and a fire than cold here with Katy, me, and the drama?"

Jenna nodded. "Good point; I'll dash to the cottage and pack while you grab Katy."

They chuckled as they went inside with their arms around each other.

Chapter Thirteen

When they went into the kitchen, Jenna set Ralph's folder on the kitchen table while she inhaled the tantalizing bouquet of oven baked chicken and garlicky sauce for the tofu. "Smells yummy in here."

"That's the advantage of coming in from outside," Layla said.

Morgan raised her eyebrows. "There you are. Petra's been asking for you."

Jenna sighed as she removed her coat.

"Just give me the word, babe, and we're outta here." Ethan took her coat.

Jenna hugged him then turned to Morgan. "Okay, I'm fortified. I presume she's in the dining room."

"She's in the living room; she said it's a confidential matter, so I'm going with you so I can take notes." Morgan picked up her notepad.

"Let's go."

"Holler if you need us," Layla said.

After they were in the hallway, Morgan whispered, "Susan told me Petra's got her shorts in a wad over losing two members who were supposed to have stories in the competition. That's a direct quote from Susan, but I really liked it. I plan to find a few more times to use it."

Jenna raised her eyebrows. "I'm surprised she didn't want to know why they left."

Morgan shrugged as they went into the living room.

Petra posed in front of the fireplace with one foot on the hearth and a hand on the mantle. She glanced at them without moving her head.

Jenna stared at her. *Why is she being so pretentious?*

Jenna strolled into the living room while Morgan waited in the doorway.

Petra raised her eyebrows. "Ah, Jenna, dear, you're here."

She glared at Morgan. "This is a private conversation."

"We understand; go ahead," Jenna said.

Morgan made a show of flipping her notepad to an empty page and hovering her pen over her pad in anticipation.

When Morgan raised an eyebrow and tapped her pad with her pen, Jenna sniffed back a giggle.

Petra cleared her throat. "I have concerns about the change from the barn to the dining room. It's been fine for happy hour and our meals, but we have our annual meeting tonight, which includes the readings for our competition. I expect the theme of the readings will be the disappearing baby, don't you?"

"It's an option. Another theme could be to follow the money," Jenna said.

Petra growled, "Why would you think that?"

Touched a nerve. "It's kind of a twist on cherchez la femme, you know, find the woman, which is in most crime novels."

"I hadn't thought of that," Morgan said. "What if you put the two together?"

Petra's face reddened. "That's ridiculous. I'm more worried that not everyone will be able to hear the stories. I can barely hear my tablemates during the meals." "Is there someone in the club who is hard of hearing?" Jenna asked.

Petra narrowed her eyes. "Why would that matter?"

"We can definitely accommodate them. We'll reserve a seat close to the readers for anyone who is hard of hearing, but we've found the acoustics in the dining room are excellent."

"Of course, everyone will have to be quiet and pay attention," Morgan added.

"Is there anything else?" Jenna asked. "We're scheduled to serve dinner in five minutes."

Petra nodded then lowered her voice. "I noticed Ralph and Lucille have not returned for dinner yet. Their stories will be disqualified for the competition if they aren't read. I have Lucille's, so I can read hers, but what about Ralph's story?"

Jenna nodded. "We can talk more after dinner, but I think your meeting will be fine."

Petra snorted. "Well, I'm not so sure; I'll hold you personally accountable if there are any problems."

Jenna nodded as she left the dining room with Morgan matching her stride.

"She's teetering on the brink of getting herself tossed out of the inn by your Operations Manager," Morgan whispered. "Did any of that make sense to you?"

"I think she's in deep trouble," Jenna said.

"I didn't think about that. What kind of trouble?" Morgan asked when they stopped at the kitchen door.

"I don't know; it's hard to decide whether she's being dramatic or if she has a real problem."

After they went inside the kitchen, Jenna inhaled. "Still smells yummy in here."

Ethan and Shane sat at the kitchen table with one of Shane's drawings between them. Shane had his laptop open and his pad of paper next to it.

"So, what's our best approach?" Ethan asked.

Shane furrowed his brow then circled an area on his drawing.

I don't need to get in the middle of this discussion.

Jenna moved away from the table.

"What was the emergency?" Layla asked.

Jenna shrugged. "We don't know."

"We have an expert opinion that her shorts are in a wad," Morgan said.

Layla laughed. "I could have told you that."

"It's seven o'clock, Boss Lady," Wendy said.

"Red is tofu, and yellow is chicken," Jenna mumbled as she hurried to the dining room door.

When Jenna went into the dining room, applause broke out. She smiled then curtsied, and everyone laughed. She held up her hands for quiet.

Morgan slipped into the dining room and stood next to Jenna.

The room became still in a hush of anticipation, as if everyone was holding their breath.

"Once again, you'll select a color for your meal. Put a yellow tag on your table in front of you for a baked chicken breast smothered with baby spinach in a creamy cheese sauce or a red checker if you prefer to garlicky sesame tofu and broccoli over noodles. We have reminder signs for you next to the markers, and don't forget to pick up your silverware and a napkin. Please stay seated after you pick up your marker so we can serve you. Bon appétit!"

Susan and Ivy were the first to the sideboard; everyone else fell into line behind them. Jenna held her breath.

Morgan elbowed her and pointed at the line and whispered, "A lot of breath-holding tonight."

"They're all rooting for Ivy."

When Susan and Ivy selected yellow evidence markers, everyone in the line simultaneously exhaled, and the chatter resumed where it had left off.

After Susan and Ivy picked up their silverware and were on their way to their table, Brittany whispered to Amanda, and Amanda smiled as they selected their choices.

When Morgan rushed to go to the kitchen, Layla dashed out with two chicken meals for Susan and Ivy.

"I peeked," Layla whispered as she swept past Jenna.

While their guests selected red or yellow, Layla and Morgan quickly delivered plates with hot meals. Jenna dropped off silverware and napkins on the tables for those who forgot to pick them up on their way through the line, and the noise in the room switched from loud conversations to the click of silverware on the plates.

Jenna relaxed near the door while she scanned the dining room. *The group dynamics have changed since yesterday.*

She studied the table with Susan, Ivy, Wanda, and Tisha sitting together, and then shifted her gaze to the table with Chris, Arthur, and Petra.

Petra must have opted to sit with Chris and Arthur, which is no surprise. Tisha probably needed a change after two days of sitting with Chris and Arthur.

While Brittany and Amanda chatted and giggled as they ate, Stan beamed.

This is the most relaxed I've seen Brittany since she arrived. Jenna furrowed her brow. *She feels safe.*

Morgan came out of the kitchen and whispered, "The two couples are in the living room. They deserve special treatment."

Jenna smiled. "It's my job."

Jenna strolled into the living room and smiled at Annie and her husband who were examining books in the bookcase, and Quinn and her husband who were sitting on the sofa chatting while they gazed at the fire.

When Annie glanced up, her eyes lit up. "Do you have time to join us?"

Jenna joined Annie and her husband near the bookcase. "I'd love to. How was your day?"

Annie giggled. "We had wonderful plans, but the weather had a different idea. We made it to the peach orchard gift shop before the storm hit, which was wonderful."

"Although we've been wet before, and we'll be wet again." Her husband's eyes twinkled, and his dimple in his left cheek deepened as he smiled.

"You are right as rain," his brother added.

The four of them laughed at the joke, and Jenna joined in.

"You're getting a head start on me with the dad jokes, bro," his brother said.

Quinn's cheeks reddened.

Jenna shifted her focus away from Quinn. *Quinn is pregnant.*

Annie glared at her husband. "We did hear the most interesting juicy morsel when we stopped at the ice cream shop late this afternoon. Two middle-aged men were sitting at a booth close to us. Tell her, Quinn. You were closer."

"We'd never heard the words 'juicy morsel' used unless someone was talking about food, so we had to listen so we could understand the context."

"You also had to listen because you two are nosy," Quinn's husband said.

Quinn nodded. "Which was our original reason. I heard Petra's name mentioned, and how many Petras could there be in Paisley? The juicy morsel is that Petra's boss was here or was going to be here, and Petra didn't have a clue. We weren't sure if that meant Petra wasn't expecting her boss, or if she didn't know she had a new boss. We've been watching for someone new, but nobody's shown up."

Jenna nodded. *It's interesting that Amanda has blended in so well, she doesn't count as new. Not that it matters; Amanda is definitely not Petra's boss.*

"One man said they didn't have to rush eating their sandwiches because they couldn't go to work until after dark, and the other man said a third job in less than a week was gravy. The other man said it was more like finishing the week with fireworks," Annie said.

"We didn't know the ice cream shop had sandwiches until the men ordered them," Annie's husband said.

"We didn't even consider looking at the menu because we were too focused on our ice cream options," Annie said.

"Ice cream is definitely a priority." Jenna chuckled. "Did they hint what their job might have been?"

"One man said it didn't take an Einstein to be a lousy mechanic, which sounded almost philosophical to me," Quinn said.

Annie furrowed her brow. "I thought it sounded creepy."

Quinn nodded. "They did look creepy, so that makes sense."

"I would have been as curious as you were, but their entire conversation was puzzling, wasn't it?" Jenna rose from her seat. "Thanks for giving me a chance to rest a minute. Enjoy your evening."

Jenna paused before she reached the doorway. "I need to know. Who tried the wine?"

Annie grinned. "None of us. We clinked our glasses and toasted each other and then inhaled the bouquet."

"And that was the end of our grand wine tasting experience." Quinn giggled.

"It still sounds like you had fun," Jenna said.

The four of them nodded.

Quinn said, "My favorite part of the day was when we didn't get drenched by the thunderstorm."

"I was going to say that," Annie said. "Now, I have to come up with something else."

They've got the right idea. Jenna smiled as she strolled into the kitchen.

"Did you go to the living room? You must have, because you're smiling," Morgan said.

Jenna nodded. "Talking to the two young couples was refreshing."

Layla snorted. "That's bordering on cheating, Boss Lady, but since Vera left, there's really no one left who can match her."

"What's our timing for dessert?" Wendy asked.

Morgan peeked into the dining room then closed the door with her nose wrinkled. "Boss Lady, you're going to have to remind people about clearing their dishes if they want dessert."

"I'll do that now. Do we know how we're handling three desserts?" Jenna asked.

Wendy nodded. "Layla and I talked. We can load up the utility cart with desserts then you and Morgan can go from table to table. Layla will be the runner to keep the utility cart from running out of the three desserts."

"Sounds like a plan. Are we ready?"

"We'll load up the cart while you make your announcement," Morgan said.

"Morgan, put a stack of napkins on each table that's ready for dessert," Wendy said. "The cupcakes might be a little messy."

Jenna went into the dining room. When she help up her hands, conversations ceased.

"We have three desserts tonight for you to choose from tonight."

"Three?" Arthur asked.

Jenna smiled as she nodded. "Our chef and sous chef wanted tonight to be special."

Jenna was interrupted by applause and whistles.

When everyone quieted down, she continued. "After everyone at your table has finished eating, and your dishes are in the bins on the sideboard that Morgan set out earlier, we'll come to your table to give you your choice of dessert. You can choose a generous piece of chocolate sheet cake with fudgy chocolate butter cream frosting, a giant peach cupcake with whiskey buttercream frosting, or a super-size vanilla bean cupcake with peppermint crunch frosting."

Jenna stepped back while the tables were cleared. Morgan pushed the utility cart with the desserts into the dining room. As Jenna and Morgan went from table to table, they dropped a small stack of napkins and forks for those who requested cake in the middle of each table and served the requested desserts while Layla kept the utility cart supplied.

After everyone had a dessert, Jenna pushed the utility cart back to the kitchen while Morgan and Layla carried the bins into the kitchen.

When Jenna's phone rang, she furrowed her brow. "I don't know who this is."

"Yes, you do, but answer it anyway," Ethan said.

He's making fun of me. Jenna glared at him and then rushed into her office as she answered. Katy slipped into the office with her before Jenna closed the door.

"Jenna, somebody is pranking me, and Lucille is in on it."

Jenna held the phone away from her ear as Vera continued to shout. "I called my sister to be sure she knew we were coming, but she was still at home and in bed with a fever. She sounds like she has a terrible cold, but I wouldn't have ridden in a car with her no matter what she has. If she has a fever, she's contagious."

"Tell her what we're going to do," Ralph said.

"I was getting to that," Vera grumbled. "Jenna, we're going to pull into the roadside park ahead and eat in the car before the chicken gets cold. We'll be back in plenty of time for Ralph to read his story."

"But if Petra pulls a fast one and calls for a vote, read my story, Jenna."

"Did you hear Ralph, Jenna?" Vera shouted.

"I heard him. I'll be ready to read if Petra tries to cut the evening short."

"Is Lucille still behind you?" Jenna asked.

"No, she pulled into a gas station a few minutes before I called my sister. That cost us more time because Ralph turned back to see if she was having car trouble and she was. She said her engine temperature went up. I didn't see why that would be a big deal, but she said it was. The gas station owner said he'd look at it, but he had to call someone to come in and take over the register first."

"If her car's still there, we'll stop to see if she wants a ride back," Ralph said.

"I don't think we should stop," Vera said.

"I can make it quick. Jenna's busy. Let her hang up, Vera."

"Ralph said you're busy. Oh, there's the rest stop." Vera hung up.

Jenna stared at the phone and exhaled as she sent Vera a text. "Let me know what Lucille's status is."

Jenna stroked Katy's back while she waited for a reply. "Maybe we'll hear something from Vera about Lucille before they return. I'd like to avoid Mr. Bentley after that insensitive remark he made, but I have to go into the dining room to keep tabs on Petra. I never use the door from the office to the dining room when guests are around. I'm stuck."

Katy nosed the door to the kitchen.

"You're right; he's probably still busy."

Jenna and Katy went into the kitchen. Jenna avoided looking at Ethan as she hurried to the dining room door. As she closed the door behind her, Shane said, "Told you."

I'll bet Shane told him how rude he was. Shane shouldn't have had to do that.

"Jenna," Morgan hissed.

Jenna flinched. Morgan stood in front of her, and her face was two inches from Jenna's face.

Where did she come from?

Morgan whispered, "What's wrong with you? You look like you want to fight the entire room."

Jenna swallowed hard then smiled. "Better?"

Morgan didn't budge. "Too scary. You look like a blonde werewolf."

Jenna chuckled. "Werewolf?"

"Much better. Thank you. Petra wants to be obnoxious. I want to toss her out. It's your turn to be the nice person."

Jenna glanced at Petra who was barreling toward them. "Here she comes."

"Thanks for the warning." Morgan hurried into the kitchen.

Jenna raised her eyebrows as Petra neared.

"Are we almost ready for the meeting to begin?" Jenna asked.

"We can't. Ralph and Lucille aren't here."

"Do you begin your meetings with the readings? I would have thought you would speak to the club members first."

"Of course I will, and then Chris will remind us of the story we used for our competition. After that, we will listen to this year's submissions then vote to determine our winner." Petra glanced around. "We always have a podium."

"We'll bring in one. Where do you want it?"

"Bring it in, and I'll show you where to put it." Petra crossed her arms.

Jenna hurried into the kitchen.

"What do you need?" Morgan asked.

"I need a podium. What do we have?"

"We could steal the guest register sign-in table," Wendy said.

"I'll get it," Ethan said.

"I'll go with you," Shane added.

Morgan glanced at Jenna, who turned to go to the dining room.

"Thanks," Morgan said as the two men left.

Morgan growled, "We'll talk later, Boss Lady."

Jenna frowned. *Why is she so irritable?*

After she was in the dining room, Jenna exhaled as she thought about Quinn to erase her cranky attitude. *Quinn will be a wonderful mother.*

Petra's face was red as she stomped toward her with her fists clenched.

Arthur rose from his table and strode between Petra and Jenna and broke Petra's concentration when she had to stop short to keep from bumping into him.

"Excuse me," Arthur said.

Petra's face became redder as she glared at him.

Jenna held her breath to keep her smile from turning into a chuckle. *Petra needed steam coming out of her ears like a cartoon.*

"We have your podium." Ethan and Shane carried in the heavy sign-in table.

Jenna exhaled. "Thank you. Now, where do you want it, Petra?"

Petra grumbled, "I don't know; just put it anywhere."

"How about right here?" Arthur pointed to where he stood.

"Works for me," Shane said.

After they set the makeshift podium down, Ethan and Shane headed toward the door to the kitchen. Ethan smiled and winked at Jenna as he went by, and she accidentally returned his smile.

Jenna glanced at Petra who glared at Arthur's back as he strolled back to his seat while Chris smiled.

Jenna sighed as she sat at the table near the kitchen door. *Dang it. I'm supposed to be mad at him, but oh, that smile of his, and then he had the nerve to top it off with a wink.*

Jenna's phone buzzed with a text while Petra was talking.

"Call please. Ralph."

Jenna quietly rose and went through the kitchen to her office and called Ralph.

"Jenna, it's your turn to trust me. As far as everyone else at the inn is concerned, Lucille is taking Vera to her sister's house, and I went to get gas. I might need your help to figure out why I was gone so long, but I'll be back in ten minutes."

Ralph exhaled. "It's unreal, but Lucille's car burst into flames at the gas station right after the owner moved it to an empty side lot so it wouldn't be taking up customer parking space. Lucille told the Georgia Bureau of Investigation agent and me you warned her about a recall for her car, which is why she stopped at the gas station. Do you know a GBI agent named Georgia? She's taking Vera and Lucille to a safe house for the night. I'm supposed to act normal, but right now, I'm not exactly sure what normal is, so I might need your help. The sheriff wants you to call him."

Morgan came into the office after Ralph hung up.

"Is everything okay?" she asked.

"Ralph's on his way back. Lucille is taking Vera to her sister's house, after all."

"Good, so it was just our usual genealogy drama."

Jenna smiled. "You got it."

"We need to talk," Morgan said.

Jenna rose. "I agree. We'll talk right after the meeting."

Morgan opened the door to the kitchen. "Shane and Ethan went to the living room to work. The kitchen is almost clean; do you want to talk to Wendy and Layla before they leave?"

"That's a good idea."

When they walked into the kitchen, Wendy and Layla were putting on their coats.

"Tonight's happy hour and dinner were an enormous hit. Everyone raved about the food, Wendy," Jenna said.

Wendy blushed and ducked her head. "Thank you."

Jenna continued, "I don't know what we would have done without your help, Layla. Thank you so much for jumping in."

"It's been an adventure." Layla grinned as the two of them left.

"I have one more thing to do before I return to the dining room," Jenna said.

"I'll be sitting at our table."

Katy followed Jenna into the office. As soon as Jenna sat at her desk, she called the sheriff.

"Tell me about the recall on Lucille's car," he said.

"I had a feeling her car was going to catch on fire, and that was the first thing that popped into my mind."

"Do you remember Clint from the GBI?" the sheriff asked.

Jenna smiled. *How could I forget Clint with his cute dimples and brand new baby?* "Of course."

"He's going to be lurking on the property tonight. Don't shoot him."

"Okay. What's going on?"

"We'll talk tomorrow." The sheriff hung up.

Jenna remained at her desk as she stared at her phone.

"Katy, Georgia from the GBI was here, and we still don't know why. Now Clint will be around, and we are still clueless. Are we being protected by GBI? From what? Or is there an active investigation going on? Does this have anything to do with the chef, or Felicia?"

Katy moaned as she rose. When she padded to the door to the kitchen, Katy stared at Jenna.

Jenna exhaled. "Back to work."

While Jenna strolled through the kitchen on her way to the dining room, she stopped to pick up Ralph's folder and snorted.

When I asked the sheriff what was going on, his answer was about as sincere as let's do lunch.

Jenna rubbed Katy's chin then went into the dining room. When she sat down with Morgan at their table next to the door, she held the folder on her lap.

"In conclusion," Petra said, "please remember to complete the surveys when you receive them, so you will have a voice in our selection of where we will meet next year."

"Will the Peach Blossom Retreat be a choice?" Susan asked.

"We don't go to the same place twice." Petra glanced at Jenna and put on her best plastic smile.

"I move Peach Blossom Retreat will be included as a choice," Ivy said.

Arthur said, "I second."

"Call for the question," Stan said.

Petra's face turned red. "Out of order. Moving on..."

Jenna examined Petra's face.

Petra's red face again. She's deeply involved, and there's my red.

"All in favor." Tisha narrowed her eyes at Petra, and Petra froze.

Jenna cocked her head. *Tisha controlled Petra with a look.*

The response was immediate. "Aye."

"I think that was unanimous," Morgan whispered.

"Opposed?" Petra squeaked.

When no one said anything, Petra sighed. "Motion passed. The Peach Blossom Retreat will be included as a choice."

Petra cleared her throat. "Moving on to our competition. Chris, please summarize your genealogy puzzle we selected for this year's competition."

Chapter Fourteen

Chris strolled to the podium with a sheet of paper in his hand. "This was a cold case of an actual event. The movie script, which was touted as factual, was based on manufactured details that were purposely created to discredit the family and their business. The lies were repeated as truth and sensationalized by mainstream media and then picked up by social media. It took very little time for the dramatic, wildly distorted stories to be widely accepted as fact. Unfortunately, the lies from the movie made their way into police records as fact. I'll read the facts everyone had as a reference for the actual events."

While Chris was speaking, Ralph slipped into the room and sat down next to Ivy. Ivy glanced at him then peered at the dining room doorway and exhaled as she leaned back and turned her attention to Chris.

I'm not the only one who won't miss Vera's drama.

Chris picked up his paper and continued with the details of the cold case. "A toddler disappeared twenty-five years ago. Her wealthy parents died in a car crash five years after her disappearance, and a distant relative of the father was the recipient of the substantial inheritance. The relative used the funds to expand his business, which prospered and grew to four times the value of the original inheritance. The man sold his company, but kept his interest in the company by keeping his majority of the shares. He placed all his wealth, including his stock, into a trust that was managed by a law firm. After the man died in a plane crash, the company was investigated for money laundering because of a tip from an unknown insider. While there were arrests of minor players in the money laundering case, the mastermind was never identified. That's it."

Susan lifted an eyebrow. "I thought it was significant that the movie focused on finding the whistleblower who exposed the crime, not on solving the crime."

Wanda added, "No one seemed to be interested in who was behind the money laundering. Also, wasn't the movie funded by a rival company?"

Ivy nodded. "After the movie came out, the same rival company bought the original company for a fraction of its worth when shareholders rushed to sell their stock in the original company."

Before he returned to his seat, Chris said, "None of those facts appeared in the movie."

Petra swallowed hard as she rose. "Well, then. This went down a path I didn't expect at all. Aren't we ignoring genealogy and the baby that disappeared? Can we briefly focus on the movie? Surely it had some tidbits about genealogy and the baby that were useful."

"The movie backers poured a lot of money into the right pockets, which is why the movie won awards," Arthur said.

Petra snorted. "We don't know that."

"But we do. It was well-documented several years later by an investigative reporter," Susan said.

Petra dismissed Susan's comment with her hand, and Ivy narrowed her eyes. "Everybody knew that so-called reporter was hired by a rival producer who had a severe case of sour grapes, but let's hear our submissions. Who would like to go first?"

"Everyone does not know that, and I'd love to know the source for your information, but in the interest of time, I'll read Ivy's submission," Susan said.

Susan rose, and Petra pursed her lips as she stormed to the nearest empty table.

While everyone watched Susan approach the podium, Ralph strolled to the sideboard and poured a cup of coffee. Jenna joined him and set his folder down in front of him. After she straightened the napkins, Jenna returned to her seat.

"Slick," whispered Morgan.

While Susan read, Jenna furrowed her brow. *Ivy thinks the kidnapping was arranged by the nanny. I need to check Mr. Thorton's notes.*

Jenna whispered, "I need a break."

Morgan nodded.

After Jenna hurried through the kitchen, Katy followed her into her office.

Jenna pulled out the folder with Mr. Thorton's notes that she hadn't read yet and scanned the pages for any mention of Briana or a nanny.

When a photo dropped to her desk, Jenna stared at the grainy, faded color photo of a woman who had her head down while she looked at the infant she held in her arms.

Jenna narrowed her eyes as she scrutinized the Caucasian woman's body structure. *That's not Louise Prentice, because she was short and slender. This woman looks more like Petra.*

She leaned back. "The woman could be a family friend or a neighbor." She looked at the back of the photo and smiled as she recognized Mr. Thorton's distinctive handwriting. "Thank you for the reference to a page number, Mr. Thorton."

She stared at the stack of papers. "Unfortunately, these are all out of order."

Jenna put all the pages into the folder and jotted down the page number from the photo on the folder. "I can put them in order while I'm sitting in the dining room if I do it quietly."

After Jenna picked up the folder, she and Katy hurried to the kitchen. Katy flopped down near the oven while Jenna slipped into the dining room.

Jenna sat down next to Morgan while Susan flipped to the last page of Ivy's story.

Morgan whispered, "Ivy's story is great."

"It would be," Jenna whispered as she quietly pulled out a stack of paper. She glanced at the page numbers of the first ten pages. *This is going to be harder than I thought.*

Morgan elbowed her and leaned close to whisper. "Can I help?"

Jenna exhaled as she stared at all the papers. She pointed to the folder. "I'm looking for this page number."

Morgan nodded as she reached for a stack of papers.

After Susan finished reading Ivy's story, everyone except Petra applauded.

While Susan strolled back to her seat, Petra hurried to the podium.

"Who is next?" Petra raised her eyebrows as she glanced expectantly at Ralph then Stan.

Stan and Ralph exchanged a look, and both of them remained seated.

Petra cleared her throat. "I have Lucille's submission. She left it with me so she could take Vera home."

"Why did Vera go home?" Wanda asked.

"Personal reasons." Petra sniffed.

"I'll bet." Wanda muttered in her raspy voice.

Petra glared at Wanda then cleared her throat. She read the title in the tone of a dramatic reader. "When The Truth Lies in a Movie."

Susan snickered. "The truth lies. I'm giving bonus points to Lucille for her surprising mastery of personification plus irony."

"Lucille's not that smart," Arthur said.

Everyone in the room laughed, including Jenna and Morgan; Arthur furrowed his brow.

He's so serious; he doesn't understand why his remark was funny.

Petra growled, "Excuse me. It's rude to interrupt."

She snapped the paper in her hand then started over. "When the Truth Lives in a Movie."

She glared when Susan and Ivy snickered then focused on Lucille's submission as she began reading the first paragraph.

While Petra read, Jenna furrowed her brow as two cars drove up the driveway and continue past the inn to her cottage. *I have to see what's going on.*

"I'll be right back," she whispered.

Morgan nodded as she continued going through the sheets of paper one page at a time, looking for the elusive page number.

Jenna quietly slipped into the kitchen and hurried to the door that led into the hallway. When she dashed toward the back door, Ethan stood in her way.

When she tried to go past him, he shifted to the side and blocked her.

Jenna growled, "Excuse me. Somebody came up the driveway. I have to check."

"I already tried, and a sheriff's deputy who was stationed at the back door stopped me," he said.

"Well, let's go out the front, then."

Shane joined them. "You can't. Let's go into the kitchen to talk."

After they were in the kitchen, Shane said, "There's a deputy sheriff at the front door. When I told him I needed to go to my car, he told me to contact the sheriff because his orders were to make sure nobody came outside."

Ethan pulled out his phone and sent a text.

Ethan read the sheriff's reply aloud. "Meet me at the back door in a few minutes, and I'll explain. Just you."

Jenna peered at Ethan's phone. "Well, that's rude, but I'm sure he meant you, Shane, and me."

When there was a tap at the back door, Katy raised her head.

"See, even Katy wants to go," Jenna said.

Shane sighed. Jenna, If you go, I'll want to go, and Morgan's radar will know something's up, so she'll show up with Katy, and none of us will know anything because the sheriff will leave in disgust."

Jenna stared. "You practically said all that in one breath, Shane. Okay, we'll wait here, Ethan."

Jenna sat at the kitchen table, and Shane joined her.

When Shane repeatedly drummed his fingers on the table, Jenna winced. *Does he have to do that?*

Jenna cleared her throat. "Tell me about your day, Shane, but only if it was good."

He snorted. "You made it too easy. Anything would be good compared to how things have gone here this weekend."

Jenna giggled. "True."

Shane furrowed his brow then smiled. "The most excitement we've had in a while was last week. After our crew put in a new sidewalk from the parking lot to the veranda at a plantation, a mama cat took her six kittens for a stroll the full length of the sidewalk while the concrete was still wet. Our burly men caught the mama cat and the kittens and gently washed their paws before they took them to the vet to have them checked out."

Jenna cocked her head. "Really? Wasn't that extreme to take them to the vet?"

"Not really. Concrete is caustic, and they weren't sure whether they had washed between the kittens' tiny pads well enough."

"That's a really sweet story."

Shane nodded. "I know, so don't tell them I told you."

Jenna bit her lip. *It's probably not true, but it was still a good, distracting story.*

Jenna opened the kitchen door and peered toward the back door then closed the door and peeked out the side window. "I don't think it's going to rain, but we already knew that. Why doesn't the kitchen have a window that looks out back? What's taking so long?"

Shane rose and paced. "I don't know; maybe we need to put a wire on Ethan."

Jenna smiled at Shane's weak attempt at a joke then watched him pace. *At least that's quieter than thumping on the table.*

When the back door opened, Jenna jumped up and opened the kitchen door. Ethan came in with a scowl. "Let's sit at the kitchen table."

After the three of them sat, Ethan took Jenna's hand and gazed at her face. "The GBI is in the middle of an investigation and has been keeping the inn under surveillance. Your friend Clint caught two men who were tampering with your car and discovered they had installed explosives. Everything within fifty feet of your car would have been annihilated by the force of the explosion the second you turned the key to start it."

Jenna felt the room spin. Ethan reached out and grabbed onto her before she slipped out of her seat.

His voice was in the distance. "Honey, are you okay? Take in a deep breath then blow it out."

Jenna inhaled then pursed her lips as she slowly exhaled. "I'm okay."

Shane handed her a cool, damp cloth. "This might help."

Jenna closed her eyes as she patted her face with the damp piece of cloth. She relaxed as the smooth texture of an old towel provided a soothing sensation, like a gentle caress.

She held the cooling cloth against her cheek as she opened her eyes and gazed at Ethan whose face was inches from hers.

"I didn't expect anything like that. I should have heard them. Why didn't I hear them?" Jenna trembled, and her breathing became ragged.

Ethan put his arm around her. "Your hearing is phenomenal, but look how much stress you've been under."

Jenna snuffled then tears streamed down her cheeks as her voice cracked. "That's no excuse. It could have all been over because I dropped my guard."

Ethan held her and stroked her hair while she sobbed uncontrollably.

When she had no more tears, Jenna buried her face in his shoulder.

"That can't happen again." Her muffled voice was hard.

"I'll make sure it doesn't," Ethan growled.

Jenna exhaled as she raised her head and touched his cheek. "I know you will."

After he examined her face, his demeanor softened. "We'll work together."

"Even better," Jenna said.

Shane shifted uncomfortably in his seat. "We have to do something now, don't we? What does the sheriff want us to do?"

Ethan kissed Jenna's forehead then rose. "GBI took the two men into custody for questioning. For the time being, we have to act like nothing happened. To quote the sheriff, those two are not independent thinkers."

Jenna dabbed at her face with the cool cloth as she watched Ethan pace. *That's where Shane got that pacing from.*

"Until we get the all clear from the sheriff, I'm staying close. Jenna, you and Katy will have a house guest until this is resolved."

"I don't know; shouldn't we check with the sheriff?" Jenna asked.

Ethan snorted. "Go ahead; the idea was his."

Jenna rolled her eyes. "The second bedroom is yours."

Shane snorted. "You may find him on the floor next to your bed, Jenna. I know that's where I'd be if it was Morgan's car."

Jenna rubbed her forehead. *Why am I a target?*

She exhaled. "I have to go back to the meeting in the dining room."

Jenna rose and headed toward the door.

"Why?" Ethan asked.

"The sheriff said to act like nothing happened, and people in the group will wonder if something is going on if I don't return."

"We'll be close," Ethan said.

Jenna nodded as she went into the dining room and sat next to Morgan while Petra continued reading.

Morgan beamed as she pointed at a sheet of paper on the table between the two of them.

Jenna's eyes widened when she saw the page number. *She found it.*

Petra finished reading Lucille's submission. "This is Lucille's submission."

"No, it isn't," Wanda said. "That's not what Lucille wrote. I sat next to her, and she didn't write any of that."

Petra clenched her fists and growled, "That must have been her first draft. This is what she gave to me as her final submission."

"It doesn't even sound like Lucille," Wanda grumbled.

Tisha glared at Petra. "Maybe the idea of a proxy reading a submission was not a good idea after all; otherwise, aren't we deadlocked into a dispute with no resolution with the author not here to defend her work?"

Petra's cheeks reddened as she pouted. "I thought you, of all people would support me. I don't think it is right to penalize Lucille for helping a friend."

Jenna bit her lip as three more vehicles passed the inn and continued to her cottage. *That last one sounded like a truck. Are they going to tow my car away?*

"I agree with Petra," Ralph said. "To make sure we don't have any confusion in the future, I move the author of a submission for the competition must be present at the time of reading."

"Second," Stan said.

"What about this submission that is supposed to be Lucille's?" Wanda asked.

"It's a submission for this year's competition, so when we vote for the competition, vote for the one you think is best," Arthur said.

Petra furrowed her brow in confusion. "Is that how it works?"

Tisha rolled her eyes. "Yes, that's how it works. Let's vote."

"All in favor of Ralph's motion to require an author to be present when their submission is read for a competition, raise your hand," Petra said.

Everyone raised a hand.

Petra lifted her chin, and her voice regained its confident tone. "It's unanimous. Motion is passed. Let's move on to our other submissions."

"I withdraw," Ralph said.

Stan nodded. "So do I."

Petra blinked. "But we don't have any more submissions."

"Then we vote," Tisha said.

Petra hurried to her table and picked up her red purse from her seat. After she pulled out an envelope, she removed pale green slips of paper and went from table to table as she handed each member a green slip.

She returned the envelope to her purse then held up the slip she had in her hand. "We are voting for the winner of this year's competition. Your choices are Ivy or Lucille."

Petra wrote a name on her slip then surveyed the room like a high school test monitor. Everyone had already cast their vote and had a folded green slip on the table in front of them.

"Arthur and Wanda, would you please gather the slips and tally the vote?" Petra asked.

After they collected the slips of paper, Arthur and Wanda sat at an empty table.

"I'll unfold the ballots, and you can put them in order, and we'll count them together, Wanda," Arthur said.

Wanda nodded. "I'll put the votes for Ivy on my left and Lucille on my right."

After Wanda had lined up all the green slips in front of her with only one on her right, she said, "Ivy has won the competition for this year."

"Correct. Congratulations, Ivy," Arthur said.

The room erupted in applause and cheers.

Susan nudged Ivy, who frowned and shook her head as she remained seated.

"You said there was a special prize this year for the winner, Petra. Tell Ivy what she won," Stan said.

Petra sniffed. "I'm sure Ivy would rather hear about her prize privately."

"Why would you think that?" Ivy cocked her head. "Let's hear it."

Petra's face reddened at the chuckles then she smiled at Ivy. "Of course. Your dues for the East Coast Genealogy Club are paid in full for the coming year, and you are the lucky winner of a three-day weekend for two at the Peach Blossom Retreat, courtesy of the East Coast Genealogy Club."

Ivy's smile vanished, and she pursed her lips.

"For two means two rooms, right?" Ralph asked.

Petra sighed. "Of course. If there's no other business…"

Morgan poked Jenna. "They can't leave; do something."

Petra paused as Jenna rose from her seat.

"Did you have something to add, Jenna?"

Jenna smiled. "We still have appetizers for you to enjoy, and we'll make a fresh pot of coffee. We'd love for you to stay and socialize at an after-party at the Peach Blossom Retreat."

After the cheers and applause died down, Petra said, "If there's no other business, the meeting adjourned."

While Petra grabbed her red purse and headed toward Jenna, Morgan swept up Mr. Thorton's notes and dropped them into the folder.

Before she left, Morgan said, "I'll put the folder on your desk; the page you were looking for is on top. If you make the coffee, I'll bring out appetizers."

When Petra reached Jenna, she sighed, "Jenna, can you change the gift from the East Coast Genealogy Club from one room for three days to two rooms?"

Jenna nodded. "We certainly can. You can duplicate your original order with your payment information, and we'll approve it. The system will send you a revised. Do you want us to copy Ivy on the receipt?"

"Yes, and I'll tell Ivy to watch for it."

Petra rushed out of the room as Morgan pushed the utility cart into the dining room and then placed three platters on the sideboard.

When Jenna and Morgan went into the kitchen, Shane was slicing a block of extra sharp cheddar cheese for a cheese board on the counter.

"The twelve-cup coffee maker is ready to go, Morgan. I'll carry it to the dining room. Do I put it wherever I can find room?" Ethan asked.

"I'll show you." Jenna opened the door for Ethan then frowned as the truck and cars she heard earlier headed down the driveway toward the road.

Morgan peered at her phone. "We just got a notification of a pending payment for the additional room for the genealogy club. I can approve it from my phone. Is that okay?"

"Sure is, and send Ivy a copy of the receipt. Petra jumped on that right away, didn't she?"

Ethan put the coffee maker on the sideboard and plugged it in. Jenna's phone buzzed with a text from the sheriff.

She groaned as she read the text then handed the phone to Ethan. "The GBI is taking your car for further testing."

"Are you okay?" Ethan returned her phone.

Jenna exhaled. "Not really; I guess I hoped they'd take photos and be done."

"I'll be your chauffeur, not that you go anywhere very often except to the inn and back to your cottage." Ethan smiled as he returned to the kitchen.

Jenna stared at the kitchen door. *Is that how dull I've become?*

"Jenna?" Arthur startled her.

He stepped back. "Excuse me; I didn't mean to scare you."

"You didn't scare me; I've just been a little on edge lately," she said.

"Wanda sent me that picture of Vera and the baby that Lucille sent to her, and I removed the fake part and made it not fuzzy. Do you want to see it?"

Why not? What's one more thing to confuse me?

"I'd like that; thank you."

"I'll send it to you when Chris and I get to the hotel tonight." When the appetizers were gone, and the conversations waned, the after-party guests slowly drifted out after thanking Jenna.

Ivy and Susan were the last to leave.

"I got my copy of the revised receipt; Thank you. I plan to return in the spring," Ivy said. "I invited Susan to come with me because I wouldn't have won if she hadn't agreed to read my submission, so the award is half hers."

"I look forward to seeing you both." Jenna smiled.

Ivy smiled then lowered her voice. "We don't think Petra will return next year. Wasn't she a walking disaster?"

Susan added, "We are obviously not the only ones who think she was over her head. When I went to the restroom earlier, I heard her talking to somebody in the living room, and she said you can't get rid of me because I know too much. For two cents, I would have gone in there and told Petra she didn't know diddly."

Ivy nodded. "I don't think anyone in the club would have blamed you if you had."

After Ivy and Susan left, Jenna locked the dining room door then picked up the last empty platter and went into the kitchen.

"Is that it?" Morgan asked.

Jenna nodded.

"I'll vacuum the dining room in the morning before breakfast," Morgan said. "We've packaged up our dinners; we're going to take them home. The meals for you and Ethan are on the counter."

"Thank you both for everything," Jenna said.

After Morgan and Shane left, Jenna hurried to her office and picked up the folder. When she returned to the kitchen, Ethan narrowed his eyes. "Are you planning on working tonight?"

"No, I just have a couple of things I'd like to check."

Ethan snorted. "While you're doing your couple of things, I'll warm up our dinner."

Ethan picked up a backpack and the sack with their dinner while Jenna put on her coat. After they left the inn, Katy raced around the backyard then dashed to the cottage as Jenna opened the door.

When they were inside, Ethan said, "Wait a minute."

He took her into his arms and held her tight. "I've been wanting to do this all night."

I think I was supposed to be mad at him; maybe I'll be mad at him later.

She wrapped her arms around him then sighed as they released each other.

"Thanks; I needed that. I'm going to dress for dinner."

Ethan blinked. "What are you talking about? We're having dinner here."

Jenna smirked. "I know. That's why I'm going to put on my most comfortable sweatpants and a flannel shirt."

Ethan grinned. "I'll have your dinner ready in a jiffy, princess."

Jenna pulled out the page Mr. Thorton had referenced on the back of the photo of the woman holding the baby. She took the paper with her as she hurried to her bedroom to change.

After she pulled off her boots and jeans, she sat on her bed and read.

"The nanny was Leanne Peterson. She disappeared after baby Briana disappeared. Her college roommate was Patricia Hollinger. The law firm that managed the trust for Gerald Prentice was the Hollinger law firm, and Patricia Hollinger was the daughter of the founding partner."

Jenna's phone buzzed with a text. She took in a sharp breath as she stared at the photo Arthur sent.

She exhaled. "It's what I thought."

This is Petra twenty-five years ago. She was the nanny. Tisha was her college roommate, and Tisha's father managed the trust. I'll bet Tisha is managing it now.

While Jenna stared at the photo, her phone buzzed with a text from Petra. "I went to the living room to get a book and locked myself out of my room. I hate to ask, but can you come let me into my room?"

Jenna pulled on her jeans and put on her boots. She threw on her coat and headed to the door.

"I'll be back in a couple of minutes."

When she reached for the door to open it, Ethan's hand flew over her head and slammed against the door.

She whirled around and raised her chin as she glared.

His eyebrows raised. "Where are we going?"

"Petra locked herself out of her room; I'm going to open her guestroom door for her."

"Do you believe her? What's her real reason for you to go to the inn?"

"Maybe she needs to talk. Get out of my way."

"Yes, ma'am." Ethan removed his hand and put on his coat. Before Jenna could close the door, he was at her side.

"What do you really think?" he asked as he stayed close to her while she rushed to the inn.

"She was Briana's nanny and kidnapped her."

"Do I know who Briana is?"

"The baby in the story Chris told."

Ethan grabbed her arm and stopped her. "That was true?"

"Yes. I'll fill you in after I unlock Petra's door."

When Ethan reached past her to open the back door, Jenna froze.

Ambush, sweet pea.

"Ethan, change of plans. Nettie says it's an ambush."

"Then we don't go in."

"Petra doesn't know we've been warned. Maybe she'll be rattled and confess. If you cover me, I'll be fine."

Ethan grumbled, "I hope I don't regret this."

"Don't talk like that; you'll make me nervous."

When they went into the inn, Ethan put his hand on Jenna's shoulder, and she stopped. After he slipped off his boots, he closed his eyes and exhaled quietly then nodded.

Jenna watched as Ethan slipped around the corner to the dimly lit hallway.

When Jenna walked from the back door to the kitchen door, her footsteps clicked on the wooden floor. After she reached the dining room, Jenna glanced down the hallway. Ethan was in the shadows of the hallway near Petra's room door and the stairs.

Jenna quietly called out, "Petra?"

She frowned as a muffled voice came from the living room. "In here."

Dame with a rod.

Jenna held up her index finger and mouthed, "One." Then pointed her finger and cocked her thumb, and mouthed, "Gun."

Ethan nodded as he mimicked her motion of pointing with one finger and then followed it with a pointed finger and cocked thumb.

"I'll open your door for you," Jenna said.

"Help me up first. My ankle," the woman whispered.

Chapter Fifteen

"I'm not strong enough. I'll get Ethan and Shane to help me," Jenna said. "I'll be right back."

Jenna clomped as she rushed toward the back door.

"Hold it!" Ethan growled.

Jenna whirled around as Tisha turned to point her gun at Ethan.

"Drop it, Patricia," Jenna shouted.

Tisha turned back and pointed her gun at Jenna. The red patches on her throat darkened as they spread upward to her face, and her eyes were black with hate.

"Put it down real slow," Jenna said.

Fire!

Jenna pulled the trigger a split second before Tisha fired her gun.

Tisha screamed and dropped her gun as she collapsed in front of the living room.

Ethan rushed to her and kicked her gun down the hall toward the kitchen. The pistol clattered as it slid on the wooden floor.

Stan, the twins, and Amanda rushed out of their rooms with their guns drawn. Ralph was halfway down the stairs.

Jenna called out, "I'm okay, everybody. Shooting is over. Everybody is safe."

Susan sauntered out of her room. "I called the cops."

Ivy peered from the top of the stairs. "I missed the action."

Jenna's phone buzzed with a text from the sheriff. "Clint's at the back door."

Jenna said, "Ethan, Clint's here."

She rushed to the back door. When she opened it, Clint wore jeans, a flannel shirt, and a camo jacket. *I almost didn't recognize him in civilian clothes.*

He asked, "Are you okay?"

"Yes. Tisha shot at me, but she missed. I shot her."

"Where is she?"

"In the hall in front of the living room."

Jenna led the way, but Clint strode past her. When Clint reached the dining room door with Jenna on his heels, Ethan stood in the living room doorway. "Petra's not here."

Jenna dashed to Petra's bedroom; when she opened the door, she gasped at the intense odor of iron. *There's so much blood.*

Petra lay on her side on the floor near the foot of the bed. Her face was gray, and she was lying in a large pool of blood. A butcher knife was buried to its hilt an inch below her sternum.

Jenna grabbed onto the doorframe and squeaked, "Ethan."

Ethan and Clint rushed to Petra's room.

Clint went into the room, and Ethan put his arm around Jenna, who was shaking.

He whispered, "Tisha is playing possum. Clint knows it. We have two ambulances on the way."

Clint stepped out of Petra's room and scanned all the guests in their doorways. Clint's clear, loud voice conveyed authority. "Did anyone see or hear anything?"

All the guests slowly shook their heads.

Clint continued, "Stay in your rooms. We have a crime scene that hasn't been compromised. Let's keep it that way."

"Can Jenna and I wait in the kitchen?" Ethan asked.

Clint nodded.

After they were in the kitchen, Ethan said, "Your hands are shaking, but that's normal. I'll be right back. You need to eat."

"I'm not sure I can eat." Jenna glared at her hands as they continued to shake, and her heart continued to pound.

You're the bee's knees, sweet pea.

Jenna's smile was weak, but her hands quit shaking, and her heart rate slowed. "Thanks, Nettie. I appreciate your help."

Anytime.

Jenna listened to the wailing sirens as they grew louder the closer they were to the inn.

When the wails were abruptly cut off, Ethan came into the kitchen with their warm food.

"Two ambulances just pulled in at the driveway."

Ethan put plates and silverware on the table then opened the refrigerator. After he poured two glasses of sweet tea and put them on the table, he plated their baked chicken with creamy cheese sauce and baby spinach.

Jenna inhaled the tantalizing, mingled aroma of garlic, basil, and thyme on her baked chicken breast. "I thought I couldn't eat, but I didn't realize how hungry I was."

After Ethan finished eating, and Jenna had only a few bites left, Clint and the sheriff came into the kitchen and joined them at the table.

"Are you just now eating?" the sheriff asked.

"The chicken was in the oven when I got a text from Petra."

Jenna handed her phone to the sheriff.

He peered at the phone then handed it to Clint.

Clint put his notebook on the table. "Tell me what happened."

"I was suspicious when I got the text from Petra."

Clint peered at her. "You had one of your feelings."

"Yes."

Jenna and Ethan told him about Tisha impersonating Petra and then shooting at Jenna.

"Her shot went into the wall next to the kitchen; two inches to the left..." Clint cleared his throat. "Do you know why Tisha tried to kill you and Petra?"

Jenna nodded. "It will be easier for me to explain if we go into my office."

An hour later, Clint had Mr. Thorton's records.

"Let's see if I can summarize this. Petra was the Prentices' nanny and orchestrated the disappearance of the baby, Briana Prentice. Petra worked for Tisha, who is actually Patricia Hollinger. The trust created by the Hollinger law firm managed the Prentice wealth and had complete control of the trust after Gerald Prentice, the only remaining heir of the Prentice fortune died."

Jenna nodded.

"Patricia Hollinger is also the mastermind behind the money laundering scheme uncovered at the former Prentice contracting firm, and it's all right here." Clint patted the stack of papers with Mr. Thorton's notes.

"Do you have anything else for me?" Clint smiled.

Jenna returned his smile. "Like maybe a signed confession along with Patricia's detailed document of how to launder money?"

"That would be nice." Clint chuckled, and Ethan joined in.

Clint cleared this throat. "What do you know about the chef who died?"

"Not much, except he couldn't hold a job because of theft and drugs."

"You'll probably hear he worked at the Hollinger law office in Atlanta. A previously minor detail that became significant tonight. I have a theory that stealing from a corporation like that could lead to an unfortunate demise," Clint said.

Jenna nodded. "Interesting theory."

"Thanks, but we still have one big question that we'll never answer. The fate of the Prentice baby."

Jenna nodded.

Clint picked up his notes and the folders with Mr. Thorton's notes. "We'll get your car back to you as soon as we can. The sheriff will keep you up to date."

Clint put out his hand and shook with Jenna then Ethan. "It was nice to see you, but don't do this anymore. You're making some of our best investigators turn prematurely gray."

After Clint left, Ethan said, "Are you ready to go home?"

"Absolutely."

When Jenna opened the kitchen door, she exhaled in relief when the hallway was empty. "I was worried everyone would still be up, but all the guests have gone to bed."

Ralph sat on the stairs. "Thank you for what you did for Vera."

Jenna stopped and gazed at him. "You're welcome."

As they strolled to the cottage, Ethan said, "I thought I'd still stay with you tonight for moral support and to listen if you needed to talk."

Jenna shook her head. "I'm too exhausted to even think right now, but I'm sure it will hit me tomorrow. I'll see you in the morning."

Ethan sighed. "Okay, if you're sure. I know it's been a long day for you. I'll leave after Katy takes her bedtime break."

When Jenna opened the front door, Katy danced then darted into the trees. Ethan went inside and came back out with his backpack.

He put his arm around Jenna while they waited for Katy.

"The sky is clear, and the stars are out. We're lucky we're far enough from town that we can see the stars," Ethan said.

Jenna gazed at the sky. "I have always lived in a city before I moved here. I didn't know what I was missing. It really is beautiful isn't it?"

"It is, but it's a waste if there isn't anyone to share it with."

He turned and wrapped his arms around her, and Jenna rested her head on his chest. She lifted her face and pulled him close.

After a slow, sweet kiss, Ethan teased her mouth open and groaned as she matched the intensity of his kiss.

When Katy whined then barked, they came up for air.

Jenna giggled when Ethan said, "I didn't know we had a chaperone."

Jenna dropped her arms and wriggled to be loose, and Ethan released her.

"Good night, sweet thing." Ethan kissed her one more time for good measure.

"Good night." Jenna and Katy went inside.

Jenna peered out the window and chuckled while she watched Ethan strut to his truck.

Jenna changed into her pajamas and climbed into bed. After she pulled up the covers, the full weight of the weekend hit her and she cried herself to sleep.

Jenna woke at five thirty and stumbled into the kitchen with Katy at her side. After Katy went out back for her morning bio break, Jenna fed her and hopped into the shower.

While she dressed, her phone buzzed with a text from Ethan. "Good morning, cutie."

She smiled and replied, "Good morning, cowboy."

"I'm 5 minutes from the inn."

Jenna chuckled. "Me too."

Her phone buzzed with a text from the sheriff. "Call when you're awake."

Jenna exhaled and called him.

"Hope I didn't wake you. Georgia rode in the ambulance with Petra last night. Petra told her Tisha stabbed her because she was the last person alive who knew Tisha was the mastermind behind the money laundering. Unfortunately, Petra didn't make it to the hospital. Georgia said it was a wonder she held on as long as she did."

Jenna sat down on the sofa and rubbed her forehead. "Thanks for letting me know."

"Tisha isn't doing well. She had an undiagnosed heart defect and is in open heart surgery. Being shot might have saved her life. They'll remove the bullet and patch up that wound later. Just thought you'd like to know." The sheriff hung up.

Jenna choked back tears as she put on her coat. "It was sad news about Petra, but I'm glad the sheriff called, Katy. I would have wondered all day."

Jenna hesitated at the door. "We have to go, don't we? At least it will be a short day. We just have to get through breakfast."

After they were outside, the mockingbird sang. Jenna smiled when a familiar truck roared up the driveway.

Katy yipped, and the two of them rushed to Ethan's parking spot as he pulled in and parked.

He jumped out of his truck and hugged Jenna. "How did you sleep?"

"It was a little rough," she said. "What about you?"

"I stayed awake all night and thought about you."

Jenna snorted. "You did not."

"I wanted to; doesn't that count?"

They held hands as they walked to the back door. Jenna shuffled through the autumn leaves and told him what the sheriff said.

"Are you going to tell anyone else?" he asked.

"No, they'll find out soon enough, and I couldn't deal with the questions."

"Smart lady."

"Not really. I cried myself to sleep."

"I'm so sorry. I should have stayed."

"No, I think that's what I needed to do. I'm sad today, but I'll be okay." A slow smile crept across her face. "Hugs help."

Ethan grabbed her into a hug, and she closed her eyes and leaned against him.

Katy yipped, and Darlene opened the back door and let her inside.

"Ahh, coffee will be ready." Ethan released her from the hug with a quick kiss, but they held hands as they hurried to the back door.

When they went into the kitchen, Darlene pointed to the two cups of coffee on the counter. "Katy told me there were two of you."

Jenna rolled her eyes. *She saw us walking together.*

While they drank their coffee, Darlene said, "Today is a light breakfast, because everyone will be traveling home. It's all buffet. We're serving fruit cups, chiles rellenos quiche, cheese quiche with fresh herbs, and a mess of bacon and sausage as side dishes for our meat eaters."

"They'll love it, Darlene," Jenna said.

"Coffee will be ready in the dining room in ten minutes," Darlene said. "I got an early start."

Morgan and Shane came into the kitchen.

"Good morning. What's the plan?" Morgan asked.

"Buffet, and I haven't done a thing," Jenna said.

Darlene pointed to the coffee she'd poured. Morgan took a big gulp then said, "I'll get the coffee going in the dining room."

"Darlene already started the coffee. We're serving fruit cups and quiche, so we need the usual."

At seven o'clock, Jenna unlocked the dining room door, and the first ones in were Annie, Quinn, and their husbands. The rest of the guests soon followed.

After listening to the chatter and speculation and answering questions, Jenna exhaled as their guests slowly left.

Amanda lingered until most of the others had left. "Jenna, this was the wildest job I've ever had, and thanks for not blowing my cover. I'm glad my girl wasn't in the middle of it. She's safe, and you've made my job obsolete."

Jenna's eyes widened. "How did you know I knew?"

"It was in your eyes. My ability to read eyes has saved my life and others more than once."

"Impressive." Jenna smiled.

Amanda returned her smile. "Takes one to know one, hotshot."

Amanda chuckled as she left.

When Jenna surveyed the room, the only guests left, Brittany and Stan, rose from their table and held hands as they strolled to the door where Jenna waited.

Stan smiled. "Thanks again for everything, Jenna. Honey, I'll carry our things to the car and wait for you. No rush."

Brittany nodded.

"If you have time, we would be more comfortable if we sat in the living room to talk," Jenna said.

"I'd like that."

As they strolled together to the living room, Brittany said, "Stan and I plan to return so we can enjoy the area and the inn."

"It would be wonderful to see you again," Jenna said.

When they went into the living room, Brittany smiled as she lightly rubbed the fireplace mantle with her fingers. "I loved the fire in the fireplace. The warmth from the fire and the flickering flames and the crackling of the burning wood were so relaxing."

"Come in the early spring; it's still cold enough at night to justify a fire."

"Thank you for the suggestion." Brittany stared at the rug as she shifted her feet. "Do you have a lost and found?"

"Not officially, but we do have one unofficially, if that makes sense," Jenna said. "Did you lose something?"

Brittany lifted her head and stared at the fireplace. "I don't know; I might have left it at home."

She exhaled and shifted her gaze to Nettie's portrait. "I have a ring that belonged to Stan's mother. I never go anywhere without it, but I can't find it. Stan's been helping me search for it and asked a couple of people if they'd seen it, but no one has. We've gone through our luggage and our room at least three times. Now, I'm not sure I brought it with me. If I did, I might have left it in the restroom across from the dining room, but I finally checked the restroom this morning and didn't see it."

Brittany bit her lip. "I'm hoping it's at home, but I don't really think it is."

"What did it look like?"

"Just a ring with a red stone, kind of like a ruby."

Jenna rose. "Sounds like a ring Wendy found when she was cleaning."

Brittany's eyes welled up. "Really?"

"I'll be right back."

Jenna rushed to the kitchen with Katy on her heels. Katy stayed in the kitchen while Jenna hurried to her office and unlocked the drawer where she kept the ring.

When she picked up the ring, it tingled her hand. "I'm taking you to Brittany."

The ring stopped tingling, and Jenna stared at her hand then remembered, *From the times before the secret.*

As Jenna strolled back to the living room, she muttered, "Do I tell Brittany?"

Yes.

When Jenna walked into the living room, Brittany jumped up from the sofa.

Jenna opened her hand. When Brittany squealed and reached for the ring, Jenna said, "The ring is from the times before the secret."

Brittany's face went gray as she dropped to her seat on the sofa. "What did you say?"

"I have a sensitivity thing I can't explain, but that's what the ring said." Jenna felt the ring tingle as she handed it to Brittany. "It's yours."

Brittany clutched it to her chest. "You're mine," she whispered.

After Brittany placed the ring on her finger, she sighed. "I shouldn't have brought it here, but I wear it all the time at home unless I'm working in the yard. I thought I'd be more comfortable around people if I had it with me." Brittany jutted out her jaw. "It's from Stan's mother."

Jenna gazed at Brittany who looked away. *You're not that great of a liar.*

"I'm glad you have it again," Jenna glanced at the ring. "It glows in the sunlight."

Brittany exhaled as she rose. "It always has. Thank you."

Brittany headed toward the hall then stopped in the doorway as her eyes welled up. "Thank you again for my ring, Jenna. It's the only thing I have that was mama's."

After Brittany rushed out of the living room, Jenna put her hand on her heart as a tear slipped down her cheek.

"Wasn't that sweet?" Jenna sniffled as she gazed at Nettie's portrait.

A sunbeam streamed into the living room and lit up Nettie's portrait, and the chimes jingled.

Ethan strolled into the dining room. "I saw Brittany leave. She looked like an enormous weight had been lifted from her shoulders."

"This might have been the scariest weekend of my life, but for Brittany, it turned out to be her best. Isn't that strange?"

"After the group that you hosted here this weekend, nothing will ever seem strange to me." Ethan put his arm around Jenna's shoulder. "Are you okay?"

Jenna hugged him. "I am now."

Did you enjoy Jenna's story?

Leave a review with your favorite bookseller and with Barrett Book Shop!

Next to read:

GRITS AND GREED

JENNA ROSS THRILLER, BOOK 4

A haunted hotel. A ghost tour queen. A death too perfectly staged.

When Jenna reluctantly agrees to attend a four-day innkeepers' conference in Savannah, Georgia, after pushy encouragement from Morgan and Nettie. She expects networking, awkward icebreakers, and an overdose of industry jargon. What she doesn't expect is death.

Check BARRETT BOOK SHOP for GRITS AND GREED and other Judith A. Barrett books to read!

BarrettBookShop.com

Browse, shop, read, enjoy!

SUBSCRIBE AND SAVE

Join the eNewsletter mailing list and become the first to know about book specials and read unpublished stories and exciting news!

SUBCRIBE to her Newsletter via her website

www.judithabarrett.com/newsletter

More About the Author

Judith A. Barrett, award-winning author, lives on a farm in Georgia with her husband, two dogs, and chickens. She writes series for her readers: thriller, romantic and cozy mysteries, historical fiction, and post-apocalyptic science fiction novels. Stories with a twist: not your typical characters from not your typical author!

Her motto: You keep reading; I'll keep writing!

When she isn't writing, Judith is meeting readers at arts and crafts fairs, working on farm chores, hiking or camping with her husband and dogs, or rocking on her front porch while she watches the sunset and plans the next plot twist in the book she is writing.

Website judithabarrett.com

VIP Readers judithabarrett.com/newsletter

Exclusive Discounts and Sales barrettbookshop.com

Not into emails, even though Judith's story-focused newsletters are interesting, Not-Your-Typical newsletters? Follow Judith on Barrett Book Shop, Her Blog on her website: The Latest Twist, Bookbub, or your favorite bookseller for news of her latest release!

Let's keep in touch!

Find your next book(s) and buy direct from the author at the Barrett Book Shop!

www.ingramcontent.com/pod-product-compliance
Lightning Source LLC
Chambersburg PA
CBHW050126030726
47505CB00007B/2052